Second

Ruchita Misra is a t... ...gold m... ...from the Indian Institute of Foreign Trade in New Delhi and the author of the bestselling books *The (In)eligible Bachelors*, for which she was awarded the Awadh Samman in 2012, and *~~I Do!~~ Do I?*. She works in London and blogs at smilethesmile. blogspot.com.

second chance at Love

RUCHITA MISRA

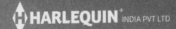
HARLEQUIN INDIA PVT LTD

First published in India in 2015 by Harlequin
An imprint of HarperCollins *Publishers*

P-ISBN: 978-93-5177-594-2
E-ISBN: 978-93-5177-595-9

2 4 6 8 10 9 7 5 3 1

HarperCollins *Publishers*
A-75, Sector 57, Noida, Uttar Pradesh 201301, India
1 London Bridge Street, London, SE1 9GF, United Kingdom
Hazelton Lanes, 55 Avenue Road, Suite 2900, Toronto, Ontario M5R 3L2
and 1995 Markham Road, Scarborough, Ontario M1B 5M8, Canada
25 Ryde Road, Pymble, Sydney, NSW 2073, Australia
195 Broadway, New York, NY 10007, USA

Typeset in 11/14 Warnock Pro
by Jojy Philip, New Delhi 110 015

Printed and bound at
Thomson Press (India) Ltd.

*In memory of Nani, who was most proud of my books,
and for Shikhar, my son. This book is an ode to the
wonderful, inexplicable way these two shall
forever remain connected ...*

Prologue

Lost

He stared at the khaki uniforms of the three men in front of him, images from the cremation clouding his vision and sense. She was gone. Gone. Gone in the most horrific way possible, with no one to blame but him.

Gone, never again to smile. Gone, never again to flick an unruly curl away from her forehead. Gone, never again to grin sheepishly at the burnt toast in her hands. Gone, never again to beg him to do her homework. Gone, never again to ask him to hold her. Gone, never again to tease him with a passionate kiss. Gone, never again to try and learn to fly kites. Gone, never again to bury her curly head in his chest. Gone, never again to run barefoot on their favourite beach in the Caribbean. Gone, never again to tell him how madly she loved him.

Gone. Gone, never to return. Gone forever. Nothing mattered now. Nothing. Nothing ever would again.

This was not how she was supposed to go. This was not how their story was supposed to end. No, no, no.

The screams inside his head grew louder by the minute.

I am responsible for her death, I am, he shouted silently, angry tears running down his unshaven and gaunt cheeks. *I am. I killed her.*

They were asking him questions. He was giving them answers. Answers that just tumbled out of his mouth in a monotone that he did not recognize as his.

'He is exhausted,' a familiar voice said. Someone placed a hand on his shoulders and he shrugged it away. His eyes fell on the bed in the corner and he longed to curl up on it and never wake up, to close his eyes and never open them again, to not breathe, to not live. To be with Mum.

A painful longing seared through his chest. To be with Mum. If only. If only he could sit beside her and put his head in her lap now. *No, that can't happen. Because she is dead too. And I am responsible for both their deaths. I killed them.*

Guilt clung to every pore in his body and he wondered if it would ever leave him. *I hope it does not,* he thought bitterly, wiping tears with the back of his dirty hand. Before he knew it, his legs had carried him out of the house towards Bandstand, towards the sea. As dark clouds gathered furiously, he started to run. He ran from himself.

She was gone. And he was lost. For eternity.

❀

How would *that* feel, she wondered, munching on a soggy corncob that tasted deliciously of the monsoon rains that lashed around her. How would it feel to love someone with a love that was more than love? To be completely, insanely, senselessly in love with someone? To be consumed entirely by it? To love with such abandon that it made living worthwhile? For that love to be the most potent force in life? For that love to burn, uplift, hurt, exhilarate – all possibly at the same time? Did such love even exist?

'Of course, it does!' a little voice murmured in her head.

'Then why have I never seen it?' she asked out loud.

'Because one day you'll experience it for yourself.'

She let the rain soak her long hair, run along her bare legs and drench her dress. This little corner in Bandstand was her personal favourite and, during the monsoons, when it was deserted like it was now, it was all hers. Her own little piece of the city of dreams.

'The worst is behind me,' she mumbled to herself, straining to hear her voice against the winds that howled angrily. 'It is. It is. I am twenty-two, enrolled in a good engineering college, Mum is okay, Urvi is with us, we are not rolling in money, but we are not sleeping hungry either. We are not perfect, but we are complete even when we are technically not complete. And who knows? I might just make it to an IIM. How cool will that be?'

In her bag was last week's mock-CAT exam paper. She had scored 99.8 per cent and was ranked fifteenth in Mumbai.

'Not bad,' she said out loud with a hopeful smile.

Hope. The four-letter word that made the road ahead seem a lot better than the one behind her, the one thing that made her not want to be a prisoner of her past.

Her eyes focused on the lone figure that had, in the meanwhile, materialized on the scene. A tall man, shoulders hunched, was running towards her.

How odd, she thought, to come out for a run in the rains. What if he is a thief running from the police? What if he's a gangster? A rapist?

She narrowed her eyes suspiciously as the man ran past her. The rain, the winds, his hair, her hair, all made it very difficult for her to see clearly. Yet she knew, without any doubt, that something was terribly wrong.

Out of breath, the man paused a few feet from her, rested his hands on his haunches, and gulped in large mouthfuls of air. Almost as if an invisible rope were pulling her towards him, she found herself approaching the man.

'Hello?' she said in a small, hesitant voice.

No response.

'Hi?' she tried again.

Nothing.

'Hey!'

And then she heard it. In spite of the winds and the rain and cars in the distance. A low, heart-wrenching sob. Like a drowning man gasping for air. She brought her hand to her mouth in surprise. A grown man crying? She looked closely. The man seemed to be in his early thirties. He looked haggard, tired and lost. He continued to look down at his hands that rested on his haunches, oblivious of the girl's curious gaze. She had to say something.

'Listen,' she said in a chatty, confident tone. 'Don't cry, okay? Everything is okay. You know what they say, don't you? It's always okay in the end. And if it is not okay, it's not the end.' The man stayed still and the girl started to feel a little unsure. 'Do you want to talk? I am very good at talking, you know. All my friends tell me about their problems *all* the time, and you know, they say I say the wisest things.' She trailed off as she sensed movement.

'Are ... are you upset about something?' she fumbled now.

The man stirred, like a cave-dragon that had been awakened from centuries of slumber. Slowly, and as if in great pain, he unfurled himself. Most of his gaunt, skeletal face was covered by hair plastered to it by the rain.

'I mean … I can help if you need to …' She was stuttering now, scared as bits of the man's face became visible to her. Dark, angry eyes pierced through her from behind long hair. 'Um, do you want me to get a doctor?' The man mumbled something. 'What? What did you say?' she asked, leaning in.

The man looked up and his eyes met hers. 'What,' he said with in a surprisingly polished accent, 'will you take to shut up?' She laughed nervously, suddenly feeling all jelly-like. 'Get lost or I'll kill you as well,' the man said in a low, dangerous growl, his X-ray-like eyes emanating fire.

Kill you? As well? AS WELL? She felt sheer terror swim through her. She gasped, tried to shriek, but no sound came out. Another look at the horrendous man, and she sprinted away from him as fast as she could.

She stopped only when she reached the main road. She looked back and thankfully saw no sign of the man.

For about two days after this incident, every now and then, she found herself wondering about the dangerous man she had met on the beach. While reading the newspaper, she kept an eye out for any murders the man on the beach might have committed. But when nothing popped up, she forgot all about the little encounter.

5

1

The atmosphere in Meeting Room Alpha of the Mumbai headquarters of India Consulting Limited was charged as Sumit Godbole and Mohit Krishna, senior VPs at IC, hurriedly got there. They had been woken up in the middle of the night by their CEO, four hours after their star analyst had met with an accident. The big project hadn't even started and something had already gone wrong.

Nothing new about that in the consulting world. Only, this time the client was the Zorawar Group. With reputation, pride and millions at stake, there was absolutely no room for error.

The Zorawar Group of industries was arguably one of India's largest conglomerates. Iron, steel, mobile phones, wind energy, housing, cars, ghee, toothpaste ... you name it and they made it. Set up in the beginning of the twentieth century by an enterprising twenty-eight-year-old, Purohit Madhav Zorawar, the group now operated in fifty-eight countries worldwide and had a reported turnover of one hundred and twenty billion dollars.

The Zorawar Group was also India Consulting's biggest and newest client, the shiniest new logo IC had acquired in a long time. The deal had made business headlines and garnered tremendous media attention. However, the honchos at IC knew that many trade pundits were avidly waiting for an epic failure, for IC to fall flat on its face.

'That email detailing the team requirement was from Madhav's executive assistant, wasn't it?' said Sumit.

Mohit sat up a little straighter and cleared his throat. Madhav's mere name carried power.

Madhav. Madhav Jai Singh Zorawar. The great-grandson of the legendary Purohit Madhav Zorawar bore an uncanny resemblance to his famous ancestor, much to the delight of the media. The two men, born over a century apart, had the same distinguished air, sharp Grecian nose and intelligent forehead. More strikingly, Madhav had, in what could only be called a genetic lottery, inherited from his most famous ancestor a dark complexion that pretty much set his grey eyes on fire. He had only to glance lazily into a camera for it to become the cover shot of a high-end magazine.

'We did briefly consider another girl for the project, didn't we?' Mohit said, steering the meeting to the issue at hand.

'Yes ...' said Sumit, chewing his lips. 'Bindiya Saran.'

'Ah, the girl with the long hair,' Mohit mumbled to himself.

Sumit nodded. Bindiya's hair which cascaded to her waist in a inky-black sheet was the first thing anyone would notice about her.

'Clever girl, good-natured and very easy to get along with, but there is a big problem.'

'Which is?'

'I get the feeling that everything is one big joke for her and she is ... um, not dependable. Brilliant in one project and mind-numbingly lazy in the next.'

'Wasn't she the analyst on that ridiculous project with the aeronautical company?' Mohit asked.

7

Sumit nodded. 'It was supposed to be a weak project. Bad company, poorly defined success factors and unpleasant people. But she turned it around well, I must say,' he said. 'However, that is just one case. She works smart, not hard. Sometimes that works and sometimes it backfires. The Zorawar Group project needs someone who will work hard *and* smart.'

'Her profile?'

Sumit said, 'Bindiya is twenty-eight, from IIM Calcutta, been with IC for two years now, has a reputation for being careless. I don't think she is fit for this project.'

'But is she the only analyst available at the moment?'

Nodding, Sumit said, 'For Zorawar we can easily pull a more suitable candidate out of the project he or she is already assigned to. We can't send Bindiya.'

'I disagree. She has a good vibe about her.'

'And of what use will a good vibe be in front of the likes of Madhav and that horrendous man who works for him ... Samar? Clever, professional and extremely thick skinned – that's the person we are looking for.'

Mohit breathed in deeply, fully cognizant of how their decision could potentially change the career path of the person chosen for the project.

'Are you still thinking of going with Bindiya?' Sumit asked, horrified. 'This is ridiculous, Mohit, absolutely ridiculous. Your choice is pretty much a recipe for disaster.'

Bindiya. Something, Mohit wasn't quite sure what, told him she would be the right choice.

'My choice is Bindiya,' said Mohit with a finality in his voice that Sumit knew only too well.

'*My* choice is certainly not Bindiya,' Sumit said. 'I have no doubt about it.'

Mohit looked at Sumit and his face broke into a smile as memories more than a decade old came rushing back.

'Do you remember the last time we reached such an impasse?'

Sumit smiled in spite of himself. Of course he did. 'Yes. At IIM Ahmedabad. Both of us wanted to ask Sheetal out,' said Sumit, talking about his wife of twelve years.

'And do you remember how we resolved the rather difficult matter?'

Sumit laughed and pulled out a coin from his wallet. 'So we toss?' he asked a little incredulously.

Mohit shrugged his shoulders. 'We both have our own reasons for our choices. Why not let destiny decide?'

'Last time we did this, you lost,' said Sumit, looking meaningfully at his best friend.

'Let's let destiny decide,' said Mohit, smiling.

'Heads for pulling a star analyst from another project and tails for Bindiya.'

'Good with me,' said Mohit.

Sumit tossed the coin.

Meanwhile, Bindiya Saran was in the middle of a heated discussion with her manager over her end-of-the-year rating, blissfully unaware of how a coin flipped and already in mid-air was about to transform her life.

2

'Bindiya Saran!'
'Aditya Joshi!'
'Shut up, Bee!'

'You shut up, Adi.'

'I am very serious, Bindiya,' said Aditya, fingering his glorious new moustache in a feeble attempt to assert authority. Only, no authority ever really worked on the madcap girl sitting in front of him.

'I have funny hair on my upper lip,' said Bindiya in a fake low baritone, mocking Aditya's voice and expression.

For a moment Aditya worried he would break into a laugh but managed to keep a straight face. 'We are not doing this,' he reiterated.

'Maybe you are not doing this. I certainly am,' said Bindiya with a wide grin on her face. She then beckoned the waiter towards their table.

Bindiya Saran and Aditya Joshi. Friends since forever.

The waiter, a serious-looking chap in his twenties, oblivious of what the immediate future held in store for him, now walked up to them.

'Hello,' said Bindiya in her serious, professional voice. Aditya already had his head in his hands and was looking away in a feeble attempt to dissociate himself from Bindiya's madness.

'Hello, ma'am,' said the waiter positioning his pen against the little notepad he carried. 'Are you ready with your order?'

Bindiya nodded and looked intently at the menu. 'Could I get one plate of idli, please?' she said in a matter-of-fact voice after a few seconds.

The waiter cast a meaningful look at the Thai menu in Bindiya's hands and said in the politest voice he could muster, 'Sorry, ma'am, we don't serve idlis.'

'Oh,' Adi heard Bindiya say in a disappointed voice. He sneaked a look at Bindiya's expression and shook his head. Hers had to be the most misleadingly innocent face in the whole wide world.

Bindiya was dressed in office formals, a simple grey shift dress and matching grey heels. Rimless glasses camouflaged large, expressive eyes and rested on a tiny nose that had caused its owner great consternation over the years. Swishing her hair, tied in an elegant fishtail, to one side, Bindiya was now studied the menu to reconsider her meal options.

'I so wanted to eat idli with coconut chutney,' Bindiya said, pouting at the waiter who stared at her in bemusement.

Aditya now let his eyes roam free over Bindiya's face, an indulgence he rarely allowed himself. He traced the intelligent curve of her dark eyebrows and the small pink mouth that moved as she mumbled to herself. Adi realized with a start that he was smiling his widest. But then Bindiya's face always filled his heart with joy; not just because to him it was the most beautiful in the world, but also because it reflected her soul which Adi knew to be gentle, kind and pure – even though her sense of humour could be wicked.

'Okay then,' said Bindiya, shutting the menu with a resigned air, 'I will have a medhu vada. Fine?'

'Ma'am?' the waiter bleated weakly.

'Yes?' said Bindiya, raising her eyebrows. 'Please make sure the sambar is steaming hot. I don't like it cold. Or warm. It should be steaming hot.'

'Er ... ma'am ...'

'Yes?'

'We do not have vada!' said the waiter in a faltering voice.

'No vada?' she asked, horrified. 'Isn't this a Thai restaurant?'

'Yes, it is. That is the whole point ...' the waiter tried.

'Do you know how many Thai people eat vada? Open up Google and I will show you,' Bindiya thundered.

Aditya shook his head, a giggle about to burst forth.

They had been banned from four different restaurants

thanks to Bindiya's great love for torturing unsuspecting waiters. Not long ago, as a waiter walked towards them with a tray laden with food, Bindiya had pointed a finger in his direction and shrieked, 'Oh my god, your fly is open!' Let us not go into what happened immediately afterwards. In short, the manager had turned red with anger and Bindiya had laughed for a good ten minutes before calming down.

Another time, she had insisted on paying the bill with Monopoly money. Once, she had a long conversation with the waiter pretending she knew him from school. And yet another time, she had insisted on calling a male waiter 'Rukamani Aunty'.

'Pad thai, for two,' said Aditya quickly before matters got out of hand.

The waiter looked gratefully at Aditya and scurried away before the mad girl spoke to him again.

'You spoiled it!' hissed Bindiya, leaning towards Aditya.

'Bee, you're impossible.'

Bindiya was mostly crazy but her craziness was interspersed with moments when she could be so sweet that his heart oscillated between sheer horror at her antics and immense fondness for a girl he had known all his life. However, of late, he often found himself worrying about her.

'And how is our man, the monster Rehan?' he asked, trying to keep the edge out of his voice.

Bindiya's face darkened with worry even before Adi finished his sentence.

'And what has upset him now?' Adi asked, all too familiar with what typically went on between his best friend and her boyfriend.

'Same old. Old same,' said Bindiya, shaking her head. 'We went out to this club where, apparently, I said something that both offended and embarrassed Rehan. I don't even remember saying anything that could have upset him so much and he is too angry to repeat it, so it is all fairly crazy—'

'Bindiya,' said Aditya, gently cutting in.

Bindiya laughed nervously and fingered a loose strand of her long hair. Aditya tried hard not to stare at the small scar running across her thumb. The sight of it made him see red. Bindiya had never told him how she got that scar, but he knew. Of course he knew.

'It's okay, Aditya, it's okay … I do sometimes do stupid things. I try to be all sensible and wise but …'

Adi looked on helplessly. Though he could not quite put a finger on the reason, Adi had hated Rehan from the very first time Bindiya got them to meet and, maybe, Adi thought, Rehan felt the same way about him. Over time, Adi had seen Rehan's behaviour towards Bindiya go from bad to worse, which left him fuming. For a couple of months, Bindiya and Adi had argued many times over Rehan, and each time they argued, Bindiya defended Rehan and that further angered Adi. How could she not see what Rehan was doing to her, Adi had often wondered. Now an unspoken truce about the matter existed between the two friends, both trying to stay away from the topic as much as possible.

As if on cue, Bindiya's phone buzzed. Aditya watched her as she listlessly read the text.

'What's wrong, Bee?' he asked when he saw her face fall after reading the message.

Silently Bindiya handed her phone to Aditya.

It was a text from Rehan. 'Bindiya, I called you thrice and you did not answer, just messaged me to say that you are busy. And now I see your check in on Facebook. You have time to eat Thai with Aditya but no time to return my call?

13

Please don't speak to me any more. I just can't put up with this nonsense.'

Aditya let out a deep breath. He looked at Bindiya and found no trace of either the smile or the cheeky glint that had her face aglow a few minutes back. She looked tired and stressed.

'So he was already angry with me. And before I could make up for the last time, he is angry again!' she groaned. 'Does that even make sense?'

Dump that jerk, you silly girl.

'He is a monster,' Adi stated in a flat voice. 'I don't get what you see in him.'

'He is not that bad, Adi, trust me ...' she said, shaking her head and putting her hand on top of Aditya's.

'Bee, has he ...' Adi hesitated. 'Has he ever ... I mean, been physically ... um, I mean, has he ever hit you?'

'Of course not!' Bindiya exclaimed. 'Why would you even think that?'

Aditya stared at Bindiya, but then, just when Adi was beginning to wonder if he had been all wrong about Rehan, she lowered her eyes. She stared at her food for a few minutes and when she looked up, the familiar smile was back on.

Aditya looked at his best friend, his heart sinking with dread and sadness. *You can fool the entire world with your smile and your lies, Bindiya Saran, but not me. Certainly not me.*

3

'Rehan, I said I'm sorry. What more do you want me to do?' Bindiya pleaded into the phone, juggling coffee and files.

She had already spent about twenty minutes apologizing to Rehan, first for having said whatever it was she had said and then for not having spoken to him the night before.

'So then it is my fault?' came Rehan's voice, low and dangerously angry. Even on the phone, the change in tone made Bindiya flinch, her stomach hollowing as it did each time Rehan got angry. Bindiya hated this moment – the moment when fear began to take over – with all her heart.

'So now you don't have time for me?' Rehan thundered.

'No, no,' Bindiya said hurriedly. ' I do … I do … I have time now …'

Time. Time. Was not she scheduled to be somewhere? What was the time now? Nine a.m. Oh no! OH NO! NO!

'Actually, Rehan … I really … um, I need to go … I have a meeting with Mohit …' Ouch.

Silence.

'I am sorry, Rehan, I am really sorry, I'll get back as soon as possible,' she pleaded, now ready to cry, feeling guilty, helpless, and angry with herself. Though she couldn't quite see it now, she was sure there was a funny side to the situation as well. After all, it must be rare to be apologizing for not one, not two, but three things at the same time?

Bindiya stared dismally at the phone in her hands and shook her head. A meeting reminder popped up.

Shit! Already two minutes late.

She ran across the office floor, patting her black trousers and straightening her powder-pink button-up shirt, her stilettos clicking noisily against the floor. She almost crashed into the meeting room door. Barely managing to control the momentum, she steadied herself and, with one final pat on her hair, she knocked on the door and entered the room.

Mohit was there, as expected, waiting for her, but he was

not the only person in the room. Sumit, another senior VP, and Jack Coster, MD, were also there.

What's going on? Are they going to fire me? What have I done now? Do I need to say sorry for something?

'You are two minutes late,' said Jack in his thick Chennai accent.

'I'm sorry, sir, client issues that ... that I couldn't put off. I'm sorry,' said Bindiya and then groaned mentally. Another sorry? No, not one but two sorrys in one sentence? Was the universe having a laugh at her expense?

'Have a seat, Bindiya,' said Sumit in a kind voice that Bindiya was instantly grateful for. 'You do seem a little out of breath.'

Bindiya gulped and sat down. *Why was Jack Coster present for this meeting?*

16

Jack looked intently at the pretty girl with long hair who sat a little nervously in front of him. A cloud of eccentricity seemed to hover around her head, making her instantly likeable. She looked intelligent and her mouth looked ready to break into a smile any time now. The eyes, he noted before hurriedly looking away, were trying to not dance with cheeky delight. Jack finally got what Mohit had been telling him about the girl all along.

'Are you aware of the Zorawar Group project, Bindiya?' he asked professionally.

Every bloody conversation in the company had to begin and end with the Zorawar Group these days, Bindiya thought to herself. IC really needed to get over the Zorawar Group.

'I do, Jack,' she said in what she hoped was an Amitabh Bachchan-ish baritone.

'Great, then you must be aware of the accident?'

'Yes, I am. It is very unfortunate,' she said, now ditching the

Amitabh Bachchan voice and moving onto what she hoped was a fairly legit impersonation of Hema Malini's.

'The team has recommended your name as the replacement and I wanted to ask you if you would be interested.'

'Aah,' said Bindiya, mighty pleased with how well the Hema Malini lilt was coming along. *What, wait, what did Jack just say?* 'I am sorry, could you please repeat that?'

'Would you like to be part of the team assigned to the Zorawar Group project?' Jack repeated.

What? What? Are you mad? 'It's a compliment to be considered for the role, Jack,' Bindiya heard herself say in a cool, collected voice.

'Would you be interested, Bindiya? It'll be a very difficult project and we have reason to believe that you could be rubbing shoulders with Madhav Zorawar and Samar Chauhan. There cannot be any slippage in the quality or timeliness of work.'

Who is this Samar Chauhan? Bindiya reached out for the glass of water in front of her and took a big gulp.

Jack continued. 'This project will erase an entire year from your life. Your day will begin and end with work. It will also, of course, be the biggest opportunity of your career.'

Bindiya stared at Jack, unblinking. In her hand was her mobile phone that contained messages from Rehan. In one of them Rehan had called her 'a sad joke of a girl' and in another 'a good-for-nothing incompetent moron'. Many others that contained more colourful language, she had deleted. And in front of her was Jack, MD, IC Limited, asking her if she would like to be part of the largest project at IC. Surely that was because he considered her worthy of such an important role? Bindiya sat up a little bit straighter but then her shoulders sagged. Rehan knew her well; what if he was right and she was not good enough to be part of this?

17

'Bindiya?'

Words from her mother rang through her head: you need to surround yourself with people who see potential in you even when you cannot. Bindiya had done the opposite and knew she was operating on zero confidence as a result. The thought made her see red. She needed to prove things.

'I will take it up, Jack.'

'Are you sure?' asked Sumit.

'Yes, sir, I am sure,' Bindiya heard herself answer.

She'd had enough of being told she was not good enough. She would prove Rehan wrong. She *had* to prove Rehan wrong.

4

Before going home that night for the celebratory gajjar ka halwa that awaited her, Bindiya met Rehan for a quick drink. Tall, lean and intelligent-looking, he could easily be categorized as 'attractive'. Her batch mate from IIM-C, Rehan, twenty-nine, was quickly working his way up in a reputed banking firm. Bindiya spent the first ten minutes saying sorry for the various things she was expected to apologize for; only then, mollified, did Rehan pull her into a hug.

Bindiya nestled in with a satisfied sigh.

Bindiya hated Rehan's hugs but she desperately needed them. She knew that the hug would not last long enough, would not be warm enough and would not make her feel wanted enough. Yet there he was holding her and that was all that mattered. Sometimes, she wanted his hugs to mean more. They never did. And Bindiya had taught herself to live with it.

There was a side to Rehan that terrified Bindiya; he could be short-tempered, pushy and unreasonable. But then, she argued with herself, there was a lot that was good about Rehan; he came from a very respectable family, he could be or at least used to be funny, and he had chosen her over a couple of other girls who had been desperate to go out with him. Most importantly, however, he had not abandoned her even after coming to know her full family history. Rehan had anger-management issues, there was no doubt about it, but he could also be incredibly sweet when he wanted. And then, as they say, no man is perfect. Bindiya could leave Rehan for another man, but then what was the guarantee that the new guy would not have other bigger, darker problems? And Rehan had stayed by her side when others would not have looked at her again. Was there anyone else who would want to be with her? Anyone half as good as Rehan?

Bindiya shuddered at the thought of being alone; she had seen at close quarters how loneliness could slowly but steadily destroy a person's soul.

19

A few drinks down, and Rehan began to kiss Bindiya's neck as he murmured congratulations. They were in full view of other guests and Bindiya felt colour rise in her cheeks.

'Um, that man there, he's watching us, Rehan,' said Bindiya hesitatingly, gently pushing Rehan away. Careful not to push too hard. *Can't make him mad again.*

'Can't I even kiss you?' said Rehan. He was still smiling, but Bindiya could see the coldness creep into his eyes. And the icy edge in his voice – most people would not have even noticed it – sent chills down her spine.

'No, no, it's fine,' she said hurriedly, mentally thwacking herself.

A few minutes later, Rehan got up and pulled Bindiya into a dark corner. 'Okay now? Am I allowed to kiss you here?' he asked, smiling.

Bindiya smiled back and Rehan wrapped his arms around her. 'Yes. Thank you.'

She looked into his eyes, searching hard, looking for *something*. While she did not quite know what the 'something' was, she knew it was as soft and earnest and beautiful as a full moon on a clear night. She also knew that she was looking in vain; Rehan's eyes were too full of lust to have room for anything else. Men and women, they will always want different things even out of a kiss, Bindiya said to herself as Rehan's mouth found hers.

❀

Once she was home and the madness that can only prevail in a household that comprised of her mother Sunaina and sister Urvashi had subsided, Bindiya turned in for the night. With Urvi holding her tight around the waist, Bindiya snuggled in her bed, and before she settled in for the night, took out her phone and composed an email.

Daddy dearest,

Wait till you hear the latest from my end. I am on the Zorawar Group project! *whoop whoop* I am so excited and I know how proud of me this will make you! I love you so much.

Love,
Bindiya

She stared at the email and tried to imagine how it would feel to actually have someone she could send such an email to. Someone real. Someone who would read the email, smile and send her an equally warm reply.

Once in a while, Bindiya allowed herself the luxury of missing him. And like every other time she did that, tonight too, soon enough, she began to feel like a traitor. Before she knew it, helpless tears had begun to stream down her face. How much pain could she bear? How much more?

'Bee Didi, are you crying?' Bindiya was brought back into the present by Urvi's timid little voice.

'No, you silly girl, I'm not crying,' she said, turning over to face her sister, hastily wiping her eyes.

A warm hand reached out and felt her eyes and cheeks. 'Your eyes are wet. And your cheeks.'

'That's because I am sleepy,' said Bindiya. 'Now, silly girlie, roll over and sleep. You have to go to college tomorrow.'

As she patted Urvi back to sleep, Bindiya heaved a deep sigh and deleted the email. There was no one to send that email to. That person did not exist. Then she hugged Urvi tight and fell into a fitful sleep, dreaming through the night of little girls and their fathers.

21

❋

A team of five consultants had been assigned to the Zorawar Group project including Atul Mahajan and Gopi Krishnan. The next few days were intense, as the team tried to train Bindiya in two weeks for a project that needed at least five weeks of training. As file after file on the project landed in her inbox, Bindiya tried her best to wrap her head around it all.

Feeling quite unprepared, Bindiya found herself saying a little prayer before she went to bed the night before the project was to start. If she had an inkling of what lay ahead, she would have said a much longer prayer.

5

It was the IC team's first day at the Zorawar Group, and Bindiya had just finished the induction session with the four-member strong HR panel. Even the Zorawar Group was taking this project seriously, she thought to herself, sitting a little straighter and swishing her plait to one side, feeling like she had already conquered the world.

'The project hasn't even started,' a little voice said in her head. 'Everyone is talking about how busy work days will soon get.'

'Ugh,' replied another voice inside her head. 'I'll finish my bits quickly and be out on time every single day. You just wait and watch.'

And Bindiya could not help but smile.

'Any questions, Bindiya?' asked the HR head, Manvi, closing the file in front of her. Manvi had taken all the IC people through the induction one by one, and Bindiya's session had, by far, been the least painful. Manvi could not, however, rid herself of the nagging suspicion that Bindiya had not heard a single word.

'Yes!'

'Go on?' Manvi said, pushing her spectacles up her nose. Manvi liked it when people asked questions she knew answers to.

'Er ... I was just wondering ...' Bindiya began a little hesitatingly.

'Yeah?' Manvi wondered what Bindiya was going to ask for. Money? Permanent role? Work for the VPs only?

'Which floor is the cafeteria on, please?' Bindiya asked brightly.

A few minutes later Bindiya found herself fervently hoping that she was indeed on her way to the cafeteria and not heading towards some CxO level meeting room. Manvi had seemed disgruntled as she gave directions and Bindiya could not quite understand why. The cafeteria was after all the hub of three very important aspects of office life – food, gossip and friends. It was a place Bindiya hoped she would be spending a lot of time in.

Bindiya knew that the Zorawar Group HQ was spread across twenty-five floors. Each floor had a distinct flavour to it and this one was decidedly more formal than the others she had seen. The décor was a subtle beige. Well-dressed people moved around with sombre faces and spoke in hushed voices. Bindiya spotted a peon and decided that he could help her with the directions.

She was about to speak out when she saw him. Or rather the flurry that surrounded him. Bindiya stared at the familiar-looking and strikingly handsome man for a few seconds before she realized who he was.

'Madhav sir,' called out someone from the crowd that trailed around him, confirming her guess.

'Yes, Amar?' Madhav now focused his grey eyes on the man who had called his name.

'Who will take the decision on the investment in Indonesia, sir?'

'Samar,' Madhav replied promptly. Bindiya could barely take her eyes off the handsome, stylish man she had read about only in newspapers. He was, if anything, better looking in person!

'Um, sir … you know, Samar sir … er …'

'Why are you all so scared of Samar?' asked Madhav,

laughing, the sides of his eyes crinkling easily, in a way that told Bindiya his face was used to smiling.

'And, sir,' someone else said, 'that CNBC interview we talked about, we really need you and Samar on it … it's going to be telecast across Asia.'

'I don't think Samar will agree, but I'll try my best to bring him along.'

'Can I take this as confirmation?' the same man persisted.

'I'll be there, can't say the same for Samar,' said Madhav, continuing to walk briskly.

'And Madhav sir, the aeronautics project meeting – are you going to chair that?' someone else shouted.

'No baba, not at all. We don't want to lose out on things before we even start!' Madhav said good-naturedly. 'Samar has a better understanding of all things related to aeronautics, I think he'll be leading that once he returns from America tonight.'

And with that, just as he had appeared, Madhav disappeared into a meeting room, taking with him the hazy cloud of people clinging on to each word he said.

Bindiya found herself puzzling over the Madhav Zorawar she had observed in these few minutes. He should have been very intimidating but he had seemed extremely approachable. Easy smile, good eye contact, a few light-hearted comments … Madhav was instantly likeable.

She shook her head, refocusing her mind on the rather pressing matter at hand – the cafeteria! And who was this Winter-summer, she mused to herself, allowing herself a little giggle at the weather-influenced name of the gentleman Madhav had repeatedly referred to.

❋

'Not Samar, Bindiya, Satan. Satan Chauhan,' said Madhulika, her voice bearing the true ring of a warning, her eyes large with trepidation.

Madhulika Banerjee was the lead accountant, and sat on the same floor as the IC group team. A rather uneventful week had passed by and Bindiya had utilized the time to make some friends.

Bindiya had just recounted her little encounter with Madhav from a week back to Madhulika.

'Satan Chauhan?' Bindiya giggled. 'Are you sure?'

'That man, Bindiya, can make you cry in a matter of seconds.'

'Really?'

Madhulika took a deep breath. 'I don't know how two people as different as Madhav and Samar can be such great friends. Madhav is super cool, really, kind and always smiling. Satan ... ugh ... he is the devil incarnate. You make one mistake, one small, tiny mistake, and he'll pounce on it even before you send your file to him. He'll then take some pliers and twist your pride till you are reduced to the smallest you have ever been.'

It dawned upon Bindiya that Madhulika was probably speaking from first-hand experience and she decided against asking probing questions.

'I hate that man, Bindiya,' said Madhulika, shaking her head, her face red now.

'You do?' Bindiya asked. 'Hate is a strong word.'

'I hate him and I'm petrified of him!'

'Oh my god, I don't like the sound of this, Madhu,' Bindiya said.

'Everyone is scared of him, Bindiya. Stay as far away from him as humanly possible,' Madhulika warned again.

25

'Oh yes, I will, of course. Why would I ever have anything to do with Satan?'

Why would I ever have anything to do with Satan?

6

Bindiya chased a runaway mushroom on her plate.

'And,' said Ankit from the Zorawar Group sales team, 'Satan is at it again!'

A couple of heads turned towards him instantly. Satan-bashing Bindiya had realized quickly, was something of an official pastime at the Zorawar Group. And Samar certainly did not shy away from providing fodder.

'He fired two people last night.'

'Are you kidding me?' someone asked in a suitably horrified voice.

'One after the other, in the same meeting.'

'Oh god!'

'Well, I heard that one of them had been repeatedly making mistakes, and Satan had, in all fairness, given him multiple warnings.'

Bindiya noted how a couple of people shook their heads in disagreement.

'Shame he's such a horror,' Arohi from HR said, smiling a mischievous smile.

'Why?' asked Bindiya.

'He's not bad looking, you know,' she said, winking. A couple of men groaned.

'He's not?' Bindiya said, surprised.

'You haven't seen him yet?' Arohi asked. The young man sitting next to her rolled his eyes.

Bindiya shook her head.

'Well ... just ignore these men, Bindiya,' Arohi whispered conspiratorially to her. 'They are just jealous of Satan. I think he's very good looking, not in the conventional way, I guess, but in an intelligent, intense way ... you know the sort who doesn't look at you but through you in one quick glance, leaving you barely able to breathe.'

Bindiya shrugged her shoulders.

'Arrey ... the sort who sits in a dark room, making cigarette swirls and thinking about poetry.'

'What?' Bindiya was laughing. 'That hardly sounds like the head of a conglomerate.'

'Only, he's not thinking of poetry but possibly planning the cold-blooded murder of another company daring to stand in the way of the Zorawar Group. Which is why,' continued Arohi, 'these guys are partially right. Satan is best admired from a distance – he does not bark, he just bites.'

Bindiya stared at Arohi.

'And that makes him even sexier!' Arohi said, looking so eager that Bindiya had to laugh again.

'That is one bad crush, Arohi,' Bindiya said.

'And trust me, I'm not the only one,' Arohi said, winking again.

News about the mysterious Satan came to Bindiya from Madhulika and Arohi at regular intervals. Samar had screamed at the regional head of strategy who reportedly fled the meeting in tears. Samar had just helmed a win that no one had thought possible. Samar had spent three days in office without stepping out of the building even once. Samar had looked very droolworthy in his smart tux at the annual dinner.

'If you want to keep your smile intact, just watch him from

27

a distance. Have nothing do with him,' Arohi warned again and Bindiya laughed.

Why would she ever have anything to do with Satan Chauhan, she wondered idly.

Someone up there smiled ...

❋

Ten days into the project, the IC group found themselves invited to a drinks-and-dinner networking event hosted by the Zorawar Group M&A team. Though no one knew for sure about that day, Samar Chauhan was known to attend the M&A networking events and that was reason enough for high levels of excitement in the IC team. All of them seemed to be desperate for one chance to speak with and impress Satan. Bindiya, being Bindiya, could not have cared less.

And it was no surprise then that Bindiya, busy chatting with Madhulika at her desk, found herself smacking her head when she glanced at her watch; the event was to start at 7.30 and it was already 8 p.m.!

'Arrgghh! I am late!' she shrieked and ran off, leaving behind a very amused Madhulika.

The event was being held in the lush expanse of the company gardens. Moving at lightning speed, Bindiya took about ten minutes to slip into a purple shift dress she had brought along, touch up her make-up, and make a dash for the gardens in her stilettos.

The party was well underway when Bindiya reached but no one seemed to have missed her. The gardens had been lit beautifully with paper lanterns and she could smell the delicious kebabs as she forced herself to ignore the food and go join a group of suited men.

Hoping that no one could hear her stomach growl, Bindiya was craning her neck to look for a waiter with a food tray when she felt the whiff of powerful cologne hit her. Unknown to her, a man had appeared beside her, and everyone in their little circle seemed to have snapped into servile attention.

Bindiya glanced sideways at him. The unfamiliar man was standing there holding a glass of wine and smiling a smile that did not quite reach his eyes as others made their introductions. He looked confident – very confident. And he exuded power. The sort of power that comes from being fully cognizant of your position in society. A flawlessly stitched suit. A sharp nose. A determined-looking chin. And X-ray-like eyes that crackled with intelligence and an intensity that was difficult to ignore.

The eyes were now looking at her expectantly. Was she expected to introduce herself?

29

'Um, I am ...'

Bindiya saw the man's eyes wander to her ID badge which screamed in bold letters the name of her employer.

'Ah, IC group,' said the man in a sophisticated, slightly accented voice that reminded Bindiya vaguely of expensive wine.

'Yes,' Bindiya mumbled and tried to force a smile. She hated hobnobbing with the biggies and this man was certainly one of them.

'Could I have a word, please?' he said as if they knew each other and had been 'having words' often. 'About IC group.'

'With me?'

'Yes, please?'

What? Her? Was this man mad? However, there was something about the manner in which the man spoke that simply ruled out a 'no' from Bindiya.

'And allow me to offer you my jacket. I am sorry we don't seem to have made proper arrangements for the chilly evening,' he said in an icy-cool, stern voice. A few of the men nodded their heads in agreement.

What was this man saying? And doing? The evening was pleasantly warm, Bindiya thought indignantly, but before she could react, the man had taken off his jacket and firmly placed it around her shoulders. Bindiya was staring open-mouthed at him, vaguely aware of the soft, expensive fabric of the jacket around her, when he gently touched her elbow.

'A word in private, ma'am?' he asked with icy politeness.

Bindiya looked bewildered but, on autopilot and not quite sure of what was happening, she let him guide her through the throng of people towards the dimly lit edge of the garden. Many people nodded at the man, displaying the same servile behaviour that Bindiya had seen in her group. The man marched on unfazed, his king-like disregard for lesser mortals very evident and, to Bindiya, quite disorienting.

As they walked towards the huge tree that marked the edge of the garden, a terrible thought hit Bindiya. Senior VP (or whatever position this crazy man held here) at Zorawar Group takes advantage of dark garden to assault and rape IC employee – the headline danced in Bindiya's head, turning her throat dry.

'Where are we going?' she asked, her voice quavering when they were a few feet away from the tree. Bindiya knew in her bones, feeling surer with each passing second, that no good was going to come of this.

'The tree,' the man said, not bothering to glance in her direction.

'Why? Wh ...'

30

'Please hurry up. I don't have the entire evening,' he said in that cold, businesslike voice, almost as if he were doing her a favour by hustling her to this godforsaken part of the gardens.

'What?'

'Now,' said the man once they had reached the tree, 'give me my jacket.'

Oh god, it was happening. Was this man asking her to undress? Maybe he was one of the sadistic men she had read about who first wrapped their jackets around innocent girls and then ordered them to take them off, including their own clothes, fulfilling some weird fantasy. The sick, rich bastard.

'I'll scream now,' she said in a voice hoarse with fear, jabbing a shaking finger in the man's face, hoping against hope that the gesture made her appear less scared than she was. 'I swear I'll scream so loudly that everyone will come running. Don't you dare touch me ...'

'What?' the man asked irritably. 'Give me my jacket, go behind the tree and sort your dress.'

'What?'

Sharp, icy eyes stared at her with growing, ill-hidden impatience. 'Give me my jacket. Go behind the tree. Sort the zipper of your dress,' he said slowly, as if speaking to a dimwit.

Bindiya put a hand inside the back of the jacket to feel her dress and felt the earth shift beneath her feet. She was not zipped up! Her fancy purple dress was gaping wide open, leaving bits of her back and her bra band exposed The jacket, for the time being, covered her wardrobe malfunction.

'Oh god!' she said, mortified, feeling a deep blush rise up her cheeks.

'Hurry up, please?' he said, thrusting his hands in his pockets and turning around to give Bindiya some privacy.

Bindiya hurried behind the tree and zipped up her dress.

31

Once done, she paused to thud her head against the bark of the tree a couple of times and then walked out sheepishly.

'Let me walk you back to the guests,' said the man, taking the jacket that Bindiya silently offered to him.

As they moved closer to the crowd, the man beckoned a waiter. 'Get the lady some water,' he said and began to walk away without so much as a look in her direction.

Bindiya was still staring at his back when he turned around and said, 'It might just be a good idea to learn how to put on your clothes,' in a voice that dripped with sarcasm. His eyes bored into Bindiya's for that one brief moment before he vanished into the crowd that swallowed him greedily.

Obviously, all that Bindiya could think about that night, as she tossed and turned in bed, was this incident. And the stranger. However, she wasn't too sure whether it was gratitude or extreme outrage that she felt towards him. Neither could she decide whether he could be called handsome or not. Well, he was handsome, probably, though in a I-am-out-of-everyone's-league way, Bindiya finally decided. She idly wondered if she would like to bump into this striking man again. She didn't even know his name.

She shook her head as her eyes finally became heavy with sleep. 'No,' she mumbled as firmly as it is possible to right before one dozes off, 'I hope I don't set eyes on him ever again. His eyes were so cold ... and lonely ... and even though he seemed so powerful, why did his eyes look so empty? I don't want to have anything to do with him.'

❀

Two days after the garden party, Bindiya, not yet recovered from her embarrassment, was still avoiding all conversation about the event. Though, of course, it was impossible to not have heard that Samar Chauhan had apparently made a fleeting appearance at the dinner party. Gopi, the only one from the IC team who'd had the chance to have a brief chat with Satan, was now telling everyone, for the tenth time, about his nerve-racking conversation with Zorawar Group's second-in-command.

'And he said what?' Atul asked, incredulous.

'That he had no time for such nonsense,' said Gopi so sheepishly that Atul guffawed.

'So not a great first impression on the mighty Satan then?' Atul said and then shook his head. 'I really wonder why anyone would hire a man as obnoxious as him.'

It was then that a clear voice cut through the din of office gossip, reaching Bindiya who was standing in a far corner, sipping coffee. 'Excuse me, could someone please tell me where I can find Ms Saran?'

Bindiya froze. Who could be looking for her? And why the hell was this voice disturbingly familiar?

Atul looked around and turned paper-white when he saw the person at the door. It was Gopi who called out his name. 'S ... sir ... Samar sir!' he fumbled.

Bindiya sputtered her coffee in unadulterated delight. Had Samar just heard Atul call him Satan? Had that really, truly happened? This was the stuff that office legends were made of.

Bindiya craned her neck to have a look.

'Ms Saran?' the voice asked again, the tinge of irritation unmistakable.

And that was when, as she sauntered across the floor towards the voice, Bindiya overcame giddy delight at her colleague's faux pas and finally put two and two together. The

33

man at the door was Samar Chauhan. The man at the door was asking for her. That meant – and Bindiya's hands grew cold as realization dawned – the satanic Mr Chauhan was asking for her!

By the time she reached the door, Gopi and Atul were fawning around the statuesque man who stood with his back to Bindiya. Tall, lean and broad.

'Mr Chauhan?' said Bindiya in what she hoped was her most sophisticated voice. At the same time, she crossed her fingers and prayed she hadn't already done something to earn Samar's wrath.

The man turned around as if in slow motion and a pair of eyes drilled into her. Bindiya stilled in utter shock. For about one-millionth of a nanosecond, a vague look of surprise crossed over the man's face, the only indication that this was as much of a surprise for him as it was for Bindiya.

'Ms Saran?' the man asked and Bindiya nodded on autopilot.

'Mr Chauhan?' Bindiya asked again, uttering each syllable slowly and staring wide-eyed. Was he really Samar Chauhan?

A slight, professional nod. The next instant, instinctively, her hands flew to the back of her dress. Just to, you know, make sure. For that man, the man who had taken Bindiya to the tree two nights ago so that she could zip up her dress, the man Bindiya had hotly warned against touching her, the man who had caustically told Bindiya to learn how to dress herself, that man Bindiya had fervently hoped she would never see again, that man was standing in front of her. And he was Samar Chauhan.

The Samar Chauhan.

Bindiya found herself swallowing with tremendous difficulty.

'Bindiya, are you okay?' Gopi asked, looking first at the ash-grey face of his colleague and then at the expressionless face of Samar Chauhan.

'Yes, yes, of course,' Bindiya fumbled and then gripped her coffee mug with all her might.

'Ms Saran,' continued Samar, 'could I have a word please?'

Could I have a word please? Memories from two days back resurfaced. *Oh god, about what?*

'Y ... yes ... sure.'

'I am given to understand that you'll be working with me, as part of a smaller core team on a branch-off of the main project. As a resource, I need you to be entirely dedicated to that one project. I thought I would come over, introduce myself and ask you if you would be okay with working on my project.'

Bindiya stared at Samar.

'Ms Saran?'

Bindiya continued to stare.

'Ms Saran?'

'Bee!' Gopi hissed.

'Yes, yes,' Bindiya said, blinking rapidly, unable to get over the shock. 'Yes, yes.'

'Great. I'll send you further details on the project. Naina is my PA and you can get information about my diary from her.'

Bindiya nodded.

'Any questions?'

'Eh?' Bindiya asked.

'I guess not,' muttered Samar Chauhan with a slight shake of his head, then nodded at Gopi and Atul, turned around sharply and disappeared.

There was stunned silence in the cubicle for the few seconds needed to recover from what had just happened and then everyone started speaking at once.

'Do you think Samar heard us?'

'If he did, he didn't show it!'

'Of course he wouldn't show it.'

'Did you see the way he looks at things – like he's going to eat it all up?'

'He looks like a hawk!'

'Oh my god, Bindiya will be working on a project with Samar!' Gopi gasped dramatically.

'Bindiya, did you know this was going to happen? Did Jack say anything to you?'

Bindiya barely heard anything that the others said to one another and to her. Hers had been, in many ways, a not-so-happy life. Unexpected good things never happened to her. A project with the country head of the Zorawar Group had to be a good thing, right? With Samar at the helm, Bindiya did not feel so sure. She took a deep breath and tried to forget about the piercing stare that still sent shivers down her spine.

Why would I ever have anything to do with Satan?

7

Sunaina Saran sat at the dining table and tried hard to concentrate on the article she had to submit that night. As a freelance journalist in a world full of freelance journalists, she knew work was hard to come by. Yet she found it difficult to concentrate; every once in a while she would glance at the clock on the wall. With the country being so unsafe for women these days, being the mother of two girls was not easy. She breathed easy only when both girls were within sight. It was already 8 p.m. and neither had called to say she was on her way home.

Sunaina's face was lined, both with worry and laughter. Life had, she often reasoned with herself, been unkind and generous to her in equal measures. With time, she had taught herself to focus only on the kindnesses around her.

Kindness. Easily the most underrated virtue. It is so important to both be kind and be appreciative of kindness. Sunaina had taken great pains to teach her daughters that, even in this day and age, a bit of old-fashioned kindness could go a long way.

The quiet house made her mind wander to places it had not visited in a long time. It had been a long journey ... a long journey that had started with that one shattering revelation many years ago. It had taken her to the darkest, unhappiest place her mind had ever known. However, as she always said, now was all that mattered. It was far from perfect but it was also far from the worst it had been.

Sunaina wrote for a few minutes but memories from the past clouded her vision. Sometimes, we go through experiences that are so bitter that the taste, an unpleasant acidic taste, lingers on even after decades. Time, they say, is the best healer. Doctors, therapists, counsellors and psychiatrists had spent hours telling her that. She disagreed then and she disagreed now.

Time can dull the ache, it can blur the images in your head, it can probably even make you forgive. But it cannot undo what has happened. It cannot erase the scars. It cannot take back the tears. It cannot decimate the consequences.

God had given her many problems but he had also given her two pillars to lean on. Bindiya and Urvi, Sunaina's daughters. Urvi was little when it had all happened but Bindiya, unfortunately, was old enough to not only understand everything but also be a part of all that had transpired.

37

Sunaina shook her head at the memory. The only reason she would ever go back into that hellish time would be to shield Bindiya better. To envelop her in her arms and not let her see the things she had seen, not let her hear the things she had heard, and not let her feel the things she obviously must have felt.

Bindiya, my darling beautiful Bindiya, I am sorry ... forgive me if you can ...

'Mom!' someone yelled through the door.

An involuntary sigh of relief escaped from Sunaina. At least one of her daughters was home, safe and sound.

'Bindiya, is that you?'

Bindiya bounded in, though she looked tired from the long day at work. She was wearing formals, fitted navy blue trousers and a sleeveless white shirt with a Nehru collar. Her long plait swinging behind her, she looked tall on her high heels.

'Mom,' said Bindiya, shaking off her shoes and plonking herself down cross-legged on the table as was her habit. 'Would you like to work with someone everybody hates?'

'Hmm, maybe,' Sunaina replied.

'Why?'

'Because it takes a little bit of daring to be unpopular,' said Sunaina with a wink.

A week had passed since Samar Chauhan had presented himself to Bindiya. She had not seen him since and was very grateful for that. The more she asked around about Samar, the more she felt unsure about working for him, though there was precious little she could do about that. Naina, Samar's PA, had dutifully sent Bindiya file after file on the project, none of which Bindiya had bothered to even open. Madhulika had gasped dramatically when Bindiya had given her the news.

'By the way,' said Sunaina, interrupting her line of thought, 'Rehan called.'

'Why? Why didn't he call on my mobile? I told him I was going to be late at work.'

'I think he was calling me to check if I knew where you were.'

Bindiya said nothing. This was not unusual.

Sunaina stared at the retreating back of her eldest daughter and shook her head slowly, sadly. Rehan was educated, from a good family, and Bindiya seemed to like him. Yet Sunaina knew, without an iota of doubt, that Rehan was not the right person for Bindiya. Her heart collapsed sometimes at the way he spoke to her ... and yet Bindiya did not leave him. Sunaina knew that at some level their past was to blame for that. For daughters, fathers become role models and Bindiya had a shitty role model, Sunaina thought, trying hard, and failing, to keep the bitterness at bay.

8

Bindiya hurried along the shiny corridor, her heels not carrying her fast enough. She looked at her watch. Two minutes past ten. Not bad, she thought to herself, slowing down, the sense of urgency disappearing. She had made it in time after all – well, almost in time – for the 10 a.m. meeting.

Today was an important day. Important-ish. She had been invited to the kick-off meeting for the project. Nothing much was expected of her, she knew; all she had to do was show up, look interested, and not make a fool of herself. That, even she could manage.

Though the meeting was to take place in the meeting room

adjacent to Samar's office, Bindiya noted with some surprise that not a single soul lurked outside. Either the meeting had started or everyone was pathetically late, she thought, smiling to herself. She glanced at her watch again. Four minutes past ten. That was as good as 10 a.m.

Nonchalantly, Bindiya pushed open the heavy door to the meeting room – and then froze. About fifteen sombre-looking people sat around a large mahogany table, their eyes fixed in front of them. She spotted Samar Chauhan standing at the head of the table, speaking with a very serious expression on his face. Dressed in a light grey suit and a sparkling white shirt, he looked sharp, alert.

Too sharp? Too alert? And the electricity that seemed to charge the air around him? What was all that about? Handsome? No, not in the conventional way. Striking? Yes, in a very intimidating way.

Bindiya was staring at Samar, thinking these thoughts, when he spotted her. She hurriedly straightened up and smiled a small smile of acknowledgement. Samar's face did not change at all. Or did it? Did Bindiya spot a slight pursing of the lips? The ghost of a frown? The shadow of disapproval?

Bindiya gulped. Slide number thirteen of a presentation was displayed on a large LCD screen. *When had the meeting started?*

'I am sorry,' she mouthed sheepishly at Samar and looked around for a chair to sit in. Never again be late for Samar's meeting, she told herself firmly.

She was about to sit down when a cool voice cut across the room. 'I am sorry, Ms Saran, you are late, the meeting has already started.'

Many faces turned around to stare at her.

'I am sorry, Mr Chauhan,' Bindiya said and again began to

sit down, deeply and painfully aware of the fact that by now every eye was on her.

'Ms Saran, people are only welcome to join in before or till 10 a.m.,' Samar said, impatience lacing his voice.

Are you kidding me? Bindiya stood still, stunned, not ready to believe this was really happening.

'Could you leave the room, Ms Saran? I don't think I can make it any plainer than that.' He picked up a set of papers and turned to face the LCD screen again. For him the matter was closed.

For a moment, Bindiya stood there, rooted to the spot, unable to move. Was she back in school?

'Just go,' someone next to her hissed helpfully.

Too shocked to respond, Bindiya turned around and left without another word. Walking out of the meeting room, like a student punished by her teacher, she bit her lips, trying hard to stop herself from cyring.

'I hate him,' she mumbled to herself angrily, 'I hate him!'

That little incident was a portent of many things to come.

As days became weeks, Bindiya began to understand why Samar was disliked with such fervour. About a week after the first meeting, in another meeting, Bindiya found herself fighting a losing battle with eyes that refused to stay open. She had, after all, woken up at six to make sure she made it to the meeting at nine with half an hour to spare. And what was absolutely hilarious was that even then Bindiya had been the last person, save the great Mr Chauhan, to enter the meeting room.

'Ms Saran.' The cool, suave voice she had learnt to dread

41

swept aside the cobwebs of sleep in a hurry. Lithe, fit and reminiscent of a powerful eagle swooping down on helpless prey, Samar came close to her and stood still, hands arrogantly stuck in his pockets. A whiff of expensive-smelling cologne hit Bindiya. Why do all rich men smell a particular way?

'Y ... yes, yes, Samar?' she mumbled.

'Would you like to give the team a full description of the beta problem faced by the project?'

Bindiya gulped; she could only vaguely recall someone talking about some alpha-beta problem that had sounded all Greek to her. She stared blankly at Samar.

'You have no idea what I'm talking about, do you?' Samar said with a slight, elegant arch of his eyebrows.

'I ... I ... um ...'

'You may not know much about it, Ms Saran – it's only the biggest issue we are facing at the moment,' said Samar, his voice dripping with sarcasm.

'Um ... I –'

'Thank you, Ms Saran,' cut in Samar, leaving Bindiya crimson with embarrassment.

Yet again.

9

'Can you pick up my phone, Adi?' Bindiya said, concentrating on the road ahead.

'Sure,' Adi said and dutifully lunged towards the dashboard of Bindiya's red Maruti for the phone.

A message was blinking on the screen. In the few seconds that it took him to hand the phone to Bindiya, he had read the message.

'Shut up, you fucking bitch,' the message read. It was from Rehan.

Adi saw Bindiya briefly glance at the screen of the phone and her face redden.

'All okay, Bee?' Adi asked.

'Yes, Adi, everything is okay,' said Bindiya, smiling her widest at Adi.

☀

A fortnight later, Samar fired a young man from another project in full view of Bindiya and others, leaving her quite shaken. Bindiya felt sure that she was next. She worried and she stressed, she had nightmares about it, she spent nights tossing and turning and, with Rehan acting up again, days doing increasingly slipshod work. On the outside, however, Bindiya continued to grin and make jokes about Samar. She had to appear cool.

On one occasion, distracted by a particularly nasty email from Rehan, Bindiya sent across to Samar a shoddily done analysis. She got a reply in about twenty minutes; that was all the time that Samar took to receive, read through and highlight thirty-seven mistakes.

'Ms Saran,' read the last line of the succinct email, 'such work might be acceptable at IC but I will not entertain poor-quality submissions at any cost.'

Bindiya debated the pros and cons of faking illness to resign from the project. As her confidence dwindled, mistakes followed mistakes, and humiliation of some sort followed each one of those mistakes. First the project team, then the IC team, and very soon the entire office began to mumble about Bindiya's incompetence. Most of the people who had worked with Samar before expected another public firing.

43

'He loves picking on people, Bindiya, and has chosen you as his target. You'll just have to put up with it. He can be an arrogant prick!' someone said to Bindiya after Samar had publicly asked Bindiya if anyone had taught her to do additions when she was little. Or should he arrange for lessons? Zorawar Group, he had added sarcastically, would consider it charity and be happy to pay.

'Madhulika,' said Bindiya, digging into her salad, 'I am so petrified of Samar that my heart starts thudding with fear when I have a meeting with him.'

'Oh, you poor thing!'

'I hate Samar,' Bindiya stated angrily, chasing a piece of tomato with a fork.

'Oh, that's okay, babe. I do too. Everyone does.'

'Really? Everyone?'

'Of course! Who do you think would like such an obnoxious man?'

Fair point, well made.

❦

A month later, Samar made Bindiya redo the slides in a presentation eleven times, a record of sorts at Zorawar.

Kindness in words inspires confidence; for the more vulnerable amongst us, more so. The opposite also holds true; for the more vulnerable amongst us, more so. Each time Samar expressed dissatisfaction with her work, Bindiya felt herself withdraw further into a hard shell. Finally, close to tears, Bindiya called up Atul and asked him to take over. That night, Atul fired an email to Jack back at IC. Bindiya was probably not the best choice for the project, they both agreed.

Before he went to bed, Jack kick-started internal processes to take Bindiya off the project.

A week later, Bindiya found herself sitting at her desk, taking a moment to herself, struck by the shabbiness of the work she had submitted to Samar an hour back. The response from Samar had been curt. 'This is not a joke,' was all he had written in his email after which he forwarded the work to someone else.

As support from her colleagues from IC dwindled, Bindiya felt her self-esteem spiral downwards into a dark abyss. Sunaina and Aditya worried, questioned and prodded. All they got in response were angry tirades about Samar. She spoke of Samar non-stop, spewing venom at him. Samar was fast becoming an ogre she didn't want to even look at, yet she couldn't stop talking about him.

45

10

Even over the din, the clock sounded like a gong when it struck eleven. Though it was the middle of the week, the Boho Bar in Bandra was teeming with people, some already drunk, many others close to it. The music was getting louder and more unpleasant as the night progressed. Rehan and Bindiya were sitting in a dark corner catching up over the week.

'Bindiya, I've been thinking,' said Rehan, slipping a hand through hers.

'Yes?'

'I think it's time for us to take our relationship to the next level now,' he said, leaning in for a quick kiss.

Bindiya sat up straight, not quite believing her ears. A

string of butterflies woke up in her belly and began their little dance. Was Rehan asking her to marry him? Bindiya mentally kicked herself (and Mum and Adi) for always doubting Rehan's intentions.

'If you are joking, please stop!'

'Of course, I'm not, Bee.'

'I ... oh my god.'

'Bindiya,' said Rehan, pulling her close, 'we've been together for some time now. I think we can take the next step ... I mean if you are ready ... er ...'

'Yes, I agree, I agree. I feel ready!'

Oh my god. Is it really happening? Is he going to go down on one knee?

'You do?'

'Yes! I do,' she said, giggling.

'Oh,' said Rehan, looking relieved, 'I thought I would have some convincing to do.' Bindiya looked at Rehan's crooked smile with renewed fondness. 'When do you want to ... er ...' asked Rehan.

'I ... it's so sudden, how can we decide so quickly – surely you and I alone can't decide the dates?'

'Dates? What dates? Let's do it tonight?'

'Tonight?'

Really, this brand-new, commitment-friendly, impulsive Rehan was so much better than the older, perpetually angry one, thought Bindiya.

'Let's do it tonight! My place, I'll tell my flatmate to sleep somewhere else. We'll have the house to ourselves,' said Rehan, his eyes shining with excitement. 'Tell your mum you are staying over at some friend's place ...'

Wait, what?

'No,' she said. Bindiya was not against having sex. However, she knew that at this stage she would only be having sex with Rehan in the hope that he would somehow love her more in return. And that was so wrong. Surely it had to feel more, well, *right*?

'Bindiya, come on!' said Rehan, getting up and pulling Bindiya by her hand. His face shone with an eagerness that Bindiya now found nauseating.

'A no is a no, Rehan,' she said pushing away his hand.

'Come on? Don't tell me you are going to go all bharatiya nari now,' he said mockingly.

'I need to go,' she loudly. The bar was crowded and people now began to turn around and stare. Rehan, flushed with embarrassment, sat mute and turned his face away from Bindiya. She snatched her jacket, picked up her car keys and mobile and fled.

After a moment, Rehan hastily followed her. 'Bindiya,' he called out in the car park. A vague glimmer of hope raised its head in her heart. Rehan had come for her.

Bindiya paused and turned back, desperate to give him another chance.

'Come on!' Rehan said, pulling Bindiya into a hug. Ready to forgive and forget, she wrapped her arms around his neck, longing for the comfort of knowing that he loved her. She felt herself calm down a bit as Rehan cradled her, mumbling sweet nothings.

Bindiya was grateful for the dark car park; it was a special moment between them and the darkness provided much-needed privacy. All she needed to hear was that he loved her. That he wanted to marry her. That even though his mother would not approve of Bindiya because of family history, he would fight for her because he loved her.

Rehan and Bindiya stood still for a few minutes, arms

47

wrapped around each other and then, a few seconds later, she felt it. Rehan's cold hands creeping up inside her blouse.

'Rehan, no,' she said.

'Come on ...' he mumbled, his voice thick with desire.

'No!' she said, pulling away. Rehan's grip was like steel and, startled, Bindiya looked into his dark eyes.

'Let me go, Rehan,' she said as sternly as she could, warning signals going off in her head.

The next instant, a strong hand clamped over her mouth. Rehan's other hand was clutching the bare skin of her stomach, his fingers digging deep into her flesh and inching upwards.

'Shut up,' Rehan hissed into her ears. 'I'll do what I want to.'

Looking at Rehan, now fumbling with her breasts and grunting, Bindiya thought that with his wild eyes and flared nostrils, he looked more like an animal than a man.

'Your boyfriend is forcing himself on you,' a surprised voice in her head whispered, 'and you are letting it happen.'

When abused patience turns to anger, it is not just anger it morphs into, it becomes a force. And it was this force that Bindiya now felt surge through her body. She began to kick furiously and bit down hard on the hand over her mouth, making him scream in pain. Bindiya fumbled with her phone; Rehan saw that and released one hand for an instant to wrestle the phone out of her grip and throw it against the wall, where it broke into pieces. That one second was all that Bindiya needed. She kicked him in the groin hard enough for him to stumble and fall over the curb.

'You bastard!' she heard a banshee-like voice scream at Rehan and realized with surprise that it was coming from her. And without looking back, she ran, shaking and shivering, as fast as her legs would carry her, to the safety of her car.

Bindiya's cheeks were wet with tears by the time she got behind the wheel of her trusted Maruti. She drove fast, recklessly, occasionally wiping a fresh avalanche of tears with the back of her hand. At red lights, she would wrap her arms around herself, hug herself tight and rock herself to and fro, all in a desperate attempt to stop her body from shaking like a leaf in a storm.

A leaf in a storm – that was what Bindiya felt like. Like a fragile, pale leaf being battered around by one violent storm after the other. All she wanted was someone who could hold her tight, somewhere she could feel safe and something that could make the world less painful. All she needed was someone, just that one person, together with whom she could survive the storms.

As Bindiya rested her head on the steering wheel, she knew one thing without any doubt. She could not hold on for much longer. She just could not.

49

❋

'Bindiya, how was your day?' asked Sunaina, bleary-eyed but awake as Bindiya knew her paranoid mother would be, when she finally reached home close to midnight.

'It was great, Mum,' she said and bent low to give her mother a goodnight kiss. 'Sorry, I got late. There was a lot of work pending in office,' she added, shrugging her shoulders.

Sunaina nodded and readied herself for bed, smiling at her cheerful daughter. Bindiya walked towards her bedroom slowly, thankful that Mum had, yet again, not been able to see through the façade.

The night was long. And lonely. So very lonely.

Bindiya changed into her pyjamas and sat cross-legged

on the bed she shared with Urvi. Urvi's gentle breathing usually calmed Bindiya like only a favourite lullaby, sung by a voice more familiar than your own, can. But tonight it was a noise, a noise she wanted to get rid of. For a long time, Bindiya stared at her baby sister's face lit by the faint light seeping through the windows, searching in vain for the peace she usually found in the restful lashes curled against flushed cheeks. Urvi, ever since she came into their lives, armed with an adorable mop of curly hair and a lopsided grin, had been more Bindiya's baby than anyone else's.

Without warning, the tears started again. They came from nowhere and they came from everywhere. They came from years past, they came from the evening that had just gone by, they came from what she had been forced to become, they came from what the future held ... they came from sheer hopelessness.

Bindiya cried silently for fear of waking up Urvi. She cried bitterly for the little girl who never had a childhood, pitifully for the girl who had been humiliated tonight by a man she thought she loved. Bindiya cried. And she cried. And she cried till she could cry no more.

She woke up weak and bleary-eyed. Her body ached from being alone, from being heartbroken, from being continuously fearful.

She sat on her bed, legs crossed, and told herself to smile. Ordered herself to smile. The Bindiya that entered the dining room a few minutes later had a wide grin plastered on her face. No one should know anything. Not her sister. Certainly not her mum.

'A fresh day, baby,' said Sunaina, giving her eldest daughter a kiss.

For a second Bindiya thought she would tear up and she fought for control. 'A fresh day, Mum,' she said. 'Don't we all need one every once in a while?'

It was this thought that she kept in mind as she walked into her cubicle and opened her laptop. And it was then that she realized that another disaster had struck.

11

'You were supposed to send out the Excel file last night by eleven,' said Atul, his usually smiling face lined with worry.

Bindiya nodded absently, her mind wrapped up in events of the night before. From the pub she had driven straight to Bandstand, desperate to hear the calming sounds of waves crashing against the rocks. It was only when the shivering had subsided that she had made her way back home. She had spent the whole night awake, alone and fearful.

'And you did not,' Atul was saying.

'Did not what?' she asked.

'The file, Bee!'

And then it hit Bindiya and she gasped in horror, everything else now forgotten.

'The team, including Samar, tried calling you repeatedly but you were unreachable. After leaving about a dozen voice mails, and getting no response from you, three people decided to stay up the whole night and they had to work out the entire Excel sheet from scratch. They did three weeks' worth of work in a night.'

Bindiya's heart was now thumping loudly out of sheer fear.

51

'One of those three people,' continued Atul, trying his best to keep his voice even, 'was Samar Chauhan, who supervised the entire emergency operation.'

Now Bindiya looked up, aghast. 'Oh god, no!'

'Yes. And he wants to see you in his office. Now.'

'Atul, I am really sorry. I ... something happened last night ... and um, my phone ... I was very distracted. I'm so sorry.' Bindiya looked pleadingly at her senior.

'Bindiya, Samar is seething. He was ready to rip our contract apart last night and I had to use all my persuasion skills to beg him not to. You, your careless attitude and lack of discipline will be responsible for the utter failure of IC's largest and most important project.'

Bindiya sat down and covered her face with her hands. She had messed up the biggest opportunity of her life and let her company down.

'Samar is waiting for you,' Atul said in a gentler tone. Bindiya looked haggard and defeated, almost as if someone had sucked the life out of the poor girl, thought Atul, unaware of how close to the truth he was.

'I'll lose my job here?' she asked weakly.

'Bee,' Atul said out loud, 'I like you. I really want you to make this work but I don't ... um ...' He looked away.

Bindiya nodded and slowly walked out of her cubicle towards Samar's, her head hung low with despair and fatigue. There was little doubt that by the end of the day she would be jobless and that meant that her family was going to have to survive without the only steady source of income it had. How many months would her savings last? Would anyone hire her after this debacle at Zorawar?

It was the first time Samar had asked Bindiya to come inside his office and Bindiya stood at the door that led to the reception, fear of what the next few minutes had in store for her writ large on her face.

'Samar wanted to see me,' she said to Naina, Samar's PA.

'Ah.' Naina nodded. 'Ms Saran, this way please.' She ushered Bindiya into a huge and, for the moment, empty office. If the high granite ceilings were meant to intimidate, they did their job well, thought Bindiya ruefully to herself.

'Mr Chauhan spent the night in the office,' said Naina chattily before she left.

Bindiya sat down and looked around, nervously fiddling with her fingers.

She could not help but peep at Samar's desk. Workstations can be very revealing and, unsurprisingly, his desk was very neat. A photo frame occupied a corner and Bindiya wondered who Samar could possibly love. Someone must love Samar; just as Samar must really, truly love someone, she thought. Bindiya shook her head; it was impossible to even consider the possibility of Samar being a normal man capable of love.

And then Bindiya wondered what Samar would have done to Rehan had she meant anything to him. 'He would have killed Rehan with his bare hands,' a voice in her head answered without missing a beat. Of course, it was a completely mad thought – for in the real world the man was about to fire her! All the same, Bindiya, for the first time since the incident, felt oddly relieved. A bit safer.

She shook her head and, very curious now, she craned her neck to have a look at the photo in the frame. No, it wasn't a photo. It was a framed poem.

'Ms Saran,' the now familiar, haughty voice reached her ears, interrrupting her line of thought, 'I am sorry I kept you waiting.'

Bindiya said nothing, felt nothing. She half suspected

Samar was being sarcastic but she had no strength to give it too much thought.

Samar now appeared before her, striding in confidently, emanating power and strength, his hawk-like eyes studying her intently as she stood up. Grey suit, grey tie and a crisp white shirt. A Rolex. Sharp. Elegant. Sophisticated. Samar belonged to a world that was a far cry from hers.

Samar looked at the girl with tired eyes who stood awkwardly in front of him, fiddling with her spectacles. She looked different somehow, afraid and insecure, as if something terrible had happened, something bigger and more serious than a missing Excel sheet ... as if she needed someone to tell her that everything would be okay.

'Please sit down,' he said slowly, thinking hard.

'Thank you,' she said and sat down, already feeling teary. She tried hard to shush the noises from last night, but even now, with Samar and the possibility of being sacked looming over her, they refused to go away.

Neither of them spoke for the next few minutes during which Bindiya stared at her hands, deeply uncomfortable under Samar's watchful gaze.

'Ms Saran,' Samar said finally, 'you must know why you are here.'

Bindiya nodded.

'Your behaviour has been grossly unprofessional and hence unacceptable at the Zorawar Group. I believe you have been warned multiple times in the past.'

Bindiya bit her lip to stop the tears. No, not in front of Samar. I won't give him the satisfaction of seeing me reduced to tears, she told herself firmly.

He's going to say it now. He's going to fire me. Quick, say it before he says it.

'Samar ... sir ...' she began, looking up finally, 'I would like to quit the project.' *Quit this project and go away ... go somewhere far ... run away, hide, disappear from the world.*

A slight frown and a vaguely surprised look flitted across his face but disappeared the next instant.

Tick. Tock. Tick. Tock. The gentle hum of the grandfather clock was the only sound in the room.

'A little difficult, is it?' Samar said finally, his elegant voice bearing the unmistakable hint of mockery. When Bindiya did not respond, he said, 'Fine.'

'I'll submit my resignation from the project to IC HR. Jack will probably be in touch with you about a replacement,' Bindiya said.

Samar's eyes grew cold, reminding Bindiya of icicles. Colder than when he pointed out her mistakes, colder than when he reprimanded her for her carelessness. She had, she now realized, crossed some sort of a line she shouldn't have even wandered near.

Why do I know this? Why can I see his thoughts on his face? Why do I feel as if I know him?

'Thank you, Ms Saran,' Samar said abruptly. 'You may leave now. The Zorawar Group is no place for quitters.'

Bindiya was taken aback. Surely this was what he wanted? He had made it abundantly clear, more than once, how clearly he despised her. And hadn't he called her to his office to fire her?

Samar clicked open his laptop. He was done with her.

Bindiya got up and, with one final glance at the great Samar Chauhan, turned around to leave the office. That was it, she thought, her time at the Zorawar Group had come to an abrupt and humiliating end.

55

12

This is no place for quitters. I am the quitter. Am I a quitter?

Epiphany. So this is the thing about an epiphany – it hits you when you are lost, wandering across an empty field, unsure of where to go next; you could take a right or a left or just keep walking straight, there is no reason to choose one path over the other. But once an epiphany strikes you, it is as if a clear path emerges out of nowhere. In that split second you have direction.

Epiphanies can hit you in many ways and in the intriguing case of Bindiya Saran it took the shape of a harmless, framed poem. As she was leaving Samar's office, her eyes fell once again on the poem and she caught some snatches of the words. And, walking out of Samar's office, it hit her.

She knew the poem. She knew the words. It used to be her favourite poem a long time back ... in that other world when Daddy was with them.

> Success is failure turned inside out—
> The silver tint in the clouds of doubt,
> And you never can tell how close you are,
> It might be near when it seems afar;
> So stick to the fight when you're hardest hit—
> It's when things seem worst that you must not quit.
> Rest if you must, but don't you quit.

How often had she mumbled those words to reassure others – and herself? And how and why had she forgotten them all this while?

'Don't quit, Mummy, don't quit. Rest if you must, but please, please, I beg of you, don't quit.'

'I will not quit on you, Urvi, I promise I won't. Even if everyone else does, I won't.'

As memories and battles from years gone by came rushing back, something changed. Everything changed. Before she knew what was happening, Bindiya was already running down the corridor, back towards Samar's office.

'Wh ... Ms Saran,' stuttered Naina, surprised to see the girl rush back, hair flowing wildly behind her. 'Please wait here, you can't run inside like this.'

'I ... er ... left my mobile phone,' Bindiya lied.

'Sorry, ma'am, we'll get it for you ... I ... no ... no ... NO!'

Bindiya had kicked off her heels and made a mad dash for Samar's office. As she barged in, Naina followed hot on her heels.

The sudden commotion in his quiet, serene office made Samar delicately raise an eyebrow. A dishevelled-looking Bindiya Saran, her hair in a mess, stood panting, her hands clutching the head rest of the chair and, Samar noticed with mild surprise, her sandals. Behind her stood Naina, Samar's secretary, a stricken look on her face.

Samar's gaze was even and cool. 'Ms Saran.'

'Samar.'

'You are back, I see.'

'Yes sir, I am back. I ... er ... need to say something.'

'I am all ears,' said Samar, taking off his spectacles and placing them on the desk.

'Samar, I told her to stop ... I'll get security ...' Naina spluttered.

'Naina,' came Samar's calm voice, 'it's okay. I'm quite sure Ms Saran is not a security threat. Could you give us a moment, please?'

Naina cast a dirty look at Bindiya and walked out.

57

Once she was out of the office, Samar shifted his gaze to Bindiya. 'Ms Saran, would you like a seat?'

Bindiya sat down. And then immediately got up. 'No ... I can't sit!'

With the back of his forefinger, Samar gently caressed his forehead, as if delicately massaging a headache, something he did when he was thinking hard. 'And to what do I owe this visit?'

Oh god! Come on, Bindiya, you can say it. Samar won't eat you.

One look at his eagle-like eyes and Bindiya changed her mind. Got up, about-turned and made for the door. But no, she couldn't run away like this; she had to tell him. She forced herself to walk back to Samar's desk, painfully aware of his steady gaze.

Samar was sitting calmly, unmoving, intently watching Bindiya's antics.

Bindiya took a deep breath and said, 'Samar, I am not a quitter. I do not quit. I know I have been horrible and unprofessional and lazy and insolent and all those things but I am not a quitter. That is one thing I am not.'

Bindiya paused for breath. No reaction on Samar's face.

And the toughest bit was still to be said. 'Can you please give me one more chance?'

Samar said nothing, his eyes scanning and registering each expression that flitted across Bindiya's face.

'I promise I'll do my best. It may not be good enough for you, in which case fire me, but please, please give me another chance.'

Samar said nothing, simply continued to stare at the earnest-looking girl in front of him.

'A second chance?' Bindiya pleaded.

Silence.

'He's going to start shouting at me now,' Bindiya thought to herself, scrutinizing Samar's expressionless face.

Silence.

'Okay,' he said finally.

'Okay?'

'Yes, okay.'

'Are you sure?'

'You might want to disappear before I change my mind.'

Bindiya stood there, shocked. She wondered if she could give Samar a hug but prudently decided against it.

'I think I'm about to change my mind,' said Samar, the barest hint of a smile on his lips.

'No! Don't! I'm leaving!' Bindiya shrieked and ran out of the room.

Naina could only stare at the girl who darted out of Samar's office, sandals still in her hands, a wide grin plastered on her face.

59

13

You could argue that people do not change and I think you could be right. People do not change. Sometimes as they journey through life they unbecome who they have become and go back to being who they are meant to be.

And Bindiya now went back to being determined.

Dogged determination was something you would never associate with Bindiya Saran. For reasons known only to her, Bindiya generally tried her best to camouflage how hard-working she could be. She laughed and she joked. She pretended to be all cool – only she was not just those things. She cared. She cared deeply about many things a lot of people simply would not bother about. It was this dogged determination that got her the call from IIM-C and enabled mother and daughters to live together against all odds. And it was the same dogged determination that now resurfaced, for the first time ever at work. So far, at the Zorawar Group, Bindiya had tried her level best to get away with doing as little as she could, simply because in the past her half-hearted work had been more than sufficient. It had not at Zorawar. For all her faults, Bindiya was, if anything, someone who felt immense gratitude towards people who helped her. And Samar had helped her by giving her a second chance. She had to, just had to, do her best now.

For the entire month Bindiya did not leave office before 11 p.m.

She started with the emails. She read and reread them, then plodded through the reports, newspaper columns, presentations – anything and everything about the Zorawar Group and the project that she could lay her hands on.

And as the days became weeks, the change began to show.

About three weeks after the episode with Samar, Bindiya found herself again in his large office, this time with the team for a weekly meeting. In the interim there had been a lot of talk about why Bindiya had not been taken off the project despite what had happened. She overheard a private conversation between Atul and Gopi.

'When I told Jack what had happened,' said Atul, 'he was horrified. He said he had already begun the paperwork to take Bindiya off the project. The latest mistake meant he would have to call Samar Chauhan, apologize on her behalf and obviously bump her off the project immediately in a bid to save the contract.'

'Then?'

'And then, about twenty minutes later, he called me again, his tone completely transformed. His exact words were – "Zorawar Group wants her to continue and don't we all deserve a second chance?" Which really took me aback. And really, since when has Jack begun to believe in second chances?'

Bindiya knew it was not Jack who believed in second chances.

Sometimes, we expect certain people to help us; they don't. Promptly, we curse our fate and promise ourselves that we'll never trust again. And sometimes, we get help from people we never expected help from. And that presents the bigger problem – what do you do in response if a 'thank you' just does not cut it?

True, Bindiya had barged into Samar's office and demanded his help, but he had said he would help and he had. He did not have to. It came to Bindiya as a slight surprise (or did it?) that the haughty, sharp-tongued Samar Chauhan was also someone who kept his word. It was both oddly disconcerting and heart-warmingly weird to know that he had, in his own way, stood up for her.

'We have the bid submission in three weeks' time,' came Samar's elegant voice, bringing Bindiya back to the present. Samar was looking around the room, his eagle eyes noting each expression and registering every movement. It was 7.45 a.m. and the meeting scheduled for 8 had already started.

Bindiya shook her head and focused on what Samar was saying. She owed it to Samar now to be at her best.

The meeting was a critical one and one discussion led to the other; there were heated arguments about costs, pricing and delivery of the project. It was while discussing competitor strategy that Samar asked, more to himself than

61

to any one else, 'So what is the Raheja Group's market share in automobiles?'

'16.34 per cent,' pat came a small voice in an instant, more out of involuntary reflex than anything else.

Samar's eyes flashed in the direction of the voice. Bindiya.

'I ... er ... think so ... I had read somewhere ...' she fumbled nervously when she saw his eyes on her. 'I mean ...'

'16.34,' someone else shouted loudly and confidently, unaware of the little exchange between Samar and Bindiya who sat a few feet apart. 'I just checked the industry reports.'

Bindiya cast her eyes away from Samar and went back to her laptop.

A few days later, Samar got an email from Bindiya at one in the morning. It contained slides, the submission deadline for which was 10 a.m. the next day. Nine hours before time.

62

That was a first.

Samar, who was about to get up from his desk and head home, sat down and opened the slides with some interest. He was curious to see how many errors Bindiya Saran had made this time.

He spent about twenty minutes on the presentation. His face was expressionless when he shut down his laptop without having found a single mistake in Bindiya's work.

And that was another first, Samar thought to himself.

Another week and another 7.45 a.m. meeting in Samar's office. Bindiya looked at the little plaque with the poem on his desk and smiled to herself. The office still felt hostile, Samar less so than before, but the plaque felt like a friend. A friend in the midst of strangers. A friend who had already helped her.

The discussion turned heated in a matter of minutes.

'Team,' said Samar, pacing the room briskly. It was not even eight in the morning but his rolled-up sleeves and slightly ruffled hair indicated he had already put in a couple of hours at work. 'Why do you think our strategy will *not* work?'

Bindiya flinched. It was almost as if Samar had read her thoughts.

Others mumbled dissent.

'Of course it will work,' someone said.

'It's spot-on!' came another indignant voice.

'We have thought this one through, there is no loophole,' said a third voice.

That Bindiya had flinched had not escaped Samar's eyes and he now turned to face her, his eyes even sharper than usual. 'Ms Saran,' he said, coming close to where Bindiya sat, knotting her hands nervously, 'your thoughts, please?'

Bindiya gulped. Samar's eyes bored into her. 'I … um … ab …'

'When you are done with the um-ing and ab-ing, let us know please?' he said his voice patient, his mind curious. She was weird. Less careless now. But still so difficult to decipher. What had that expression meant?

'I … I think there is a flaw,' Bindiya blurted out and immediately regretted it when everyone turned around to stare at her. She had been reading up extensively not only on the Zorawar Group but also on its competitors. She had taken out the time to talk to people across the various verticals within the group who had bid against their main opponent, the Aniket Group, and she felt there was reason to worry. At the moment, however, Bindiya was squirming with discomfort.

All eyes in the room were now focused on her. That was unpleasant in itself, but all of them put together did not cause as much discomfort as did that one pair that seemed to bore right into her and read everything that crossed her mind.

'And that is?'

63

Bindiya's mind blanked.

'Ms Saran?'

Oh god!

'Ms Saran, you were saying?' said Samar. Bindiya's wide-eyed expression reminded him of a deer caught in the headlights of a speeding car and to his surprise Samar found his voice softening of its own will. 'What flaw do you spot?'

'I think ... and ... er, I might be wrong obviously ... but I feel the Aniket Group ... um, is misleading us in the open bid.'

'And what do you mean by that?'

Bindiya took a deep breath. She had been trawling through massive volumes of data on what the Aniket Group had been up to in recent times and had spotted a disturbing trend.

'Well, we have made an estimate of the number we think the Aniket Group will present to the customers. We know that the Aniket Group have recently acquired White Feathers, a small consulting company. What we also need to take into account is that White Feathers have some assets that, if used properly, could help the Aniket Group drastically lower their prices.'

There was silence in the room.

And for Bindiya this was an out-of-body moment. Surely it was not her standing in a meeting room in the Zorawar Group headquarters and talking about why Samar Chauhan's strategy was all wrong?

Samar who had wanted to hear Bindiya's point of view just out of mild curiosity now paused, surprised; she had the facts right and she made sense.

'What do you propose we do?' Samar was by now standing right next to Bindiya's chair. She caught a whiff of his expensive cologne and was surprised that she recognized the distinct smell.

'Ms Saran?' came Samar's voice.

'Eh?'

'What do you propose we do?'

'I think our pricing is way off. We need to be a lot cheaper than we are at the moment.'

There was silence for a few seconds and then everyone started speaking at once.

'I think this is ridiculous,' said Vinay, speaking above the din.

'Why do you say that, Vinay?' said Samar, now turning around to face him.

'For starters, this is conjecture,' said Vinay, 'coming from someone who is new to the industry.'

Bindiya looked down. Why the hell had she spoken up? Why? That stupid plaque and its stupid friendly stare.

'And,' continued Vinay, 'I do not think the Aniket Group will use those assets because we believe they are engaged elsewhere.'

'We do not know for sure,' Bindiya said in a small voice, feeling the confidence begin to ebb. 'I read some reports about ...'

'If we go in with reduced margins, we will just end up with business we were anyway going to win but with a heavily reduced bottom line,' interrupted Vinay.

'Bindiya?' said Samar, raising his eyebrows. For a moment Bindiya was lost in the perfection of the exquisite arch of his brow.

'Bindiya?' Samar prodded her again.

Oh. Oh no.

The confidence from a few minutes back was now lost in the woods. There was no way Bindiya could get it back. And there was no way that Bindiya was going to argue with Vinay.

'Um, no ... I mean ... You must be right, Vinay. It was just conjecture on my part ... and ... you are right, I don't have much experience in the industry, this is just academic research and ...'

That Bindiya's confidence had collapsed was clearly visible to Samar and he jumped into the conversation, feeling oddly protective of the girl he knew was trying hard. 'Vinay, can you proceed with our current strategy?' He turned to her. 'Bindiya, could you run a parallel response to bid with your strategy? Where we go as low as we possibly can?'

'Okay, sir!' said Vinay smartly, excited about Samar picking him to lead the project. This would definitely help him get the promotion he badly wanted. The Bindiya girl was too silly to be taken seriously by anyone; even Samar had publicly humiliated her enough on previous occasions. The stage was set for a glorious win for him.

Bindiya stared wide-eyed. 'Run the project?' she whispered to Samar.

'Akshay,' said Samar, gesturing towards senior VP Akshay Singh, 'will help you. And that's all, ladies and gentlemen. We have five weeks to go before the submission of the bid. Vinay continues the work we are doing, Bindiya branches off with Akshay to take up another strategy. Closer to submission we'll choose one course.'

Bindiya came out of the meeting room in a trance and bumped head-on into Naina who was entering Samar's office.

'You mad girl!' said Naina, laughing.

'I'm sorry, Naina. It's been a crazy day!'

'You are so crazy that you make the world around you go crazy,' said Naina, shaking her head.

As she walked towards Samar, Naina wondered why she had begun to like this slightly whaky, pretty girl with the long hair. She didn't know it, but at that very moment someone else was wondering the same thing.

14

Transformations are interesting, more so if they happen to people you know well. Sunaina could only watch in mute surprise and fascination as her eldest daughter went through a transformation.

The work-phobic girl now even spent her weekends staring at her laptop and BlackBerry. She refused party invitations because she had conference calls to attend. When she did go to one, she was typically the last person in and the first one out.

'This one project, Mum,' she would say, 'this one project. Just this one thing.'

Sunaina wondered what it was about the project that had consumed her daughter. Was it fear of Samar? Fear of losing her job? In the end, Sunaina decided it was neither. Bindiya had been made responsible for an idea that was hers in the first place. It was like having a baby. One day you are young and carefree and then suddenly you are responsible for something that is more your own than anything you have ever known.

Then you can't take any chances. Then you don't want to take any chances. Then it consumes you. In a good way.

※

Akshay, Bindiya realized within a matter of a few hours, was a godsend. As a VP with over twenty years of experience in the industry, he was an invaluable guide. Kind and patient,

67

Akshay seemed to be Samar's opposite and Bindiya breathed a sigh of relief. One Samar Chauhan was enough.

Oddly enough though, on the only occasion Akshay spoke of Samar, he did so with immense fondness.

'He is probably the most misunderstood man in the world,' Akshay said one day, gazing out of the window, lost in his own thoughts, 'but it's nobody else's fault. People see what Samar chooses to show. It is easier to believe in the superior sneer on his face than it is to see beyond the façade and at the man he truly is ... and ... I think he likes it ...'

'Likes what?'

'Likes it when people hate him. He's more comfortable with people thinking the worst of him than he is with them getting to know the real Samar. Those who know him well will take a bullet for him and some of them work in this very office,' said Akshay cryptically as he shut his laptop. A thousand questions sprang up in Bindiya's head but she knew that the conversation was now over.

'Mysterious Mr Chauhan,' mumbled Bindiya to herself with a giggle, though she kept wondering what pain the rich, successful Satan could possibly have endured.

In the days that followed, Samar remained distant, taking updates on the project from Akshay. Bindiya sometimes saw Samar walk by her cubicle on his way to Madhav's office, a flurry of activity clinging to him like a sticky haze. Bindiya had noticed how everyone stopped what they were doing when Samar walked past, seemingly oblivious of the effect he had. While most people spoke ill of him behind his back, the same people talked deferentially *to* him, eager for a scrap of attention from him. Samar would nod his head, speak quietly, briskly, and take instant decisions. He wasted no time being nice. He wasted no time tolerating mediocrity.

Try as she might, she could not help but eye his lithe frame, sharp suit and alert face. And the eyes. The eyes that did not miss anything. The intelligent eyes that sometimes, Bindiya thought to herself, glowed.

One time, Samar caught her looking at him and Bindiya had to hurriedly look away, embarrassed. That fleeting moment stayed with her long after she left home for office. What was it about him, about the way he had looked at her across the floor that made her feel not just nervous, but ...very ... conscious of herself? Did he make every girl feel that way?

Bindiya shook her head. Naina was right; she was crazy.

❋

It was the day of the bidding.

Samar had declared that he did not intend to choose between Bindiya's and Vinay's strategies until the last moment. Hence two complete sets of offers were being constructed. Twice the work. Twice the stress.

As days flew past, curiosity about which project Samar would select for the final submission began to mount. Most people, including Bindiya, were confident that it would be Vinay's offer that would be the Zorawar Group's final submission. Yet Bindiya soldiered on. On multiple occasions and often in front of Samar, Vinay challenged Bindiya's strategy. While initially her defences had been weak, with Akshay's help, she soon began to gain confidence. Each time one of the open debates began, Bindiya knew they had Samar's full attention. On a couple of occasions, Vinay asked for Samar's views but each time Samar simply said that he did not know and was relying on the two of them to tell him which strategy would work better.

Work can become an addiction – it was an intoxication Bindiya had spectacularly fallen prey to. Even though Bindiya was aware that all her hard work might be in vain, the episode with Rehan was still painfully raw and work kept her sane. Bindiya had not told anyone what had happened; she was too ashamed of it even though she knew it was Rehan who had been at fault. But she had let things happen, and that she felt acutely guilty about.

At around three that afternoon, Akshay came running to her, his face expressionless. 'Samar chose your numbers,' he said.

'Oh god,' she mumbled and sat down. The stress of the last few days was beginning to take its toll now and Bindiya could feel a fever creep up. 'And? We lost?' Bindiya felt that her worst nightmare was coming true.

'Yes,' said Akshay.

70

'Oh god,' Bindiya gasped. All that hard work? And whatever would Samar think?

'Just kidding!' Akshay now grinned his widest and pulled a very surprised Bindiya into a quick hug. 'We have been shortlisted! You did so well, Bee! I am proud of you!'

'Are you serious? Samar chose my numbers? And we got shortlisted?'

Akshay laughed and nodded. Bindiya felt her shoulders sag with relief before disbelief began to kick in. Samar had used her numbers! And they had been shortlisted! Had she really done it?

As the news spread Bindiya's team members, including Vinay who took his loss sportingly, came to congratulate her. Akshay informed the team that Samar wanted to take everyone out for a celebratory dinner.

Later that night, Bindiya, who had not gone because of a splitting headache and another pending deadline, was wrapping up work before heading home when she heard someone clear his throat. Bindiya looked up lazily but bolted straight up from her chair, toppling over a glass of water, when she saw who it was. Samar was standing there, hands in his pockets, looking at her.

'Relax!' said Samar, walking briskly towards her desk and picking up the glass, much to Bindiya's embarrassment. 'Are you okay?' he asked as he placed tissues on the spilt water.

'Y ... yes,' mumbled Bindiya, not moving or helping Samar, just looking on, horrified. Why did she always have to behave like an idiot in front of him, she wondered.

'I hear you have a headache?' Samar asked, taking in her flushed face and red eyes. She probably had a temperature too and didn't even know it, he thought.

'Oh no ... I mean yes ... I mean it's okay ...'

'Go home,' he said quietly.

'Yes, I mean ... I'll just call the company cab ... I ...'

'My driver will drop you home,' came Samar's reply, steeped in quiet authority.

What?

'No, no, I'll ... I ...'

'I insist, Ms Saran.'

Bindiya could only stare as Samar made a call for the car, then nodded a wordless goodbye and began to walk out of the cabin. Once at the door, however, he turned around and, with eyes boring into hers, said, 'Well done, Ms Saran.'

'Um, I ... you ... Thank ... you ... er ...'

'It's good to have you on the team,' said Samar and turned around to walk out.

'Samar,' Bindiya bravely called after him. Something had been troubling her since Akshay had given her the news earlier that day and she needed to ask him.

71

'Yes?'

'You always knew, from the very start, that the Aniket Group would use the assets belonging to White Feathers, didn't you?'

For a moment Samar's eyes held Bindiya's.

'Rest well' Ms Saran,' he said, 'You look tired.'

And with that Samar thrust his hands into his pockets and disappeared into the hallway. Bindiya stood rooted in her place for a long time, thinking. Although Samar had not answered her question, she had her answer.

Sometimes all that we need – and need desperately – is knowing that someone sees the good in us when we have lost all sight of it ourselves.

72

15

The next stage of the project now began in earnest. The Zorawar Group and the Raheja Group – two conglomerates with very similar profiles had been shortlisted. They had locked horns in the past in many an ugly, gory corporate battle and there was little chance that this would be any different.

First meeting for Stage Two.

Clad in a formal black skirt and mauve shirt, black heels, her long hair straightened and falling against her back like a waterfall, Bindiya Saran looked around Samar's office. The team had already gathered, a good twenty minutes before the meeting was due to start.

Bindiya had been the first to arrive.

The door opened and, along with a gust of air, came in Samar. Hushed silence greeted him. Long, purposeful strides. Confident. Serious. Sleeves characteristically rolled up at eight in the morning. It was said that Samar began work at four and Bindiya was quite sure it wasn't just a rumour.

Before the hour was up, the team of eleven had been divided into groups, each dealing with one aspect of the bid. Samar walked around the room, pausing to talk to each group, listening to their ideas and giving his inputs.

Bindiya had been paired with Akshay, whose attitude towards her, over the course of this bid, had become positively avuncular, and Feroze, senior VP at the Zorawar Group. Akshay and Feroze's friendship was as legendary as were their fights. They had not been a team for ten minutes before the first disagreement cropped up.

'That is absolutely ridiculous,' said Feroze, slapping the desk with one hand to make his point.

'No, it's not. Why don't you suggest something better?' the quiet Akshay challenged his senior.

'Guys,' said Bindiya, desperation in her voice, 'really guys, let's not ... not ...'

'No, Bee,' said Akshay, 'let's see what the grand Mr Feroze has to say.' The belligerence in the usually sedate Akshay's eyes was as amusing as it was alarming.

Bindiya, oblivious of the pen in her hand and of the world around her, was focused entirely on the battle that raged in front of her. She gestured wildly, begging the two men to stop bickering like little kids, at the same time trying her hardest not to burst into laughter. Bindiya's hands flayed about expressively, an old habit, and then she felt them hit something.

Someone groaned. For a moment, the world stood still.

Bindiya turned around, her face pale. Since her face had already lost colour, it could not get any whiter when she saw who she had hit. If it could, it would have. For, doubled up in agony, hands clutching his left eye, was Samar Chauhan.

73

'Oh my god! Oh my god! Oh my god,' mumbled Bindiya, horrified.

Impulsively she reached out to Samar, her instincts as the protective older sibling taking over. 'Show me,' she commanded him. Obediently, or perhaps shocked that anyone could order him around, Samar obliged.

Bindiya, gulping with difficulty, mouth dry, heart beating loudly, put a gentle hand on Samar's temple. It was hotter than she had expected. Yet soft, like a baby's skin. An angry, red mark was rapidly appearing next to his left eye.

'Your eye is okay,' she said, breathing out with relief.

'Oh my god!' screamed Naina who had just come in. 'What happened?'

'Nothing, Naina, I'm fine,' mumbled Samar, gingerly touching his eyes. 'My team members just enjoy poking me in the eye.'

Bindiya blushed crimson, mortified. She could hardly believe she had actually, physically, hit Samar. Could it get any worse?

'Here, let me have a look please?' said the efficient Naina, pulling out the first aid box. She smiled reassuringly at the white-faced girl standing a few feet away. Bindiya tried to return the smile but all she could manage was a grimace. She had hurt Samar! In the eye! In full public view!

The commotion soon died down and everyone, including Samar, went back to work. In the end it was little more than a scratch and the meeting continued as if nothing had happened.

Bindiya, however, could not shush her wildly beating heart. She spent the next two hours replaying the little scene in her head and trying hard not to look at Samar. When, finally, the meeting ended at eleven, exhausted from the manic session, the team dispersed quickly, eager to get back to their emails and workstations.

Bindiya, fiddling with her hands, stayed back. It took every bit of her courage to not scamper away with the rest.

Samar was sitting at his desk, immersed in his laptop. The plaque with the poem stood erect and smiling, offering mute encouragement to Bindiya.

Bindiya cleared her throat.

Samar looked up, startled at the noise. 'Ms Saran! You haven't left? How can I help?'

Bindiya's heart was in her mouth even before she uttered her first words. 'Um ... er ...' She fidgeted.

'Yes?' said Samar, gingerly touching his eye again. He took in the nervous-looking girl in front of him. He had seen her smiling widely at the beginning of the meeting but now her face was clouded with worry.

'Samar,' babbled Bindiya, wringing her hands nervously. 'I wasn't looking. Akshay ... Feroze ... I wanted to get them to stop squabbling. I didn't see ... I mean, I saw but later ... and then there was your eye ... It hurt ... I mean, does it hurt? I mean, does it hurt very much? I mean I am sorry! Sorry! I ...' She trailed off, looking lost.

Samar's face remained expressionless, eyes fixed on the visibly agitated Bindiya.

'I am sorry,' said Bindiya, looking everywhere but at him. 'I'm sure it hurts.'

'It's okay, Ms Saran, please don't worry.'

'I am sorry.'

'It's okay, Ms Saran.'

'No, I am sorry.'

'Ms Saran!'

'I am really sorry.'

75

'Bindiya!'

Bindiya froze. *Bindiya*. It was the first time she had heard Samar call her that. Her name sounded weird, funny-weird, funny-nice-weird, coming from Samar.

'I am fine,' he said in a gentler voice. 'I am fine.'

Bindiya looked around. 'I'll go then?' she asked stupidly.

Samar stared at her.

'Oh ... yes ... I'll go.' Bindiya answered her own question.

'Good day, Ms Saran.'

'Good day, Sata ... Samar,' mumbled Bindiya, her eyes growing to double their size as she realized what she had almost said. Ready to burst into tears now, Bindiya gave herself a big imaginary kick.

'I'll leave. That's the best thing to do,' she added and scuttled away.

76

Samar stared at the retreating form of Bindiya Saran. Only when the door had closed behind her did he allow himself the chuckle that had been threating to burst forth all the while.

16

They say that time heals, that it helps you forget. What they don't tell you is that, like most well-meaning friends, it can only help you heal if you let it.

Bindiya had not allowed time to help her. There was something so persistent about those morbid memories that she could not let go. Over the years they had become part of her being. Vicious memories that, she sometimes felt, no joy could make her forget. Memories that hit her out of the blue, unwarranted but, at some sadistic level, not wholly unwanted.

She saw it all now. Curled up on the bed, reading another

abusive text from Rehan, she saw it all come back in a torrent of misery.

The sprawling building. The cream-and-white walls. Those barren walls.

Even though she had been only twelve then, the sadness in the walls extended arms out towards her and tried to drag her in. She had shuddered as she was ushered into the room.

'Wait here, we'll get her,' someone said to the twelve-year-old Bindiya, pushing her into a chair. The chair. The steel chair. The clanging noise it made that jarred in the morose silence of the building.

She looked up when she heard footsteps.

There she was, staring into the void.

'Bindiya is here,' someone said to her. 'You remember her?'

'Sit down. No, not on the floor, here on this chair.'

'Don't do anything, just sit. Do you know this girl? No? This girl here?'

Bindiya stared at the woman in front of her. Her face was more familiar to her than her own. She even recognized the blue shirt, the loose brown trousers. Yet the woman in front of her was unfamiliar. Her soul was alien. Strange.

Bindiya stared at her. The woman looked blankly at the walls. Her eyes were empty. Scarily empty.

Neither of them recognized the other for very different reasons.

A kind woman put a hand on Bindiya's shoulders. 'It may not look like it, but she's getting better.'

This is better? Tears strung her eyes. Even now, years later, Bindiya could feel them cascade down her cheeks in silent, unadulterated misery.

'She doesn't recognize me,' Bindiya mumbled to no one in particular, trying to take in the horror.

77

'She will, beta, bit by bit, it was all a big shock for her ...'

'Mummy?' Bindiya tried, and she put a hand on her mother's arm. The unfamiliar woman in Mummy's body jerked it away – the only reaction she got from her.

The memory faded as abruptly as it had appeared. But as happened each time it visited her, it left her face soaked with tears.

And yet again, Bindiya cried herself to sleep.

17

It was rare that anyone else caught her attention when Samar was within sight. Hence, it was with surprise that Malika Oberoi tried hard not to stare at the tall, slim girl with long hair.

Really long hair.

Malika knew instantly that she disliked the girl. She did not like her peaches-and-cream complexion; she did not like the way her hands moved animatedly when she spoke; she did not like the innocence in her face; she did not like the sparkle in her eyes. And she certainly did not like the way Samar was leaning in, all ears, listening to her.

Malika had known Samar since both of them were fifteen. To most people, Samar's face, at the moment, would appear expressionless. Malika, however, could clearly see the sides of his lips trying hard not to twitch into a smile. His eyes were hard but there was a ghost of a laugh in them. Samar from ten years back would have by now thrown his head back and laughed a big throaty laugh. The Samar he had become tried hard to not even smile.

'Who is that girl?' she asked her PA.

'Bindiya Saran, consultant from IC.'

Malika nodded her head dismissively. Her Louboutins clicked against the polished floors as she walked purposefully towards Samar.

'Is that all you disagree with, Ms Saran?' Samar was saying in his elegant voice. The sinful elegance of Samar's voice. How she had missed it! It never really sounded the same on the phone and Malika had been starved of it. She walked faster.

The girl's eyes grew wide and then she blinked a few times. Nervously, she fiddled with the cuffs of her shirt. Malika despised nervous people but there was something endearing about this girl's nervous movements and Malika could see that it was not lost on Samar.

'No ... no ... I agree with everything else,' Bindiya said hurriedly, words tumbling out one after the other.

'Thank you for your inputs, Ms Saran, I shall keep them in mind.'

'Thank you, Samar.'

'Samar!' exclaimed Malika when she was a few feet away from the two. She had hoped to catch his eye before she reached him but Samar had been too engrossed in the conversation to notice.

'Malika!' said Samar, surprised but happy and smiling. 'You weren't supposed to be back till late in the evening!'

'Surprise, surprise!' said Malika, throwing back her thick, glossy, perfectly coloured and blow-dried hair.

'It's so good to see you!' he said, coming forward.

Malika felt the familiar tingle of excitement as Samar wrapped his arms around her. The hug was quick; Malika knew it would be quick. She had anticipated it and was prepared. As her face rested on Samar's chest for a brief second, Malika quickly memorized everything. The strength in his arms, his rock-solid body pressing against hers, his smell ... Samar filled up her senses. As always.

Samar pulled away all too quickly and then looked at her. 'You look well,' he said, scrutinizing her. 'Paris suits you.'

'No place that doesn't have you in it can suit me,' said Malika, laughing.

Bindiya cleared her throat. She had watched the little scene with wonder. Statuesque at five feet eight inches, Malika was dressed in a bright red power suit and black heels. Bold colours. Bold, powerful personality. Stunningly beautiful, perfect makeup, not a hair out of place, obviously successful, Malika looked like someone who was used to getting her way.

Unpleasantly intimidating. Bindiya wanted to not be around her.

Samar obviously seemed to think differently.

'Malika, meet Ms Saran. Bindiya, Malika, Malika Oberoi, Chief Marketing Officer of the Zorawar Group.'

Oh, the Malika Oberoi.

The women shook hands. Bindiya had heard and read about Malika Oberoi's hugely successful career. She appeared on TV shows on Women's Day, extolling the virtues of being a working woman.

'She has been living in Paris for the last year, doing a course that she really did not need, but is now back to join us.'

'Come on, Samar, I needed that experience, it's such a fantastic, specialized course,' insisted Malika. 'Why don't you just say you hated not having me around?' She gave Bindiya a meaningful look.

'Welcome back, Malika. And nice to have met you. I'll catch you both later,' said Bindiya. She scampered away but not before having noticed the menacing, though brief, look Malika had shot in her direction.

✹

It was well past 11 p.m. and Samar had just finished updating Malika on the latest projects at hand.

'Now that you are up to date, Malika, and ready to take charge, I can book my holiday,' Samar joked as he shut his laptop. 'Have a good night's rest and I'll see you tomorrow.'

'What if I don't want to go, Samar?' asked Malika, getting up and walking slowly and seductively across the room towards him. Staring intently into his eyes, she placed a gentle hand on his shoulders.

Sexy. Sensuous. Suggestive.

Samar smiled. 'I'll have to push you out then.'

By now Malika had inched as close to Samar as she dared and their faces were a few inches apart. She was close enough to feel his breath. But not close enough. Never close enough.

Those who have wanted someone they haven't got would know this feeling of utter despair and infinite hope. Despair that slams you to the ground beneath your feet and hope that uplifts you to the skies. Both typically at the same time.

She took his hands in hers. 'I missed you, Samar.'

'Malika, we were on the phone all the time.'

'Shh ... Samar, let's not think right now,' she mumbled dreamily and wrapped her arms around his neck, willing him to pull her closer. She smiled when a few seconds later she felt Samar's arms, strong and powerful, steal around her waist.

'Kiss me, Samar,' Malika muttered into his ear, pushing her body into his, slipping a hand up his shirt and digging her nails into his skin. 'Now!'

She felt his hands tighten around her waist. Their lips were a few inches apart and Samar leaned in for their first kiss.

Their first kiss. Fifteen years too late.

She pulled him closer, needing him, wanting him. 'You can have whatever you want,' she promised him.

Samar's eyes locked into hers and Malika exulted in the desire she saw in them. *He wants me.* This was it! Samar was about to kiss her.

Picking her up with ease, Samar gently turned Malika around so that she could sit on the table. Malika hitched up her skirt and wrapped her legs around Samar's waist, not believing that this was finally happening. Samar tugged Malika's face closer to his, his eyes blazing, and brushed his thumb across her lower lip. Malika felt a delicious shiver run through her body. She had been with many attractive men and very rarely had she slept with a man and not pretended that it was Samar who was making love to her. Malika knew that her body craved Samar and had been craving him for the last two decades. He was all she had ever wanted – and tonight she would have it all.

Malika closed her eyes, ready to savour their first kiss. She knew, without an iota of doubt, this would be the best kiss of her life.

Now. Now! Now?

When nothing happened Malika opened her eyes. Samar was still breathing unevenly but his eyes were open. Clear. All desire from a few seconds back had vanished.

He still held her face and she still had her arms and legs wrapped around him.

'Samar?' she whispered pulling him closer. 'Don't stop, please.'

'Malika ...' Samar said gently.

'No, Samar, no!'

'Malika ...'

'Don't think, Samar, please, please don't!'

'I don't think this is a good idea, Malika. I am sorry for what just happened,' he said in his clear accent. Not even an iota of doubt.

'No, Samar!' Malika said, already disgusted with the desperation in her voice.

Samar planted a chaste kiss on Malika's forehead, pulled away from her and walked out of the room.

Humiliated, Malika slumped into her chair and tried hard to bite back the tears.

On his way out, Samar shook his head, trying to figure out what had just happened. Malika was stunning, educated, smart, witty – and madly in love with him; always had been. She would be the perfect partner. Why, now that he felt remotely ready for a relationship, of some sort at least, hadn't he been able to bring himself to even kiss Malika?

He shook his head again and tried to get that one face out of his mind.

18

Flying in his private plane and being made to sit in the front row of auditoriums – these were Samar Chauhan's top two pet peeves.

The organizers of the annual pre-Diwali event at Ujala knew this and had made sure Samar had a seat in the corner of the fourth row. Almost in the dark. Almost invisible. Almost not there.

The lights dimmed and Samar settled in to watch the

83

performances. Ujala, which provided support to families of the mentally unwell, was part of the Zorawar Group's CSR initiatives but it held a very special place in Samar's heart.

'And now,' said the young lady presenting the show, 'we bring to you a very spectacular dance performance by our little girls. And they all want to thank their dance teacher, Bee didi, for her help.'

A loud cheer met the announcement. A group of six little girls, all of whom Samar knew by name, now appeared on the stage. Dressed in pristine white salwar kurtas, hair tied in plaits and wide smiles plastered on their faces, the girls looked angelic.

As the beat began and the song streamed in, the girls began their well-rehearsed and beautifully choreographed dance. Samar had not heard the song before. It spoke of a lonely bird looking for her mother's nest. All because she wanted to meet her mother once more – just once more – to thank her for having brought her into this wonderful world. It was unfamiliar, beautiful. Something about it made the hair on Samar's hand stand up. The pathos, the innocence, the longing ...

The lady sitting next to Samar sniffed away some tears. That was when, the spell broken for Samar for a split second, he noticed her. She was at the far corner of the stage helping the girls with the steps, giving beats.

Clad in a similar white salwar suit like the other little girls, her hair in a plait that flew around her, Bindiya Saran smiled widely as she now danced with the girls. Her movements were measured and elegant. The unmistakable grace of a trained dancer.

Samar's eyes followed Bindiya. He saw her pirouette with the girls, he saw her steady little Anjali when she was about to stumble, he saw her mouth the song, he saw her hands move rhythmically, he saw her smile, oblivious of the world, focusing only on the song and the little girls around her ...

Bee didi. Bindiya Saran.

Few things now surprised Samar; seeing Bindiya here had to be one of them. Every employee associated with the Zorawar Group was contractually required to work closely with at least one NGO on the Zorawar Group CSR roster. Very few people chose Ujala. Initially this lack of interest had irked Samar, but with time, he had realized he preferred it this way. Ujala was too special and too sacred to be shared with an unwilling employee.

But now, after all these years, here was Bindiya Saran.

The performance ended amid enthusiastic applause and the girls bowed prettily. Then they ran and hugged Bindiya who hugged them back, delight writ large on her happy, flushed face.

85

❀

Shaheen wrapped her plump fingers around Samar's and planted a wet, sloppy kiss on his cheeks. He had come to the green room to congratulate the kids on their fantastic performance.

'You danced so beautifully!' exclaimed Samar, pulling her to his knees. The spunky Shaheen, whose mother had recently tried throttling her neck in a fit of schizophrenia, was one of his favourites.

'You saw?' Shaheen's eyes widened with happy surprise.

'Yes, of course I did.'

'But I didn't see you.' She pouted now.

'But I was there.'

'No, you weren't! I was looking for you all the time.'

Samar smiled and tousled her hair. Children and their priceless innocence always made him drop the walls he had built around himself, making him vulnerable. The thought was an uncomfortable one and Samar drew no solace from it.

'Bee didi!' Shaheen yelped, breaking his train of thought.

'Yes, she was great too,' said Samar.

'No! Bee didi is here!' The little girl jumped out of Samar's lap, ran towards Bindiya, who had appeared at the door, and hugged her legs. Laughing, Bindiya picked up Shaheen and walked towards Samar. The moment's hesitation before she took the first step in his direction had not escaped him.

'Hi,' she said shyly, putting Shaheen down.

'Hello, Ms Saran,' he said, putting his hands in the pockets of his Gucci suit.

'I didn't expect to see you here,' she said, pushing back a strand of hair.

'I can say the same,' said Samar.

'Samar Uncle,' said Shaheen, putting a hand on Bindiya's cheek, 'Bee didi taught us the dance.'

'So I figured,' said Samar.

'And she danced with us onstage.'

'Yes, I saw.'

'And we had classes every morning at seven. Rufus bhaiya,' she said, referring to the centre in-charge, 'said Bee didi worked very hard with us.'

'I'm sure.'

'We had six people for the first class and now eleven girls will be in the class with Bee didi.'

'The classes will continue?' asked Samar, looking at Bindiya, a little surprised.

'Yes,' said Bindiya, 'it's good for the kids to channelize

their energy into something creative, particularly when they are dealing with difficult situations at home. Art is powerful therapy.'

Samar nodded, absorbing the idea. 'Are you sure it won't be too much work for you?' he asked.

Bindiya shook her head. 'It's okay. We all need that one person who's ready to take out time to hear, to see and listen to us. Even if it's a stranger who comes once a week for an hour to teach dance,' she said in a soft voice, a faraway look in her eyes, 'it can be life altering.'

That's an odd thing to say, Samar thought to himself and, seeing Bindiya getting ready to leave, he got up himself.

'I'll walk you to your car,' he told her.

'Er ... it's okay ... I mean ... I ...'

'This way, Ms Saran,' said Samar, voice steely and face expressionless again. For the few minutes Bindiya had hidden behind the door – to get over the shock of seeing him here – and observed Samar with the kids, he had looked different. Alive. Happy. Smiling.

Now, however, the mask was back on. She wasn't even sure which was the real Samar. The relaxed man with a child on his knee or the strict, sharp man who called her Ms Saran.

The two of them walked on the gravel path in silence, both lost in thought. The little path, lined on either side by low shrubs, was deserted. Dusk had fallen, the orange-blue sky bestowing upon the two of them its glowering beauty.

'Ms Saran,' said Samar after a few minutes, 'I wanted to ask you something.'

Bindiya looked up at him, surprised.

'Why did you chose Ujala for CSR?'

Bindiya took a deep breath. She thought for a minute and then spoke, 'A few years ago ...' She seemed to change her mind. 'I closed my eyes and put a finger on the roster. Opened them to see that fate had picked Ujala for me,' she said, shrugging her shoulders.

Liar, thought Samar.

'Why did you chose Ujala for your CSR?' asked Bindiya, looking at him from under her long lashes.

'Closed my eyes and put my finger on the list,' said Samar dryly.

Liar, thought Bindiya.

They walked towards the parking lot in companionable silence.

'That's my car,' said Bindiya, stopping beside her reliable red Maruti.

Ever the gentleman, Samar pulled the door of the car open for her. And then waited patiently for the car to start, which it did after four failed attempts.

'Um, sorry ... this just takes time to heat up,' said Bindiya after her third attempt.

Samar shook his head. This girl was a nutcase.

'It was a good performance, Ms Saran,' said Samar, once the engine was running.

Bindiya smiled. A shy, small smile. 'Thank you,' she said.

'Have a good night, Ms Saran.'

She cleared her throat. 'Good night ... er ... Samar,' Bindiya replied, gulping.

As Samar turned around and walked towards his waiting car, she dropped her head on the steering wheel, exhausted from the little interaction with Samar. Her head hit the horn and she saw him turn around abruptly at the blare.

'It's okay, it's okay,' she mouthed sheepishly at him from behind the wheel.

She saw Samar shake his head.

'Why do I have to always, always, always behave like an idiot in front of Samar?' she mumbled to herself. And then had to brake with all her strength as she almost drove her Maruti into his shining chauffeur-driven, exclusive Mercedes-Benz!

19

Bindiya was in Rufus's office at Ujala discussing that week's dance class timetable when a polite 'Hello, Rufus' interrupted their conversation. Bindiya looked up to see an elderly, distinguished-looking gentleman standing at the door, a warm smile on his face.

Rufus almost jumped out of his skin the moment he set eyes on the gentleman, making Bindiya chuckle to herself. Much to Bindiya's amusement, Rufus got up hurriedly, clumsily scattering a pile of files, raced to the door and dived straight for the man's feet. When he finally got up, after much coaxing from the older man, Rufus kept his hands folded in the most servile manner.

Must be an important man, Bindiya thought with a smile, observing the two men talk. From what she could make out, the elderly gentleman seemed to be very aware of all that was going on at Ujala.

'And this lady here?' said the man, now extending a hand in Bindiya's direction.

'I am Bindiya Saran,' said Bindiya, grinning and shaking his hand. For some reason, she already liked this man.

'Nice to meet you, beta, I am Ojas Chauhan,' said the man. Bindiya noted with mild surprise that his voice, like his face, was vaguely familiar.

'Samar sir's father,' said Rufus, bobbing his head.

89

'Wa ... what?' fumbled Bindiya, shocked. The idea that Samar actually had family seemed to be fairly revolutionary. So this was the man who had probably taught Samar how to tie his shoelaces or throw ball or maybe eat with chopsticks? Or maybe the super rich have servants to do all this? Or maybe Samar, being Samar, came into the world knowing everything? Bindiya shook her head to stop the mad stream of thoughts. Of course, this had to be Ojas Chauhan. Ojas Chauhan, now retired, was one of the best-regarded businessmen of his time. Bindiya had often read about him, especially when she was doing her MBA.

'Do you work at Zorawar too?' asked Ojas, smiling at the funny look on Bindiya's face.

Bindiya nodded, now tongue-tied. Rufus's behaviour didn't seem funny any more.

'With Samar?'

Bindiya nodded again. Ojas took a few steps towards her and patted her shoulder in mock sympathy. 'My condolences,' he said and winked.

Bindiya blinked and then stared at Ojas Chauhan. When, a few seconds later, Ojas burst into laughter, Bindiya hesitated for a second before joining in with gusto. Before long, thanks to Ojas's easy demeanour, Bindiya found herself telling him all about her little dance class. And before their brief encounter ended, Ojas had invited Bindiya to the slums where he did most of his charity work.

Both Bindiya and Ojas parted ways with wide smiles on their faces. Bindiya decided there and then that she liked Ojas tremendously and would love to be friends with him. What she did not know was that with time Ojas would become a lot more than a friend; it was the beginning of a friendship that would last both of them their lifetimes.

20

Arguably, the biggest problem with us Indians is that we have learnt to adjust. We have adjusted to potholed roads, dirty water and unsafe cities. We have adjusted to corrupt politicians, female infanticide and blaring horns on the roads.

We have also learnt to live with terrorism. Cities pride themselves on bouncing back quicker, much quicker than the last time. Another day. Another city. Another attack.

Later, a little-known terrorist outfit would accept responsibility for the bomb blast at India Gate. By then, seventeen people would have been declared dead and another two would be in critical condition; both of them, a thirty-three-year-old man and a two-year-old girl, would subsequently succumb to their injuries. TV channels would go crazy, covering every little detail of the attack, and the pathos of the injured, the empty promises of the politicians, the way Mumbai comes together in the face of adversity.

Yet again.

How many times more? These questions will crop up but later, much later. For the time being, a tired team of twelve people sat holed up inside the Zorawar HQ.

The clock had just chimed half past six when Naina rushed in, her heels clattering against the polished wooden floors of Samar's office.

'Samar,' she said breathlessly.

'Yes, Naina?' asked Samar, not looking up from his laptop.

Naina ushered him to a corner before giving him the news. 'There's been a terrorist attack at the India Gate,' she whispered. 'The police are worried this might be the first of a set of serial blasts and our security team has instructed that we all stay inside the office premises.'

Samar hurried out of his office and dialled the number of a family friend, ACP Shukla. Yes, there had been an attack. Yes, they were concerned about serial blasts. No, they did not know for sure. Yes, please stay inside the Zorawar HQ. No, no one should leave.

Armed with all the information he could gather at such short notice, Samar rushed back inside and, after a quick chat with Naina and Malika, he addressed the team.

'Guys,' said Samar in a loud, clear voice, 'there has been a terrorist attack at India Gate which is not too far from here. The police are jamming all the networks to make sure the terrorists are not able to communicate further with each other. So please, before the systems get jammed, immediately get in touch with your families to make sure all is okay. We've been instructed to stay the night in the office. It might be a good idea to let your families know you are okay and will spend the night here.'

No one in the room waited for Samar to finish his last sentence. Phones were whisked out and trembling hands dialled familiar numbers.

Samar looked around and saw with relief that most people seemed to be able to get in touch with their families.

'Are you okay?'

'Oh, thank god, I was so worried!'

'I'll be spending the night here, but don't worry, don't panic.'

'Hi, can't hear you, are you okay, please text me! Text me!'

'Chintu is okay? Ma? Everyone okay?'

Malika, who was following Samar's eye, flashed a warm smile at him. She hated seeing him stressed. After that night in Samar's office, Malika had thought hard about her feelings for Samar. She was in love and she hated what it was doing to her. Her love, unrequited for the moment, was madness. Her heart beat and broke for Samar. Yet, she knew she could do nothing. Even if Samar did not love her back, she at least had the consolation of knowing there was no one else in his life either. Malika Oberoi would not give up. She still wanted Samar more desperately than she had ever wanted anything. Was there any shame in wanting? In wanting so obviously, not covering it up with a façade of irreverence?

No, there isn't, Malika said to herself. Wanting is easy. It is getting that requires the machinations.

'It's okay, they are all okay,' she said to Samar.

Samar just nodded, his mind preoccupied. He had just spotted Bindiya Saran who had retreated to one corner and was desperately punching in numbers. Feroze, who had spoken to his family, stood next to her, a worried look on his face.

In a second Samar was by Bindiya's side. 'Were you able to get in touch with your family?' he asked.

A deathly pale face looked up at him.

'N ... no ... I ... I can't ...'

'Use my phone,' said Samar, thrusting his phone into Bindiya's hands.

'Who else has not been able to reach out to his or her family, please let me know?' shouted Samar over the din. Thankfully, everyone else had managed to get through to their families.

'Right, then, we have instructions from the assistant commissioner of police to stay the night in the office premises. He's sending more security to guard the building from outside. As you are all aware, we are dangerously close to India Gate and travelling on the roads at this hour is not advisable at all. Any questions?'

'Dinner?' came Atul's voice.

93

Weak laughter met his feeble attempt at humour.

'The kitchen staff has promised to cook something for all those staying the night,' said Malika, smiling encouragingly at everyone.

'Malika, your mum's okay?' Samar asked, turning to face her.

'Mum is in London, Samar, I told you,' she said, rolling her eyes. Samar cared, she knew and loved that he did.

'Oh right, okay,' said Samar. From the corner of his eye, he could see Bindiya still punching numbers on his phone, her face getting paler by the second.

'Everyone, please gather your belongings. The Internet is being shut down and phones might stop working. Let's all move to the auditorium.'

As the team began to troop into the other room, Samar walked up to Bindiya. Naina and Feroze were standing with her, worried.

'Any luck?' he asked.

Bindiya swallowed and shook her head. 'I need to go,' she said in an unsteady voice.

'Bindiya,' said Samar in an urgent undertone, 'listen to me. Phones lines have been jammed by the police. I just got off the phone with the ACP. There's probably nothing to worry about. I can't let you go out of the building.'

She looked up at Samar and a big fat tear rolled down her cheeks. Samar stared at it, lost in its tragic perfection. It looked out of place on Bindiya's face.

'Samar,' came Malika's voice, sounding higher than usual, 'let's make a move now, please.'

'You will not go anywhere,' said Samar, unequivocal authority returning to his voice. 'Just follow the rest of the team to the auditorium.'

Samar had walked but a few steps in the direction of the auditorium when something made him turn back. He saw Bindiya look around and punch another set of numbers on her phone. When nothing happened, she mumbled something to Naina who looked startled. And with that, before Samar's disbelieving eyes, she darted out of the room.

'That mad, mad girl!' Samar mumbled angrily under his breath and was about to dash after Bindiya when he felt a firm hand clasp his arm.

'Let her go, Samar. However stupid she might be, she is an adult and entitled to make her own decisions,' said Malika. Something told her she should do whatever it took to keep Samar away from Bindiya.

For a moment Samar stared at Malika and then glanced at her hand clamped around his. 'Excuse me, please,' he said in a low growl and gently but firmly shoved her hand away. 'Take everyone inside the auditorium. Call Madhav, he's still in the building. Make sure he's in the audi with everyone,' he said and dashed after Bindiya.

Malika could only stare – and feel her heart break again.

21

Samar finally caught up with Bindiya in the car park. That girl runs fast, he thought ruefully to himself.

The car park was dimly lit and deserted. Bindiya stopped when she heard footsteps following her and groaned out loud when she turned around and saw Samar.

'What do you think you are doing?' Samar growled at her, his eyes burning with fire at Bindiya's stupidity.

A scared yet determined girl stared back at him. 'Samar, I need to go,' she said firmly.

'It's not safe outside.'

'I have to make sure my family's safe.'

'Bindiya—'

'Samar, Urvi is just twenty-two — what if she's stuck somewhere, what if ...'

'I—'

'And Mum ... she had to go to her office today, I don't know if she's back — what if something's happened to her?' asked Bindiya, her eyes darting everywhere, a look of sheer panic on her face.

'Bindiya,' said Samar, placing a hand over her arm, 'everyone is fine and you are not going outside. It's not a good idea.'

'Samar, that's why I have to go. It *is* unsafe and my family is out on the roads!'

'Stop it! Bindiya Saran. Stop this theatrical nonsense this very minute. I am not going to stand in the middle of a deserted car park close to midnight and convince you to come back inside. Call your brother or your father and tell them to find out where your mum and sister are. Do that right now and then we go right back in. NOW,' he said, yanking her arm in frustration.

Samar paused to breathe.

And that was when he saw Bindiya's expression shift. Deep yearning replaced anger and defiance, and without quite knowing why, Samar immediately regretted his remark.

'I am my sister's father and my mother's son, Samar,' Bindiya said, her voice breaking, eyes fixed on his.

Oh. 'I ... I ...' Samar fumbled to find the right words.

'It's just been me, Mum and Urvi for the longest time.

Mum won't know what to do ... she ... she has not been well for years ... and Urvi's just a baby,' she said in a small voice, her shoulders low and defeated and tears pooling in her eyes.

Samar felt something cold clutch his heart. For some reason, he had always presumed that Bindiya came from a happy home where she was relentlessly pampered. The princess of the household. The her highness. Not the father to her sister and son to her mother.

'Please, Samar, I have to go ... I'll die if anything happens to either of them,' she said helplessly, gulping back tears and turning around to walk towards her red Maruti, parked a few feet away. Samar stared at the slowly retreating back of Bindiya Saran, her long plait swishing. The image of Bindiya almost ramming the rundown car into his Mercedes-Benz at Ujala came back to him.

He jogged towards her and wrapped his fingers around her wrist.

'Wh ... what?' She turned around to face him, her teary eyes wide with surprise.

With his other hand, Samar pulled out his phone. 'Surat,' he barked into it, 'please bring out my car. Yes, now.'

Bindiya could only stare wordlessly as Samar, staring straight ahead, led Bindiya by her hand outside the car park where his car was waiting. 'I'll take the car,' said Samar to Surat. The two men who went back more than three decades, were more friends than employer and driver.

'No, Samar,' said Surat with a decisive nod, 'it may not be safe outside and I know the roads and this car better than you do.'

'Surat ...' said Samar, shaking his head. Why wouldn't anyone listen to him tonight?

'Please get in,' said Surat, looking sympathetically at the tear-stained face of a girl he had seen around the office grounds often in the past few months.

Bindiya, incapable of words at the moment, could only stare at Samar. She wanted to tell him to go back in, to not do this, no, not for her ... but nothing came out. Except for tears. Big fat tears. Tears born out of fear. Tears born out of gratitude for Samar. Tears born out of gut-wrenching worry. They rolled one after the other down her cheeks.

As Samar sat back and the car whizzed past the office building towards the gates, he glanced at Bindiya who was still staring at him, tears streaming down her cheeks.

He had to look away.

Inside the office grounds and outside it were two different worlds. The tree-lined peace of the grounds shockingly gave way, all too soon, to unimaginable chaos on the streets. The road was chock-a-block with vehicles, people, police and mayhem. Horns were blaring, people were shouting and sirens were piercing through the restless night.

Samar's car moved painfully slowly. Too slowly for Bindiya.

Her heart racing, she sat silently glued to the window, stupidly scanning the scene for her mother and Urvi, even though she knew they were miles away. She craned her neck to make sure the woman walking past the tyre shop was not her mum and that girl standing by the policeman was not Urvi. Nervously, she licked her dry lips. She had never known such mind-numbing anxiety.

Something hit the window.

Bindiya screamed and instinctively reached out to Samar,

burying her face in his chest. In a matter of seconds, before anyone could understand what was happening, half a dozen young boys had surrounded the car and were pelting the windows with whatever they could lay their hands on – shoes, sticks and even stones. Probably belonging to a street gang, they appeared to find hitting an expensive car and hurling abuses at the occupants, on the day their city had been attacked by terrorists, a source of great entertainment.

As the boys continued, Samar noticed with some alarm that Bindiya was shaking with fear. 'Bindiya ... Bindiya, look here, at me,' he said, looking down and gently lifting her chin.

'What's happening?' Bindiya asked, trembling. Two large fear-filled eyes gazed up at Samar.

'Relax,' came Samar's soothing voice, calm even now. 'The car windows are bulletproof, okay? They can't hurt you.'

Bindiya looked blankly at Samar, staring at the black of his eyes. The peaceful, calming, powerful black of his eyes.

'They are bulletproof, so no one can hurt us while we're in the car, okay?' Samar repeated in a gentle voice, as if he were speaking to someone very precious.

Surrounded by the worst of humanity, Bindiya clung to the goodness of Samar. She was vaguely aware that Samar's face was a few inches away from hers. She was close to him. Very close. He had an arm around her. It should have been awkward. It was not.

His arms felt strong and familiar; they belonged to a soul hers knew. Bindiya was the most scared she had been in a long time, yet once Samar told her all would be okay, she immediately believed him.

The car was moving slowly because of the boys who continued to hit the windows and bonnet, laughing loudly. Samar felt Bindiya's body tense each time an object hit the car. Her eyes would then find Samar's and Samar would tell her, without words, not to worry.

With some help from a policeman standing nearby, Surat tried to navigate around the young men but without any success. He then turned around, asked Bindiya and Samar to 'hang on' and boldly accelerated through the gang, much to Bindiya's shock. Caught unawares, the boys jumped out of the way and let the car pass.

'Phew!' said Surat, looking in the rearview mirror to make sure Bindiya and Samar were okay. Samar caught his eye. Bindiya had her face buried in Samar's neck.

'Is Bindiya ma'am okay?' he asked.

Samar nodded. 'Do you want to look up now, Bindiya?' Bindiya heard Samar say a few minutes later, a hint of a smile in his voice.

'Yes ... yes,' she said, letting go of Samar, a tad embarrassed, but not, Samar noted, moving back to her original position close to the window. She sat next to Samar, not touching but close enough, almost as if physical proximity to Samar was reassuring for her.

Samar saw Bindiya's body language change as the car turned into a residential street, steeped in darkness now, with the street lights switched off.

'Stop! Please stop,' she shrieked.

Surat had barely braked the car before Bindiya dashed out towards a small house. 'Urvi, Urvi! Urvi, are you inside? Open up,' she screamed, banging on the door with one hand and pressing the bell with the other. Samar jogged after her and reached the door at the same moment it opened and something whizzed past him and leapt into Bindiya's arms.

That something, Samar realized, was a young girl.

Samar observed the little scene that unfolded before

him with no small degree of amusement. The girl, obviously Bindiya's little sister Urvi, seemed to have wrapped ten hands and twenty legs around Bindiya. Unbelievably, the girls seemed to be hugging and crying and laughing at the same time.

'Bee didi,' Urvi cried, 'are you okay? I was so, so scared!'

'I know, I know, darling, everything is okay now,' said Bindiya in a soothing tone, wiping tears off Urvi's cheeks even though, Samar noted, her own cheeks were as wet as they could possibly be. 'Mum, where's Mum?'

'I don't know,' said Urvi, worry returning to her face. 'She's not home.'

'You said she was at work?' asked Samar, his elegant voice cutting through the room.

'Yes,' said Bindiya. 'She works as a freelance journalist for *Times of Today* and was supposed to be at their head office till nine ... but we can't reach her number ... I ... I don't know what to do.'

'Your mum's full name please?'

'Sunaina Saran,' said Bindiya.

Samar pulled out his phone, dialled a number and spoke briefly.

'Thanks, ACP Shukla, Yes, my number please. Yes, Sunaina Saran, *Times of Today* head office,' he said and hung up.

Two expectant faces were staring at him when he looked up. 'They are trying to find out and will call—'

Samar's phone rang before he could finish his sentence. 'Yes. Wonderful, thanks, Mr Shukla,' he said into the phone.

'Your mum is at the HQ of *Times of Today*. She is absolutely fine and safe,' Samar said to the girls.

And at those simple words, all hell broke loose.

'How do you know?'

'Will she stay the night?'

'Can I speak to her?'

'Ladies,' he said, his voice cutting through the din, 'I'm sending my car to the *Times of Today* head office and Surat will pick her up and bring her here, safe and sound. And no, the phone lines are still jammed and I don't think you can speak to her.'

'Thank you, Samar,' said Bindiya, grinning from ear to ear.

'Thank you, Samar bhaiya,' said Urvi a little shyly, looking wide-eyed at the powerful man she had heard so much about. Samar stared back at Urvi with some surprise; it had been years since anyone had called him 'bhaiya'. It was the warmth in the word and the innocence with which Urvi had spoken that made Samar uncomfortable.

'No problem,' he said in a curt, crisp voice. 'Things are under control now. I'll get Surat to drop me at the Zorawar Group HQ on the way and he can then go and pick up your mum and get her here.'

102

And with that Samar Chauhan about-turned and left.

22

Something shot through the door, disrupting the calm of Samar's office.

A whirl of the red of a silk shirt and the black of a pair of trousers. And a long, loosely braided plait that swished from one side to the other.

Before Samar, standing by his desk, a file in hand, could figure out what hit him, two slim arms had wrapped themselves around his neck in a surprisingly tight, fierce hug. 'Thank you, thank you, thank you,' a voice whispered fervently in his ears.

Samar looked down into dark brown eyes fanned by the longest eyelashes he had ever seen. Funnily, Bindiya seemed as surprised as he imagined he appeared. 'Did I just do that?' her shocked eyes asked him.

And with that, just as she had shot into the office, she ran out of it, leaving a bewildered Samar shaking his head in disbelief.

A few minutes later, when Naina walked in to brief Samar on his next meeting, a surprising sight met her eyes. Samar was sitting at his desk, tapping away at the keyboard and smiling to himself. A wide, happy and very rare smile.

❋

There are some experiences which bring people, however different in nature, closer. The night of the terrorist attack was one such for Bindiya and Samar.

103

From that night on, there seemed to exist a silent camaraderie between them that neither needed nor wanted words. Both Bindiya and Samar were surprised by it. As was Malika Oberoi.

Malika had paced around the auditorium, not unlike a hungry tigress, for all the four hours Samar was gone with Bindiya, consumed by thoughts of what they might be up to. Samar came back at five in the morning, dishevelled and tired, and mumbled 'she's okay' to Malika who couldn't have cared less for Bindiya's well-being. He spent the next couple of hours with various people cooped up in the auditorium, helping them however he could. Through the long night, Samar remained oblivious to Malika who sat cross-legged in a dark corner, seething with anger.

Over the next couple of weeks, Samar and Bindiya barely spoke to each other, yet Malika could sense a shift in their relationship. She felt that there now existed an always-on, always-charged connection between Bindiya and Samar. There were little signs, signs that no one else would notice – the restlessness in Samar's eyes till he spotted Bindiya, the little smile she reserved for him, the way he ... ugh ... Malika's heart distorted and contorted each time she was witness to one of these moments.

Yet, she said nothing, did nothing. Like a snake on the prowl, she sat and waited for the right opportunity.

❋

Samar and Bindiya's friendship was not the only relationship that shifted gears during this time. Friendship between the unlikely duo of the sixty-eight-year-old retired business tycoon Ojas and the twenty-eight-year-old madcap business analyst Bindiya had been steadily brewing and was now beginning to take concrete shape. Initially they met at Ujala where a common interest in charity got them talking. Ojas, kind and easy to talk to, was instantly likeable. And Bindiya's desire to help others warmed the cockles of Ojas's heart. A genuine, warm friendship had begun to develop between them.

Before long, Ojas invited Bindiya to a maths class where he taught underprivileged children in a school in the slums. It was after that, over a cup of steaming chai at a tiny shop outside the slum, that Bindiya and Ojas began to talk, really talk.

Ojas had, till not long ago, been one of the stalwarts of the Indian mining industry. He told Bindiya all about how he began his mining career, and how it all seemed to fall apart at one point, only to become better and bigger with time.

'Why don't you work now, Mr Chauhan?' Bindiya asked, sipping her chai. 'Sixty-eight is the new thirty-three.'

Ojas smiled. 'I work, Bindiya, I work very hard, only no longer for money, power or fame.'

'Because you already have so much of all that?' asked Bindiya, smiling.

'Because I have realized that if money, power and fame are your only earnings, you are a very poor man. And at this age, I do not wish to be poor.' he said, smiling back.

'And when did you realize that?' she asked slowly, mulling over his words.

'Certain things, when they happen, change the course of your life, Bindiya. They ... make you question everything you thought your life stood for and then, after resisting for some time, you change, you decide to flow with the river for it tires the soul to swim against the tides of time.'

105

Bindiya took a deep breath and nodded. She understood every word Mr Chauhan had just said. 'And ... and what happened in your life – if you don't mind my asking?'

Mr Chauhan was silent for a few moments and then said, 'I lost my wife. She was and is the biggest love of my life.'

'Oh, I am sorry.'

'It's okay, it was a long time back ...'

For the next few minutes the two sipped their tea in silence, both lost in thought. When Bindiya looked at Mr Chauhan, he was smiling.

'Um, you know, I've been thinking,' said Bindiya, 'and worrying ... Samar, I mean, he's so senior at work ... do you think he'll have a problem if I became friends with you? Will he get angry? I mean, I have no intention of stepping out of line – '

'Bindiya,' Ojas interrupted. 'Why would Samar decide who you become friends with?'

Bindiya paused and thought for a moment. 'My friends call me Bee,' she said, grinning.

23

'And why are you packing a suitcase?' Adi asked Bindiya as he plonked himself on Bindiya's bed. A million pieces of clothing were strewn across the bed.

'Have you ever been to Shimla?'

'Are you going to Shimla?'

'Yes!'

'Why?'

'Work!'

'Who goes to Shimla to work?'

'Well, the Zorawar Group has a yearly outbound trip and this year it's in Shimla. People will stay in groups in different cottages and take part in team-building exercises and so on.'

'Which group is Hottie in?' Adi asked.

'Hottie?'

'Samar,' chuckled Adi.

Bindiya rolled her eyes. 'Don't know.'

'Is he going?'

'Don't care.'

'Ha ha, very funny,' Adi retorted. 'You can't lie to me, darling.'

'I don't know,' said Bindiya, pouting now.

'But you hope he is?' said Adi, narrowing his eyes at Bindiya. Bindiya blushed in spite of herself. 'Oh my god! Are you blushing, Bee? Are you?'

Bindiya pretended to hit Adi who yelled and ran out of the

room, Bindiya close at his heels, dangerously armed with a clothes hanger.

❋

Pretend as she might that she did not care, Bindiya found herself on the constant lookout for Samar on the flight, during the drive to Shimla and then the quick bus ride to Kufri where the group was staying in a beautiful camp. She told herself to behave; when that did not work, she silently scolded herself, and then when that did not work, Bindiya, overcome with frustration, rolled up a newspaper and thwacked her head with it.

Lalita, from marketing, who was sitting next to Bindiya, wondered if Bindiya had finally lost it. 'Not surprising – after all, she works so closely with Satan,' the wise Lalita reasoned with herself.

Kufri, about twenty kilometres from the hustle and bustle of Shimla, was nestled in the Himalayas. Windy, cold and gorgeous, it stole Bindiya's heart from the word go. The low rolling hills in the foreground and the humongous mountains in the background, the landscape buffeted by the howling wind – Bindiya fell in love with the place in a matter of seconds.

Theirs was a group of a hundred and twenty people spread across twenty beautiful cottages. Bindiya's cottage was a large spacious house with six rooms and magnificent bay windows overlooking the valley. On a sheet of paper stuck on the main door were printed the names of the six people the cottage had been allocated to. Bindiya grimaced when she read the first name: Malika Oberoi. And her heart skipped a few beats when she read the last: Samar Chauhan.

However, soon, euphoria turned sour. This arrangement meant only one thing: Malika wanted to be with Samar. Or worse, Samar wanted to be with Malika.

Much to Bindiya's growing annoyance, two days passed by without any sign of Samar (or Malika). Rumour had it that they both were abroad for an urgent meeting and would join the group later in the week.

Through the day the team took part in umpteen games and activities. Bindiya trekked, built fires and danced with the locals; all the while thinking only about Samar.

Just after midnight the second day, Bindiya lay on the couch in the living room, working on an Excel sheet by the soft yellow light of a table lamp. The cottage was still, dark and empty. Her housemates had gone to Shimla to dance the night away at a disco. As the night wore on, the numbers began to blur, and Bindiya was toying with the idea of curling up and dozing off on the sofa when a voice broke through the dimly lit room. A familiar voice. 'Hi,' it said.

Bindiya sat bolt upright instantly, her heart beating fast. Samar.

'Oh hi,' she said, acutely embarrassed by her dinosaur-print pyjamas. And the loose Hello Kitty shirt. And the messy hair.

'I'm sorry, I didn't mean to startle you,' said Samar, coming closer to her, the light from the lone lamp bathing him in a warm shade of yellow. Samar's usually alert face was tired and his eyes held the unmistakable redness that comes with lack of sleep. Standing there, in the middle of the room, seemingly exhausted and in need of a hearty meal, he looked vulnerable. Bindiya immediately shook the thought away; Samar and the word vulnerable could not be used in the same sentence, she told herself.

Samar stared at Bindiya, taking in her eyes that were wide with surprise. Something about this girl always made him want to smile. He found his amused eyes straying to the pink and yellow dinosaurs on Bindiya's pyjamas but sensing her embarrassment, he hurriedly focused them on her face.

'N ... no ... I am fine ...' she was saying as she tied up her hair in a neat bun, settled her spectacles and stood up.

'Do you know which one is my room?' Samar asked, looking around. The house seemed to be empty.

'Yes, yes, sure,' said Bindiya.

'Where is everyone?' Samar asked as he followed Bindiya.

Oh my god, I am alone in the house with Samar! 'They've all gone dancing ...'

'You didn't go?'

'No ...' she said, shrugging and smiling a nervous smile, 'I had work.'

Samar nodded and Bindiya pointed to an empty room. 'There are two empty rooms – this one has a better view.'

'Thank you,' said Samar.

Bindiya had turned around to leave when a thought struck her. 'Have you had dinner, Samar?'

'No, I'll fix something for myself in the kitchen. I am guessing you've eaten.' Samar's voice remained polite and formal.

'No, not yet.'

'In that case, I'll fix something for both of us,' said Samar.

'No ... no,' Bindiya mumbled hurriedly. 'Why don't you freshen up and I'll fix dinner.' She hurried out to change into something more presentable, rubbing her arms to rid them of the goosebumps and frantically switching on all the lights on her way to her room.

Approaching the kitchen with the intention of helping

Bindiya with dinner, Samar stopped in his tracks at the door. Bindiya, wearing a light pink chikan salwar kameez, hair in a loose bun and face refreshingly makeup-less save for a little silver bindi, was standing by the cooking range. She was humming to herself and swaying gracefully to the tune as she stirred something in a frying pan. As Samar looked on, she brought her hand to her forehead to push back a strand of wayward hair, and in the process smeared a bit of gravy across her cheek. Samar thought of pointing it out to her, but decided against it. The simple beauty of the scene appealed to him.

Sensing eyes on her, Bindiya looked up. Much to her surprise, she found Samar standing at the door, leaning against the wall, hands crossed against his chest. Both his coat and his tie were missing. He had rolled up his sleeves and opened an extra button in his shirt. He was looking at her but seemed to be lost in his own world. Arohi's words from months back came rushing back to Bindiya. Samar could look strikingly handsome in his own unconventional way, she thought, and tried hard to not blush.

'I am sorry, I had to get on a call which took longer than expected. How can I help?' Samar said breaking the silence.

'It is okay, I am done here. Let's eat? Bindiya asked.

A little later, Bindiya found herself seated opposite Samar at the dining table in an empty house a few hours from Shimla.

'I'm afraid this is a very simple meal,' she said, looking at the dal, mixed vegetables and chapattis.

'I like simple food,' said Samar, attacking the meal with a gusto that Bindiya found oddly satisfying.

'Are you very tired?' Samar heard a small, concerned voice speak up a little later.

'A little,' he said, looking up at a worried face staring

intently at him. He noted how her forehead was scrunched up in a frown. 'I'll be fine, Bindiya. I just need a good night's sleep,' he said after a moment's pause, his voice gentler than usual and eyes less harsh.

'Yes, yes, of course,' she said hurriedly, embarrassed at the colour that she knew was steadily rising up her cheeks. The hardest part, Bindiya thought to herself, of pretending that you don't care is finding out how much you actually do.

Samar had not slept a full night in the last decade and there was no reason for this night to be any different. He tossed and turned through it, images from a past that he would not and could not forget tormenting him, as they had every night for the last ten years. Occasionally Bindiya's face would crop up too, and he would toss and turn more. He finally got up at six, very late by his standards, but continued to lie in bed. The house began to wake up and sounds from outside reached him every now and then. Whenever someone talked loudly, Bindiya's hushed but firm voice would reach his ears.

'Please,' she would beg the perpetrator, 'can you keep your voice down? Samar needs to sleep, he's very tired. If we're too loud he'll wake up. Please?'

Every time he heard that, Samar tried very hard not to smile but failed each time. He was a man hardened by circumstances and life, but Bindiya's sweetness touched him. Why did she care for him?

24

It was barely 10 p.m., yet most people at the camp had retired to their cottages. It had, after all, been a very long day full of activities and sessions. With Samar and Madhav in the campsite now, the group, eager to please the bosses, seemed re-energized. It was not every day that you got to spend time with the two big bosses!

Since their little dinner together Bindiya had seen Samar only in the presence of others, mostly in sessions that he chaired. Binidiya sat transfixed and unmoving along with the rest during one such session where Samar spoke at length about his association with the Zorawar Group, his passionate, carefully chosen words making a huge impact on the audience. It earned him a standing ovation, led by Madhav himself. Bindiya noted with a certain distaste that Malika, who had finally come that morning, stayed glued to Samar's side throughout the day.

Now, late in the night, Bindiya sat in a little corner of the camp overlooking the valley, wrapped in a light blanket and her thoughts. The night was cold and it compounded the loneliness that clutched at Bindiya's heart, bringing stinging tears to her eyes. The moon hid behind the clouds and the mist added an aura of melancholy to her mood. She had tried Adi's number but poor connection at the camp had made conversation virtually impossible. Bindiya knew that she felt the way she did for a reason.

It was her dad's birthday. A gentle reminder of what was no more.

Dad.

Bindiya wondered what that word meant to other girls and felt a pang of self-pity surge through her. Maybe, at some level, it was her fault. She thought about all that Rehan had done to her, her soul and her spirit – the continuous verbal abuse, the debilitating disparagement and then the attempted rape. A shudder went through Bindiya when she considered what could have happened that night in the car park. Rehan had never apologized; instead, Bindiya had been receiving some nasty texts from him, abusing her and her family. She wondered if she should tell someone about Rehan. But whom could she trust? Who would bother to do something, anything, about the mess that was her relationship with Rehan?

'Ms Saran,' the now very familiar voice reached her, interrupting her thoughts. Bindiya hurriedly composed herself and turned around. Samar stood there, hands in the pockets of his jeans, looking a lot younger than he did in a suit. She felt mildly surprised that Samar even owned a pair of jeans.

'Samar, hi,' she said, getting up.

Something about Bindiya's face made Samar stop in his tracks. 'Are you okay?' he asked in a gentle voice that took Bindiya by surprise.

'Yes just sitting here.'

'Mind if I join you?'

Bindiya hurriedly got up to offer him the only chair around but Samar sat down on the ground, leaving the chair for her. Bindiya sat down next to him and Samar smiled and shook his head at that.

The two of them sat on the ground looking at the valley below, the empty chair beside them.

After a few minutes Samar spoke. 'Thank you for sorting out my dinner last night. I was so tired that I don't think I even thanked you properly.'

'Oh that's not a problem,' said Bindiya.

'And also, thank you for making sure the noise levels this morning were kept down.'

Bindiya now blushed a deep shade of red and looked at her hands. 'Um, I knew that you ... you ...'

113

'Do you like Kufri?' he asked to change the topic and stop Bindiya's nervous mumbling.

'Yes, I do ... it's almost as if it's easier for me to breathe here,' she said.

'I spent a lot of my childhood here. You see that hill there?' said Samar, pointing to the dark outline of a hill that did not seem too far away.

Bindiya nodded.

'That's Mahasu Peak, the highest mountain here. We own some properties there that we used as holiday homes during the summer months.'

Bindiya smiled and tried to picture a school-going Samar Chauhan. 'Samar's summer holiday,' she said, giggling, her hand covering her mouth.

Samar snorted with laughter, taking the little joke in his stride. 'You know, there's a little stream down below,' he said, pointing into the darkness of the valley below them.

'Is there?'

'Yes, the water is ice-cold but crystal clear. You can actually see the fishes swim in it.'

'Can we go?'

'Now?'

'Yes!' exclaimed Bindiya, her eyes shining with excitement. But the next moment, her face registered deep distress at having possibly crossed a line. 'I mean no. I mean ... it's okay, we can do it later sometime ... or not. I mean ...'

The nervous fumbling, thought Samar to himself, feeling a tug inside somewhere, which Bindiya always resorted to when she felt she had asked for too much. That she was not entitled to things seemed deep-rooted in her, and Samar wondered why.

I am my sister's father and my mother's son.

'Let's go now,' Samar heard himself say.

'No, I mean, it's okay, I just said that impulsively. It's late and dark and ...' said Bindiya, giving Samar some excuses to choose from.

Samar ignored Bindiya and called out for Vishnu who managed the camp. He was requested to accompany them down to the stream and he promptly agreed. He ran and got an electric light and the three of them set forth.

'How far is the stream?' Bindiya asked, walking closely behind the two men as they began their trek down the hill.

'A twenty-minute walk.'

'How do you know?'

'I used to go there all the time when I was a kid.'

'Will there be animals there?'

'Yes!' said Samar, turning around and fixing very serious eyes on her.

Bindiya laughed nervously, not sure if Samar was being serious or just kidding.

'You know, I'm very afraid of snakes,' she said confidingly a little later. Samar was already smiling and he hoped that the darkness hid his expression.

'And?'

'And what?'

'What else are you afraid of?'

'Owls.'

'Owls?'

'Yes.' She nodded her head vigorously.

'And?' he asked, skirting a piece of rock.

'Bees!'

'What rubbish, who's afraid of bees?' said Samar, laughing openly now.

'When I was little, I used to think that bees were baby

tigers,' said Bindiya sheepishly. 'So I stayed away from them because there was no way of knowing if a bee near me was old enough to suddenly morph into a tiger!'

'Who fed you all this rubbish?' Samar asked, laughing harder now.

'Adi,' she said. 'Adi is my childhood friend. Growing up, he fed me a lot of rubbish, literally and figuratively.'

Samar laughed.

'Ouch!' Bindiya groaned out loud as her foot hit a stump of root that was jutting out. She lost her balance and had it not been for Vishnu, who immediately lent her a steadying arm, Bindiya would have taken a tumble.

'Are you okay?' Samar asked her, concerned, flashing the light on her foot to make sure she was not injured.

'Yes, yes, I'm okay.'

'No twisted ankle or anything?'

'No,' she said.

'Are you sure?' Samar asked.

Bindiya mumbled a yes, touched by his concern.

For a minute the trio walked in silence. Samar expertly manoeuvred around another uneven bit of rock.

'Bindiya,' he said, turning around to face her, 'this part of the hill is quite uneven. I'm used to the hills but I realize that you are not. Why don't you hold my hand – don't want you falling flat on your face here.'

Why don't you hold my hand? Why don't you hold my hand? *Why don't you hold my hand?*

Samar extended his hand. For a second Bindiya froze.

'Come on? Quickly now?' prodded Samar. 'I'll feel better knowing that you are not going to topple over.'

In spite of the darkness that engulfed them, Bindiya felt very self-conscious as she took his hand, feeling strong, long fingers clasp hers immediately. In Samar's large hand, Bindiya's felt small and delicate. His hand was hard, like that of most men, Bindiya thought to herself, yet his elegant fingers curled around hers gently, as if they held delicate china.

Both Bindiya and Samar hardly spoke now, and it was Vishnu who chattered nonstop, talking about the vegetation and the week's weather forecast. Bindiya realized that Samar was as aware of her hand in his as she was. He tightened his grip when her steps threatened to falter and loosened it when she seemed okay. Steadier and stronger, with Samar there for support, the rest of the distance was covered much faster.

Before long, the narrow stream, ink-blue under the moon, glistened through the shrubs.

'Oh my god!' said Bindiya, staring at the gorgeous snake-like stream. 'It's beautiful! Do you remember the river like this from your childhood?' Gently, she pulled away her hand from his.

'Yes,' said Samar, looking around, taking in the beauty, 'it looks exactly the same.'

Bindiya took off her socks and shoes and jumped into the stream, the clear waters barely reaching her ankles. 'The water is sooooo cold,' she gushed happily, twirling and extending her arms to embrace the beauty around her, oblivious of Samar who sat a few feet away, drinking in her joy. Vishnu had wandered off somewhere.

Samar was, for the moment, finding it difficult to peel his eyes off Bindiya. Seeing her like this, oddly enough, made him feel very peaceful. The sight that met his eyes was the gentle balm his soul had been craving. And that was when he realized he was smiling.

With her, for her, thankful for the joy on her face.

117

When Bindiya finally stepped out of the water, wordlessly Samar offered her his handkerchief to wipe her feet before she put on her shoes.

'Thank you for bringing me here,' said Bindiya, coming to Samar and sitting comfortably on the boulder, vigorously wiping her feet.

'My pleasure.'

'And why did you stop coming here?' she asked, pausing for a minute to look up at him.

'There was no Mum,' he said.

Bindiya now remembered Mr Chauhan telling her about having lost his wife many years ago. Mrs Chauhan, Samar's mum. For some reason, Bindiya had not made the connect till now. She looked at Samar's expressionless face and tried to imagine what he must have felt then and struggled to find the right words.

'I am sorry,' she said finally.

'And Kufri was her favourite place,' continued Samar as if he had not heard her. 'I never felt like coming back here once she was gone.'

For a few minutes neither spoke.

'What was your mum's name?' A timid voice reached Samar. That she was scared to ask this question was so obvious that Samar had to smile.

'Diya.'

'Diya,' whispered Bindiya.

'Diya Madhuri Chauhan,' said Samar.

'It's a beautiful name.'

'She was beautiful too.'

Bindiya smiled.

'It was her kidneys that took her away from us. I was twenty when both her kidneys failed. We got her a transplant and it all seemed okay for a short while but then her body rejected the kidney ... and that was that,' said Samar, mildly surprised even as he spoke that he was actually sharing such personal information with someone from work.

'What was she like?' asked Bindiya a little later, her gentle voice blending with the gurgling of the stream, the only other sound in the vicinity.

'Very strong.' The words came out of Samar's mouth before he could stop them. 'Very strong and very beautiful. She was a banker and, like you, a dancer too.'

'Really?'

'Yep,' said Samar, nodding and looking at Bindiya, who now sat on the boulder hugging her knees.

'What kind of a dancer?'

'Bharatnatyam.'

'You used to go watch her performances?'

'I never missed a single one.'

'And Mr Chauhan?'

'My father and I used to buy her a lovely bouquet and I'd hand it to her in the green room after the dance recital. Over time it became a ritual for us. A sort of family tradition.'

'How sweet,' said Bindiya, smiling. 'I am sure it meant a lot to your mum too.'

'You know, she helped with two dance recitals after her transplant even though she had stopped working. Dance was her biggest joy even in her last days.'

'Art can be like a lifeboat sometimes, the only thing you can cling to when life throws you into choppy waters,' said Bindiya, and Samar turned to look at her, surprised. He just knew that she was speaking from first-hand experience.

The moon hid behind low-lying clouds and something hooted somewhere, breaking the spell.

119

'Animal!' shrieked Bindiya, clutching the sides of the boulder in shock.

Samar laughed. 'Let's get going?'

'Yes,' she said, smiling.

When they approached the hill again, this time to climb it, Samar offered her his hand silently, without even glancing in her direction, almost as if it was the most normal thing to do. And this time Bindiya did not hesitate to put her hand in his.

That night Bindiya dozed off thinking about and trying to understand why she had felt so much stronger and safer with Samar's fingers clasped around hers. The simple complexity and beauty of two people, strangers still but not quite strangers, holding hands while negotiating a hillside, under a duvet of stars and the moon, was not lost on her.

120

Not unlike Bindiya, Samar too went to bed thinking of their little trip to the stream. Bindiya's shy smile. Strands of her hair that she had to continuously push away from her face. The joy that radiated from her ...

Sometimes you don't quite know why you connect with a person. For Samar, Bindiya and the ease with which he was able to connect with her was turning out to be an enigma. Only for the second time in about a decade and a half since her passing away had Samar voluntarily divulged information about his mother. He had not spoken about this either with his father or Malika or Madhav. Was it because Bindiya, with her open smile and honest expression looked so innocent and harmless? Or was it something deeper, more complex? Why did it seem okay to talk to her about things he would not normally breathe a word about to anyone else? Why did she not seem like a stranger when she was one? Why did something in him recognize something in her? Why did he feel that he knew her from before, from another world?

25

The next morning, Bindiya found herself trying hard not to continuously stare at the door to Samar's room, impatiently waiting for it to open and for him to emerge.

At 7.30 a.m. he came out. But he was not alone.

Malika, looking stunning in a white salwaar kameez, was standing next to him, laughing and gazing up at him. For Bindiya, the earth stopped spinning for a few seconds. How long had she been in his room? What had they been doing inside? Had she spent the night with him?

Bindiya stared at the piece of bread in her hands and then shook her head. Even douchebags like Rehan were not interested in a meaningful relationship with her and this was Samar Chauhan, super rich, super successful and ten years her senior. What had she even been thinking?

121

❋

'Bindiya Saran,' Firoze exclaimed, looking appreciatively at her, 'you look stunning!'

'Thank you, Firoze, you don't look too bad yourself,' Bindiya replied with a warm smile.

It was the last night at the camp and everyone had collected under the colourful marquee for the gala dinner co-hosted by Samar and Madhav. The dress code was 'formal, bring out your glamorous best'. Unlike the other girls who were wearing dresses, Bindiya had chosen to wear a Satya Paul off-white sari. A generous dab of her trusty eyeliner completed her simple look. However, as the only girl in an Indian outfit, she felt extremely out of place. Compliments such as the one from Firoze had flowed freely but Bindiya knew better than to believe them. She found herself toying with the idea of rushing back to her cottage to change into a simple black dress no one would notice.

Lost in her discomfort, she failed to notice Samar's reaction when he spotted her. He stared unblinkingly at the vision in white. The ivory of the sari set off her peaches-and-cream complexion beautifully, and the low back of her blouse added just that hint of sensuality. Bindiya's hair was tied in an elegant chignon and decorated with white flowers Samar had seen growing around the camp; her expressive, kohl-rimmed eyes shone bright and intelligent. Breathtakingly simple, entirely unaware. Samar told himself not to stare and then promptly sneaked one more look.

The music was just beginning to pick up and Malika came to him, smiling widely. She had never referred to that night when Samar had refused to kiss her; instead, Malika had become more attentive to his mood and let him be when she sensed that he needed to be alone. For the moment, she stood next to him, slipped a hand through his and looked expectantly at him.

'No compliments, Samar? Where are your manners?'

'You look beautiful, Malika,' he said, smiling but barely glancing at the tiny black dress Malika wore.

'You don't mean it.'

Samar smiled and said nothing. Malika was about to pester him but fortuitously for Samar, the familiar beats of Frank Sinatra's 'Stardust' trickled in.

'Can I at least get a dance if not a compliment?' Malika asked.

'Of course, come on,' he said and led her to the dance floor.

Bindiya lost track of what she was saying when she saw Samar lead Malika to the dance floor. He was impeccably dressed in a tux and radiated power, strength and wealth.

Malika's LBD, rumour had it, was an Alexander McQueen. It probably cost more than what Bindiya earned in a year. Together, Malika and Samar looked stunning.

'The power couple,' someone standing next to Bindiya muttered.

Couple.

Samar and Malika were the only two people on the dance floor except for some men who had gotten drunk too early in the evening and were dancing the bhangra to Frank Sinatra. Malika delicately put a hand on Samar's chest and Bindiya saw Samar glide his arm around her waist. The two swayed to the music, moving in unison. Malika was of course a fantastic dancer (was there anything she was not perfect at?) but the surprise was Samar. He moved rhythmically to the beat, with the ease of someone who knew what he was doing.

There was no denying it: Samar and Malika looked perfect together, custom-made for each other. Bindiya hated what she was seeing.

From the corner of his eye, Samar saw Bindiya stare at them for a few minutes, excuse herself from the group and walk away. Malika gave a deep, satisfied sigh and snuggled in closer.

Bindiya walked fast, her legs racing with the thoughts that created havoc in her head.

He is one of the most powerful men in one of the largest companies in India. Powerful like Malika is, successful like Malika is, rich like Malika is. Not insignificant like I am.

He hardly knows me. I hardly know him.

He has helped me once, spoken to me twice and looked at me thrice. There is no reason for me to expect anything else. I shouldn't be upset because he is dancing with a woman he probably loves. I have absolutely no grounds to be upset. Yet I am. Very, very. Why?

Bindiya stopped walking when she felt she was far enough. Only faint strains of the music now reached her. She sat down on a bench overlooking the forest and took a deep breath, taking in the fresh smell of the kind deodars. As the stillness of the forest calmed her, she shook her head.

What was wrong with her? How could she be so irrational? So petulant?

He probably loves her and, really, there is no denying that they look perfect together ... anyone can see that. You mean nothing to him, it's stupid to even think otherwise, Bindiya Saran! Stop these thoughts. Now. Now!

'Ms Saran?' came a smooth voice, and Bindiya could have cried with relief.

'Samar?' She turned around sharply, eager – too eager – to see him, to reassure herself that it was indeed him and not her imagination playing tricks on her.

'Are you okay?' The concern in his voice was unmistakable.

'Y ... yes ...'

You are looking beautiful tonight, he wanted to say, *and I saw the expression on your face when you left the marquee. I had to come check on you.* 'Have you met Madhav?' he asked instead.

Bindiya shook her head. 'I mean, I have of course seen him from a distance but ...'

'Come, let me introduce you to him. You'll like him,' he said, smiling a rare smile. The two of them got up and started walking towards the marquee. For a brief moment, just a very brief moment, Samar placed a protective hand on the small of her back.

His warm hand against her cold waist. For as long as his hand was there, every inch of her was focused on the sensation of him touching her. She shook her head. *I've lost it.*

As Bindiya and Samar chatted with Madhav, at a distance, Naina looked on in wonder. She had rarely seen Samar talk so much, laugh so much and look as animated as he did now speaking to Bindiya and Madhav. Bindiya giggled while covering her mouth with her hand, she pouted when she heard something she did not like, made faces that drew that precious smile from Samar, gestured passionately with her hands, threw her head back and laughed ... in short she exuded life. And Samar basked in its glory.

'Bless you, Bindiya Saran,' Naina mumbled to herself, unable to take her eyes off the smiling face of Samar Chauhan, the man to whom she owed her life. 'God bless you!'

❋

125

Back in Mumbai, Samar was staring intently at a presentation Atul was walking him through. Bindiya looked at his intense eyes and intelligent face, and an odd thought crossed her mind.

With such an intense expression even while listening to a colleague, how would Samar look, um, say, telling a girl that he loves her? Er ... not me, of course, he's not in love with me ... like, whichever girl he ... um ...

And she decided it would be best to get back to work and not think any more about Samar's intense eyes or the girl that he loved.

26

It was 5.30 a.m., and Samar was on the treadmill. Madhav was on the adjacent treadmill and the two friends were, as had been their habit for the longest time, getting their money's worth out of the editorial sections of the seven newspapers they made it a point to read through each day.

Madhav slowed his speed and Samar looked up quizzically. 'I like her too,' he said decisively, his green eyes dancing with anticipation of a reaction from Samar.

'Like whom?' asked Samar, though of course he knew.

'Bindiya.'

'And what's that supposed to mean?'

'Why would that mean anything, Samar?'

'So this is just a casual remark?'

'Absolutely!' said Madhav. 'Unless of course you have reason to believe that it should mean more, in which case I am all ears.'

'Are you done? Can I get back to my newspaper now?'

'Of course. I am just wondering why an innocent comment got such a reaction?'

'Madhav,' said Samar, turning around to face his childhood friend. 'Do you want me to get off the treadmill and hit you?'

'You were the boxing champion at uni, my friend, I don't wish to tempt fate,' said Madhav in a pretend-meek voice, laughing to himself.

❀

As time progressed, so did the project, and so did Bindiya and Ojas's odd friendship.

Ojas Chauhan, whose details were included in the 'Alumni of Note' section of the Wharton website, spent a lot of time each week with children in slums across Mumbai. Over time, whenever Bindiya had a few free hours in a weekend, she found herself accompanying him and sitting through some of the most entertaining elementary maths classes she had ever attended. Ojas had a very unique, interactive way of teaching. He used trees, pebbles, pet mice and dollops of fun to acquaint kids with the magic of numbers. Enthralled, Bindiya watched the kids develop a love for numbers. Ojas Uncle was like a master artist, moulding each child, taking her away from the physical filth around them to a dream which was happy, safe and possible.

Soon, the endearing crowd of happy faces that yelped 'Twenty-five!' in unison to Ojas Uncle's 'How much is five times five?' began to take on specific names and characteristics for Bindiya. There was Raju who always got the two times tables wrong even though he could rattle tables upto seven. There was Pinky who wanted to become a tree when she grew up. And there was Pankaj who lisped 'Humpathy dumpathy' much to her delight.

127

Mr Chauhan was their beloved Ojas Uncle, which was what Bindiya started calling him as well. She herself soon became Bee didi.

Helping others less fortunate than you fills you with hope. It is, as they say, an exercise for the heart. In helping others, you give more to your soul than to the person you are helping. Bindiya was among those lucky ones who had realized this very early on in life. In her darkest years others had helped her and now that she was stronger, Bindiya tried her best to help whomever she could, be it the girls from Ujala or the kids in the slums with Ojas Uncle.

'You know Ujala is Samar's baby?'

'You mean he set it up?' asked Bindiya, surprised.

'He conceptualized and set it up,' said Ojas Uncle, a hint of pride in his voice, 'many years ago.'

'I didn't know that.' She wondered, why something like Ujala?

'He's silent about most things.'

'You know what, Ojas Uncle, we should ask Samar to attend these maths classes with us!' she said, getting excited at the idea.

Ojas looked a little uncomfortable. 'I don't think he'll come anywhere with me,' he muttered.

'Why? Because he won't have the time?'

'No, Bindiya, he won't want to come with me,' Ojas repeated in a quiet voice.

'Oh,' was all that Bindiya managed in response, her brain working fast. She had never seen the two men talk to each to other, or heard them talk much about each other. Were father and son not on speaking terms, she thought, horrified.

'Let it be, Bee,' Ojas said, reading her expression.

Bindiya knew better than to ask why.

128

❀

'Samar,' said Malika, 'I think we need to talk about that ... um, what's her name, you know, the Saran girl.'

Samar's eyebrows shot up. The two of them had just wrapped up an important meeting that Bindiya had also been a part of, and were gathering their files before leaving the room.

'You mean Bindiya Saran,' he said, a note of icy politeness creeping into his voice.

'Yes, yes, the Saran girl,' said Malika dismissively. 'I'm very worried.'

'About?'

'Her and Ojas Uncle,' said Malika.

'What about them?'

'Do you know they are friends?' she said, using air quotes for 'friends'.

'Yes.'

'Ojas Uncle even takes her to some of the maths classes he conducts in the slums.'

'I know.'

'And you're not worried?'

'About what?'

'Samar, what makes you think that a sixty-eight-year-old man and a twenty-something girl can be friends?'

'What do you mean?'

'Oh Samar, don't you see what is happening? Bindiya is just pretending to be friends with Ojas Uncle ... just to ... you know ...' She left the sentence incomplete and looked at Samar meaningfully.

'Just to what?'

'Samar, Bindiya is not exactly super rich. Who knows what kind of a plan she is hatching to squeeze money out of Ojas Uncle? You have to be very careful with such girls who have grown up without money. These girls, from small families, are all alike and equally dangerous. There was this maid Mum had—'

A polite cough, and Malika stopped short. Bindiya stood shuffling at the door, the tips of her ears a bright red.

'Um, I left my phone here,' Bindiya mumbled to the floor, lunged forward to where her phone was lying, and fled.

'Damn it,' mumbled Samar and, pausing only to shoot Mallika a thunderous look, dashed out of the meeting room after Bindiya.

Vaguely aware that Samar was walking briskly after her, Bindiya, in no mood to have anything to do with him, rushed into the ladies' room, the one place she knew Samar could not follow her into.

Once inside, Bindiya planted her hands on either side of

129

the sink and took several deep breaths, trying and failing to calm herself. Malika's voice rang in her ears, humiliating and disparaging. Bindiya looked up into the mirror to see a red-eyed, flushed-looking girl staring back at her. The tears, angry and helpless, now began to flow down her cheeks.

She hurriedly turned on the tap and splashed cold water all over her face in an attempt to stop the sobs that threatened to burst forth.

'Ms Saran?'

Bindiya looked up, startled. Samar stood a few feet away from her, inside the ladies' room, both hands thrust in the pockets of his trousers, face serious.

'You can't come here!' she exclaimed, horrified.

'No one tells me what I can or can't do, Ms Saran,' came the cool response.

'Samar, this is the ladies'!'

'And what makes you think I care about that?'

'Samar ... I ...'

Bindiya stopped short. A girl with a long ponytail was standing at the door, staring unblinkingly at Samar.

'Get out,' snarled Samar, turning around to face the unsuspecting girl.

The girl stared at him, her mouth open, stunned. 'This ... th ... is ... the ... ladies' ...' she mumbled heroically.

'Out!' Samar's growl now held a sinister threat of things to come. The girl, intelligent enough to sense it, about-turned and scurried away. Samar walked over to Bindiya and stared intently at her face, taking in the flushed cheeks and wet eyes.

Bindiya sniffed and then wiped her nose with the back of her hand. Samar pulled out a white handkerchief from his pocket and offered it to her. Bindiya shook her head.

'I insist,' he said curtly.

One look at Samar's stern face and Bindiya found herself petulantly accepting the little white cloth. She stood there, her back against the sink, facing Samar, strands of wet hair stuck to her temples and cheeks, her eyes and nose red from crying. She fiddled with Samar's handkerchief and stared at the floor.

A few minutes passed in silence. Bindiya stared at the floor and Samar, hands crossed across his chest, stared at her.

'Most people,' he began and Bindiya looked up, 'born with a mouth can, unfortunately, speak, though a lot of them shouldn't be allowed to.'

Bindiya nodded. Samar now leaned in, his eyes gleaming. 'If anyone ever has a go at you or your family again, don't you dare leave and go scurrying into the ladies' to cry your eyes out!'

Bindiya stared at him, her eyes locked into his.

'You stay put, look them in the eye and give it right back to them a hundred times worse,' he said. 'Got it?'

Startled, Bindiya barely managed a slight nod of her head.

'You want to wash your face? We can go out together afterwards?'

'No one tells me what I can or can't do,' said Bindiya in a watery voice, a poor imitation of Samar's powerful baritone.

A small smile appeared on Samar's face as he leaned across to turn on the tap for her.

That afternoon Adi met Bindiya for lunch. He could feel his heart thump in his chest as she walked in. After all these years, he had finally decided to tell her everything, get it off his chest.

He hoped that even if Bindiya said no, their bond was strong enough to ensure that their friendship remained the way it was. Their friendship, so precious to him, had been the main reason Adi had never brought this up, never sure what was going on in Bindiya's mind. And then in front of his eyes Rehan had happened. Adi had never liked him and had hated seeing Bindiya look so unhappy with him. She hit her lowest when she broke up with him. Adi had a strong feeling that Rehan had treated Bindiya terribly, but Bindiya had never shared with him what had really happened. In a way, that worked with him; he was better off being ignorant of the exact details, scared of what he would do to Rehan if he found out.

Now finally, Bindiya seemed to be in a better place. She smiled often and had a healthy glow about her. It was, Adi knew, time for him to come clean.

'He came after me,' Bindiya said, even before she said hello, 'straight into the ladies'!'

'Eh?'

'Samar!'

And Adi breathed deep. For the next twenty minutes Bindiya talked non-stop about Samar and with each passing second Adi felt his heart sink further. 'Do you like him, Bindiya?' he heard himself ask. How had he been so blind?

'What ... erm ... no ... I mean, you know ... he's Samar Chauhan, the Samar Chauhan. He's on magazine covers, Adi, television channels interview him and he breakfasts with politicians, like, every day ... why would he ever be interested in me?'

'That was not my question, Bee,' said Adi calmly. 'Do you like Samar?'

'Shut up!' she yelped and threw her napkin at him. Bindiya had not answered Adi's question in words but he did not need them any more. The deep blush on her face told him, plainly and clearly, all he needed to know.

'You wanted to talk about something verrrrryyyy important?' Bindiya asked, teasing, desperate to change the topic.

'Yeah ...' he said and paused, and then continued, 'my job, Bee, I think I should start applying elsewhere ...'

For the next one hour Bindiya and her friend of two decades spoke at length first about Adi's job and then again about Samar. A lot about Samar.

Before they bid goodbye Adi looked silently at the animated girl in front of him. *It hurts, you know, to know that you'll never look at me the way I look at you. Should I be happy that you are my friend? Or mourn that you'll never be anything more?*

133

27

Samar looked out of the car window and stiffened. It almost felt like he had been caught red-handed when he spotted the long plait resting against the now familiar thin frame; Samar had just been thinking of Bindiya and how she had looked up at him in the ladies' when he had barged in. That look on her face had taken him elsewhere; he had forgotten everything for one mad minute. Her vulnerability was as scary as it was all-consuming. Seven long days packed full of meetings and decisions had since passed without as much as a glimpse of Bindiya ... and yet he remembered every bit of her expression as if it had all just happened.

Bindiya, waiting listlessly for the company cab to arrive, was thinking about Samar. She had not seen him in a week and was now desperate for a glimpse.

'Where's he been?' she mumbled to herself, tapping her

foot impatiently. As if on cue, a formidable-looking black Mercedes-Benz AMG G stopped in front of her and Samar rolled down his window. Bindiya knew her face had reddened with embarrassment and she dug her fingers into her palm in a desperate attempt to look nonchalant.

'Hello, Ms Saran. Are you waiting for the company cab?' Samar asked.

'Yes,' said Bindiya, pushing her spectacles up her nose and trying very hard to ignore her heart which had begun to thump mercilessly at the sight of Samar Chauhan.

'Can I drop you home?'

'No ... it's ...'

'Not okay, come on in.'

'No ... no.'

134

'Ms Saran,' Samar said in a stern voice, 'It's close to midnight and it will simply be safer if I drop you home.'

Bindiya meekly got into the car. For a few minutes neither of them spoke. Bindiya was, Samar noted, barely able to sit in her place. She looked around restlessly, bit her lip and at one point actually sat on her own hands.

'Out with it, please?' Samar said, raising his eyebrows.

Bindiya shot him such a deeply wounded look that Samar almost smiled.

'Out with it!' he insisted.

'Actually ... I am very hungry!' she said, fiddling with her fingers.

'What?'

'Yes!'

'What "yes"?'

'I need to eat. Now,' she said, pouting. 'Otherwise I'll probably die of hunger. No, not probably, most definitely!' she finished dramatically.

'What about the office canteen? Why didn't you eat something there?'

'They had nothing.'

'Nothing?'

A sheepish look crossed Bindiya's face. 'Well, nothing I like,' she said finally.

Samar shook his head. 'Surat, can you please take us to ... um, let's see what's closest ... Grand Hyatt? Ms Saran is dying of hunger.'

'Surat bhaiya!' Bindiya yelped and then shut up the moment she saw Samar's expression. 'I mean, Surat bhaiya,' she began again in a more dignified voice, 'sorry I forgot to say hi. How are Pinku, Chitku and Bottle?'

'Who the hell are Pinku, Chitku and Bottle?' Samar asked, looking first at Bindiya who was sitting at the edge of the car seat and then in the rearview mirror at Surat.

'My new dogs,' said Surat, grinning widely.

'Surat bhaiya took three of the eight pups we had at Ujala after Ojas Uncle told him about them.'

'Oh. And who named them?'

'Chitku and Pinku were named by my son,' said Surat. 'And Bottle—'

'Let me make a really wild guess,' interjected Samar, rolling his eyes at Bindiya.

Bindiya grinned and then laughed.

'Bottle is not Bottle's full name, of course,' added Surat, winking at Samar in the rearview mirror.

'Do I even want to know what Bottle's full name is?' Samar said, shaking his head.

'Yes,' said Bindiya, 'of course you want to know what Bottle's full name is.'

'What is it?'

135

'Bottle of Milk.'

Samar ran a hand over his forehead. 'The pup is called Bottle of Milk?' he repeated.

'Yes,' she said assertively.

'Oh god,' said Samar, now laughing. 'And that is because?'

'Because he looks like a bottle of milk.'

'A pup that looks like a bottle of milk?'

'Yes!'

Samar shook his head and looked so bewildered that Bindiya couldn't help but dissolve into peals of uncontrollable laughter. Surat joined in too and before long, for the first time in almost a decade, Samar found himself laughing out loud.

Samar and Bindiya dined at that rather odd hour at the exclusive, exorbitantly priced Grand Hyatt. On spotting Samar walk in, the waiters mumbled to each other and hurried to get the manager. The manager who, Bindiya noted, behaved in the most servile manner imaginable, took them to 'your favourite table, sir' which was a lonely table at the far end of the room, in a dimly lit, cosy corner.

'That way I can steer clear of people,' said Samar as he helped Bindiya take her seat.

Bindiya rolled her eyes. Steer clear of people, indeed.

Samar sipped his coffee and watched, with no small degree of amusement, a large, cheesy, calorie-rich lasagna disappear at record pace from Bindiya's plate.

It's strange the way, sometimes, conversation can flow as easy as a lazy, meandering river between two people who seem to have precious little in common.

'How's Urvi?' Samar asked, sipping his coffee.

'She is fine,' Bindiya replied turning over the glossy menu 'You have to be kidding me. This tiny little cup of coffee costs Rs 1200?'

'It's not the coffee's fault, really, you know.' His eyes were laughing.

'Can I take a sip?'

'Of my coffee?'

'Yes, of your coffee,' she said confidently and then she began her fumbling. 'No, of course not ... I mean ...'

'Here you go,' said Samar and handed her his cup.

Bindiya put aside her fork and spoon and took a cautious mouthful. Her face was contorted into a grimace when she handed the cup back to Samar. 'Nothing special about it,' she said, giving the coffee a final, dismissive glance.

Samar smiled. 'So this coffee does not get your approval, but tell me, what does?' he asked.

'Ice cream.' Pat came the reply, making Samar smile. 'When I was little, I could eat ten ice creams in one go. Not kidding, mind you. At one point, people around me were worried I had ice cream gushing through my veins instead of blood.'

'What rubbish!' said Samar, laughing.

'And you?'

'Me?'

'What did you like when you were a little boy?'

'That was such a long time back.'

'Come on, tell me.'

'Okay, let's see ... I think I used to like mountains the best.'

'OMG.' Bindiya spelt out the letters.

Samar was already smiling again. 'What now?'

'Ice cream was my most favourite thing, and mountains second most,' she said, slapping the table.

'You are just making that up,' said Samar.

'No, I swear. So Adi told me that if you draw something on the wall of your living room, it'll come alive in the night. I thought hard the whole day and after due deliberation I drew huge brown mountains on the walls.'

'And what happened that night?'

'A glorious thrashing from Mum,' she said, laughing hard.

Samar found himself staring at the girl in front of him as she laughed uncontrollably at the memory of being thrashed for scribbling on walls.

'Can I ask you something?' came Bindiya's voice.

'Of course you can.'

'Which perfume do you wear?'

Samar rolled his eyes at Bindiya. 'Really?' he asked, looking incredulous. The questions this girl asked.

'Please?'

'Essenza Di Wills Mikkel,' he replied, shaking his head.

'Have you ever gotten your IQ tested?' she asked after a pause.

'What?' Each question seemed weirder than the previous one.

'Yeah?'

'Why do you ask?'

'Your eyes.'

'What about my eyes?' Really, sometimes this girl made no sense.

'They are very intelligent,' she said, looking critically into his eyes.

Samar laughed and Bindiya stared at Samar laughing, an odd look on her face.

'Do you want to eat more?' asked Samar, eyeing her empty plate.

'No, thank you,' she said primly.

'I heard you took some of the Ujala girls out for lunch over the weekend,' said Samar.

138

'Yes, I wanted to take them some place healthy but all they wanted to eat were McDonald's burgers and French fries.'

'It's nice, what you do with them.'

'It's nice, what you do with Ujala,' said Bindiya.

'I understand that you teach some kids over the weekends too.'

'Yes, with Ojas Uncle,' she said, brightening up at the thought of her friend.

'Why? Most people your age are busy partying or shopping or whatever it is that young people these days do.'

'Life has to mean a little bit more, Samar, sometimes at least,' she said, staring at her plate.

Samar found himself analysing Bindiya as he watched the overtly obsequious waiter clear their table. She was a mix of contradictions; one moment Samar felt he had her figured out and the next he felt completely stumped. She was as mad as she was sincere. She could be the mother one moment and the helpless baby the next. She was a shield of fierce protection now and heartbreaking fragility a moment later. Who was she? He looked at her.

Sensing eyes on her, Bindiya, who had been fiddling with her phone, now looked up. The shy, small smile was back on.

'Let's go?' Samar asked, looking at his watch. It was close to one now.

They left the restaurant and made their way through the vast, well-kept lawns of the hotel to their waiting car. Ornate yellow lamps cast a warm glow on the green grass that glistened under the full moon.

'Samar,' came a soft voice.

He looked down and saw a pair of large, innocent eyes staring at him. 'Hmm?'

'You look very nice,' she said simply, 'when you laugh. You should laugh more.'

He looked at her and into her eyes, feeling, for some reason, something tug at his heart. Her words were unpretentious and she did not expect a response. He saw her gulp and then a shadow of apprehension darkened her face. The wind picked up a strand of her long hair and began to dance with it.

What power did this girl have on him, Samar wondered. Too mesmerized by her to even think about consequences, Samar instinctively reached out and brushed the hair behind her ear. Her hair was soft. Very soft. The back of his fingers touched her temple and then her right ear. It was ice-cold. He looked into her eyes questioningly. And she looked into his eyes, transfixed, not comprehending, but lost in the moment. He knew her. She knew him. They were strangers. They were bound with something they could not see.

'You have a very pretty face, you should show it more,' he said and watched, with the delight of a connoisseur, a deep blush rise on Bindiya's face.

For one wild moment, Bindiya allowed herself to wonder how it would feel to have Samar's arms wrapped tightly around her. But she shook her head; there was no point in going there, she told herself.

Yet, as they walked in silence, the air between them was charged with an undercurrent Bindiya had never experienced before. It seemed like the world consisted of just the two of them, connected to each other in more ways than logic or science could explain. She could still feel Samar's fingers brush against her ear. Gentle, tender and so intimate that she could still feel the goosebumps. His eyes had bored into hers, searching, finding, exploring ... Would her heart please stop thumping NOW?

Her hand brushed against Samar's by accident and, horrified that he should think she was doing this deliberately, she hurriedly pulled away. A moment or two later, she felt warm fingers wrap themselves around hers.

Artistic, elegant fingers. Familiar even when unfamiliar.

Bindiya did not pull away. She did not look up. She forgot to breathe. She knew intense eyes were on her, scrutinizing every thought that crossed her face. It was old-fashioned to feel so shy when a guy held your hand, yet she did. She also felt inexplicably happy – very happy, very, very happy.

Later in the night, Samar found himself trying hard to concentrate on the complicated business matter in front of him but the numbers made little sense. He would pause every once in a while and think about Bindiya.

A voice in his head warned him to stay away from Bindiya, more for her sake than his, but just for once, he wanted to listen to his heart which had begun to speak to him for the first time in a decade.

141

❀

'Bindiya,' said Malika, walking into the meeting room.

'Malika, good afternoon,' said Bindiya, trying hard to forget what she had heard Malika say about her a fortnight ago. Malika always made Bindiya feel unduly anxious, mostly because of the way she looked at her. She wondered if Malika wanted to apologize to her.

'Thank you for accepting the meeting invite,' Malika said curtly, giving her freshly blow-dried hair a pat.

'Not a problem, Malika. How can I help?' said Bindiya, opening her laptop.

'How about,' said Malika, sitting down across her and

leaning forward to shut Bindiya's laptop, 'for starters, leaving Samar alone?'

'I'm sorry?' said Bindiya, not sure she had heard Malika right.

'Leave. Samar. Alone.' Malika's eyes stabbed into Bindiya's face. The low pitch of her voice added a sinister touch, and Bindiya shivered.

'I ... no ... I have ... nothing ... I ...'

'Bindiya Saran,' said Malika, now getting up and walking towards Bindiya, 'girl to girl. Woman to woman.'

She now sat down right next to Bindiya. A waft of Malika's expensive perfume hit Bindiya.

'I love Samar, have loved him for decades now,' said Malika. 'I will not let anything come between us.' She had been informed of how Bindiya had gotten into Samar's car two nights back and Malika had not slept properly since. It was, Malika knew, time to have a straight conversation with the Saran girl.

'B ... but ... I ...'

'Stay away from him, Bindiya. Just stay away. You'll regret it if you don't,' said Malika.

'I ... I ...'

'Just because he looks kindly at you does not mean he has time for filth like you. If he wants filth, trust me, thousands of girls are lined up, legs spread wide apart for him.'

Bindiya blinked, again not sure she had heard Malika right. Then she stopped the silent blubbering, feeling foolish and weak. She should retort with something suitably hurtful. Why, instead, were tears beginning to gather in her eyes?

'Don't think for a minute that you mean more to him than ... um ...' Malika looked around and finally tapped the meeting room table, 'than this table. No one, I repeat, no man with any self-respect would have anything to do with a girl with as colourful a family as yours is, Ms Saran. I am sure you are well aware of that?'

Bindiya stared at Malika. She knew? Had she told Samar?

'One gets enough whores in this city, Ms Saran, there's no reason why he would be interested in you. If you spend any more time with Samar, trust me, you will regret it,' Malika finished, her steely eyes burning with anger.

Bindiya bolted out the room, angry and more humiliated than she had ever felt before. Not so long ago, Samar had told her to give it back if someone tried to put her down. Yet, all she had done this time too was burst into helpless tears.

Malika sat in the meeting room for a long time after Bindiya had left, thinking hard about the person she had become. Had she really uttered the mean, heartless words? Oddly enough, her heart now went out to Bindiya. The poor Saran girl had just sat there and listened when she should have gotten up and slapped Malika. Malika wondered if she was that desperate for Samar and that insecure about Bindiya's unassuming charm.

'Yes and yes,' she said out loud, sparing a hand over her forehead. 'I hate the person I am becoming ... I hate her,' she mumbled helplessly.

28

For Bindiya it had been just another dance recital. A rather sad, lonely one.

Urvi had another interview to prepare for and Mum had a cold. Adi should have come but he had, for reasons that Bindiya could not fathom, begun to distance himself from her. Bindiya made a mental note to find out if she had offended him in any way. Meanwhile in the green room, the air was abuzz with the excitement that inevitably comes after a successful performance.

Being alone is okay; being lonely is not. And it was with a deep sense of yearning that Bindiya looked around as parents, boyfriends, and siblings hugged the other dancers. She was, yet again, the only girl without a guest. Only, for some reason, tonight it hurt more than usual.

'I am not alone,' she mumbled to herself, 'and even if I am, is that such a bad thing? I like being alone.'

Most people who tell themselves that they like being alone, actually, desperately need someone. And Bindiya was no exception. Yet she valiantly kept trying.

Be happy for the others, not sad for yourself, she told herself firmly, and began to pack her bags.

Bindiya walked out of the green room, telling herself that she was feeling a lot better. She tried hard to focus on all that was beautiful around her. It was a lovely evening, pleasantly cold, with just that hint of approaching winter. Bindiya knew that right outside the building was a pretty walkway. She was planning to dump her stuff in the car and then take a long leisurely walk in the company of the trees that lined the walkway on either side, listening to their rustling leaves, a sound that always brought her great peace.

Yet she heaved a deep sigh as she lifted her bags and had to make an effort to smile a goodbye to the girls who continued their excited chatter. Try as she might, she found it tough to get rid of the heaviness around her.

She toyed with the unthinkable idea of texting Samar, looked up briefly, sensing someone's eyes on her, and then went back to the phone.

And then she stopped in her tracks. Looked up again. Had

144

she just seen someone familiar? Was her mind playing tricks on her?

For in front of her, a few feet away, face visible intermittently as people milled around, stood Samar, a huge bouquet of white and lavender lilies in his hands.

'Hello,' he said in a soft voice when he was close enough. 'Your dance was beautiful,' he said, handing her the flowers.

'You are here?' Bindiya asked stupidly, accepting the flowers.

'It does seem like it,' said Samar, smiling but continuing to look intently at her. What was it with the way Samar looked at her? Like if she were the sun, everyone else was but a faint star. Like if she were a star, she was the only star in a moonless night. Like if she were the moon, she were the full moon poets waxed lyrical about. Something – no, everything – about the way he stood there made her feel that her heart would burst. She clenched her fists with all her might and bit her lip, desperate not to lose her composure.

145

'My first post-dance recital bouquet,' she said instead looking at the flowers.

The red nose. The red eyes. The flushed cheeks. She had definitely been crying. Why did his chest tighten at the thought of her crying alone? Had someone said something? Should he ask?

'Fancy a walk?' he heard himself ask instead.

'Yes! There's a lovely walkway just outside. Aren't you supposed to be travelling?'

'Meeting got pushed around,' he said briefly. What he didn't want to tell Bindiya was that he had proactively changed the location and time of the meeting to attend her recital, the invitation to which he had been given, most shyly, a week back. Seeing her like this, he felt glad he had come.

The wind picked up speed and the two of them walked in

silence. Already feeling a lot happier, Bindiya untied her hair and gave it a shake so that it cascaded against her back.

'You should let the wind play with your hair while you still have some,' she said, winking.

Samar smiled and stuffed his hands in his pockets, happy in the knowledge that the familiar chirpy Bindiya was back.

'Samar,' she said a moment later.

'Yes?'

'Do you look like your mum?'

Samar shook his head. This girl asked the weirdest questions! 'Why do you ask?'

'Because you don't look like Ojas Uncle.'

Samar laughed in spite of himself. 'I've been told that I get my eyes from Mum,' he said, smiling.

'Oh, your mum had beautiful eyes, then,' said Bindiya and then promptly turned tomato-red.

A small smile played on Samar's lips for a good few moments before he spoke. 'Yes, she did. Would you like to have a look at her picture?'

'Yes!'

Samar flicked open his phone and went into the photograph folder, amazed at how easy it was for him to share his mother with Bindiya.

In her excitement, Bindiya put her hand on Samar's arm to lean forward and have a look. 'She was beautiful,' she said softly, 'you must miss her so much.'

'I do, every minute of each day.'

Bindiya nodded; she knew how that felt.

'Bindiya,' said Samar after a few minutes as they walked side by side near the trees.

'Yes?'

'You were upset when I first saw you today?'

When she said nothing he probed further. 'What happened? Did someone say anything?'

'No ... no ...'

'Then?'

'It's silly ...'

'I want to know.'

'Um, I ... just a little lonely,' she said. 'Everyone had guests with them and they kept on asking me who was coming to watch my dance. Usually I lie but you know I sometimes, it's nice to have someone, I mean ...'

'I was there,' said Samar.

'Yes,' she said, smiling. 'I know that now.'

'Does that make it better?'

'Yes,' she said shyly. 'In fact, I want to go back in and tell the girls they might have heard of a business whiz by the name of Samar Chauhan? He's my guest.' She was laughing now.

Samar grinned. 'Business whiz,' he scoffed good-naturedly. 'Business whiz has something important to tell you.'

'What?'

'I'll be travelling now – for four weeks.'

'But you just came back!' The distressed words were out before Bindiya could stop them.

'Yes, I have to travel quite a bit though not typically for as long as four weeks but ... um, we have another important deal to close in Canada. Malika finally managed to set up some key meetings. It all happened this morning – all very last minute.'

Malika. Bindiya wondered if she should tell Samar about her conversation with Malika.

'She requested you to go to Canada?' Bindiya asked.

'I wouldn't exactly call it a "request",' Samar said.

Bindiya smiled a weak smile, trying her best to camouflage her sadness, for something else had just struck her.

'By the time you come back, I would have finished my project at the Zorawar Group,' she said softly, looking down.

'No, we have requested IC to let you stay an extra two weeks to wrap up the project ... the whole team, I mean,' Samar added hurriedly.

'Oh, have you?'

'Yes, because, of course, the project needs you lot for some more time,' he said. 'That was another reason why I wanted to come to the dance—'

'To say goodbye?' Bindiya broke in, her eyes large and sad. Samar nodded.

'You know, goodbyes are hard for the person leaving, but they are harder for the person staying behind,' Bindiya said.

Samar looked away, gobsmacked by both how profound some of the things Bindiya said could be and how difficult this little goodbye was turning out to be.

'I'll see you in four weeks' time ...' she said quietly. 'Try not to fire anyone,' she added with a weak smile.

The kind of smile that breaks your heart and at the same time makes you want to smile right back.

'I'll try not to,' he said, smiling. 'Take care, Bindiya. If ... you need anything, Dad, Madhav and Surat will be around,' he added.

Bindiya nodded and began to walk towards her car, Samar watching in silence. It was weird but the rickety red Maruti somehow suited Bindiya. They were alike in many ways – a bit crazy and ridiculously loyal. Samar looked away when Bindiya reached her car, distracting himself with his phone, which he knew would already have about a hundred unread emails.

Work. Work. Work.

Work when you want to withdraw into a shell. When the real world puts in front of you something that you haven't experienced in a long time. Something that makes you realize you do have a heart. That people around you have a heart. Work, the best remedy for it all.

I travel all the time. I hardly stay in one place for more than two weeks. Stop this now. She is not your girlfriend. You don't owe her your presence. You don't need to say or do anything more. What the hell is wrong with you?

And then something hit him.

A fierce energy, as two lean arms wrapped themselves around him in a tight hug.

'I'll miss you,' she said urgently, on her tiptoes so that she could whisper in his ears. She was turning to run away when Samar reached out and pulled her back into a hug.

An arm around her waist and another around her shoulders, Samar held Bindiya close. He felt her hesitatingly wrap her arms around him once again and then bury her face in the nape of his neck. Her hair smelled of strawberries and apples. She felt delicate and soft. Gentle. Like a delicate ball of cotton that he could not handle gently enough.

149

When Bindiya finally looked up, her eyes met Samar's. She quickly looked down. His eyes traced every feature on her face. 'I'll be back soon,' he finally managed to say.

Bindiya looked up again but said nothing.

'You take care of yourself, okay?' Samar said again.

Bindiya nodded. 'Can I call you sometime?' she asked in a small voice that made Samar smile.

'Yes. Of course you can.'

'Even if I don't have work to discuss with you?'

'Even if you don't have work to discuss with me.'

'Even if it's not important?'

'Even if it's not important,' said Samar. 'I'll give you my number.'

'I have your number.'

'That's the work number, the whole world has it. I'll pass my personal phone number to you.'

'The one the whole world does not have?'

Samar smiled. 'Correct. Now eight people will have that number,' he said.

Bindiya smiled and unconsciously began to fiddle with the collar of Samar's shirt, lost in thought. She looked so innocently beautiful that Samar found it difficult to peel his eyes off her.

He leaned in, meaning to kiss her, desperate to kiss her, when another face from another life swam in front of his eyes. A face that brought with it a gush of excruciatingly painful memories. He looked at Bindiya, aghast.

What the hell am I doing?

150

'I'll get going now,' he said, his voice devoid of emotion, almost pushing a surprised Bindiya away. Bindiya could only stare.

29

'Bindiya, are you okay?' asked Adi the moment his eyes fell on a tired-looking Bindiya. He was seeing her for the first time since he had asked her about her feelings for Samar and the change in her appearance was as unmissable as it was worrying.

Bindiya looked sad, very sad.

'I am fine ... I am fine,' she said dismissively and sat down, propping her bag next to her.

'I ordered a glass of wine for you,' said Adi, smiling fondly.

'Thanks, Adi, I could probably do with a whole bottle.'

'What's wrong, Bee?'

'Nothing.'

'Liar.'

'What rubbish!'

'I'm asking again — what's wrong?'

Bindiya took a deep breath and looked at Adi. 'You won't let it go, will you?' she asked, smiling a weak smile.

'No, I won't. Mainly because I know you need to and want to talk it out. Out with it now, please?'

For a moment Bindiya stayed silent.

'Go on?'

Bindiya slumped in her chair, suddenly feeling drained of energy. Like a balloon that had been pricked with a pin. 'I don't know what to do, Adi, I just don't,' she said, shaking her head.

'About?'

'Malika's after my life.'

'Oh god, what did she do?'

'She picks on me all the time. She's giving me work I am not supposed to do, then shouting at me in front of everyone, blaming me for things I have nothing to do with — called me irresponsible and juvenile the other day and screamed at me for a mistake I had nothing to do with. It's like she's bent on making life hell for me.'

'Bee ...'

'Adi, she spoke to Atul and has recommended the lowest grade as my rating.'

'What!'

'Yes, I know I was careless in the beginning but after that ... I have worked my hardest.'

'What did Atul say?'

'Nothing, he hasn't decided yet but doesn't help if someone so senior has recommended a poor grade.'

151

'Bee, relax, why don't you talk to Samar about this?'

Samar.

Bindiya shook her head and looked like she could cry any time now.

'What happened, Bindiya?' asked Adi, horrified.

'Adi, I don't know why but Samar is not talking to me.'

'What?' he said, trying to look upset, but somewhere deep inside him a little candle of hope lit up. Adi instantly felt ashamed of his selfishness.

'Yes. He is travelling for four weeks. We met the day he left for Canada and he promised to give me his personal mobile number. But ... but ... just as we were saying goodbye to each other, his face ... it changed, almost like he had seen a ghost ... and he left so abruptly ...'

'He gave you his personal number?' A twinge of jealousy shot through him.

'No, he said he would but he never did ...'

'Oh.'

'And it's been nearly two weeks now, Adi, and I haven't heard anything from him ... not a word. The only emails I get are group emails for the project. I don't know if it was something I said or did that upset him but ... but ...'

'Bee, relax. I'm sure it's nothing. He's just busy.'

'No, the way he left ... there was something so ... so ...' Bindiya trailed off, unable to find the right word to express the anguish she had sensed emanating from Samar when he had pushed her away.

For a few minutes neither spoke. Too many thoughts were running in Adi's head, colliding with each other and creating an unfamiliar havoc.

'Bee,' Adi finally said in a low, serious voice that made Bindiya look up. 'I'll ask you again. Are you in love with Samar?'

152

'I don't know,' she lied this time.

Later that night, Bindiya pulled out her phone and typed an email to which she would never get a reply.

Hi Samar,

I don't know if I said or did something that upset you. I want to let you know that my intention was never to hurt you. I am sorry.

Bindiya

Bindiya reached for a shirt on her bed and clutched it close to her heart. The shirt was hers but she had dabbed generous amounts of Samar's favourite Essenza Di Wills Mikkel perfume on it. And now, as she hugged the shirt, it felt like a bit of Samar was with her.

At some level, Bindiya knew this was pathetic, but how was she supposed to ask her vulnerable heart to behave sensibly when all she could do was think about Samar?

153

She rolled over on her bed, lay stomach down and opened Google images on her phone. She typed in 'Samar Chauhan' and waited patiently as the slow Internet connection threw up tons of images of Samar. She stared at them one by one, taking in every detail. The arch of the brow, the hair, the sharp nose, the eyes that bored into her face through the mobile phone screen.

She then clicked on videos and opened the third link. Here Samar was speaking at a leadership convention in Geneva two years back. Confident, sure, articulate. Accent clipped and smart. Sexy in his own way. Bindiya chose this one because she knew this was the only video in which the camera stayed focused on his face all throughout the twenty-three minutes.

Bindiya did not hear anything Samar said; she did not need to. She had watched the video more than thirty times now and could easily recite the entire speech from memory. She simply stared at the man, finding odd comfort in the images that streamed from the Internet.

She pulled her pillow close to her and soon drifted off to sleep.

30

Sundays, for Bindiya, had now grown synonymous with mathematics, slum kids and hot samosas at Raj Samosawala's street-side shanty.

They had also grown synonymous with long, meandering and delightfully wise conversations with a man Bindiya had grown to truly respect and love: Ojas Uncle.

154

'You know, Bindiya,' said Ojas, taking another sip of cardamom tea from the paper cup in his hand, 'when I was setting up my business and long before I tasted any kind of success, I figured one thing out.'

'And that was?' asked Bindiya, settling in her chair.

'I learnt to celebrate whenever I did not get something I badly wanted.'

Bindiya smiled, all ears, for she knew enough about Ojas Uncle to know that wise words would follow.

'I would try, then fail, then try again and then fail again. I would keep trying till I knew for sure that I had tried as much as I possibly could. And if I still failed, I would celebrate. I would go out and buy myself a beer or a new pen or a cinema ticket or whatever it was that finances then permitted.'

'Why?'

'Because then I knew I was not meant to do what I had been failing at and was now available for something else.

That something, I told myself, would be bigger and more meaningful than what I had been pursuing. And more often than not, I was right.'

Bindiya nodded, taking in every word.

'I achieved all that I did simply because many of my plans did not work out. So remember, dear girl,' said Ojas, reaching across the table and tapping her lightly on her head, 'that sometimes, it is your path that chooses you. Not the other way around. And to let your path, your destiny, choose you, you must do one thing.'

'And that is?'

'You must allow life to surprise you.'

'Surprise me in which way?'

'In any and every way,' said Ojas, 'whether it is career, ambition, or love.'

Love.

155

Bindiya looked up sharply at Ojas. Was he trying to say something?

'Ojas Uncle,' said Bindiya, munching on the Parle G biscuit that came with the chai, 'does Samar do that? Does he let life surprise him?'

'I wish he did, but no, I don't think he can.'

'Why?'

'Life has sprung too many harsh surprises on him for him to welcome them any more.'

'Like?'

'Diya's death for starters.'

'Yes, he told me about that – just a little bit – and he showed me her picture,' said Bindiya.

'Did he?' Ojas asked, sounding very surprised. 'That's a first.'

And then he stopped talking to me. That's another first.

'Samar is lucky,' said Bindiya, looking wistfully at Ojas and thinking about her own relationship with her father, 'because he has you for a father. Your words always make me feel so much better about life, Ojas Uncle. I can barely imagine what a fantastic influence you must be in your son's life ...'

Ojas stared at Bindiya through his glasses, his face expressionless. 'Haven't you noticed, Bindiya?'

'Noticed what?'

Ojas remained silent for a few minutes during which Bindiya, try as she might, was not able to read his face.

'That Samar and I don't talk at all.'

'What? No, I've never ... oh ... yes ... I mean, I've never seen the two of you talk ...' mumbled Bindiya as the realization hit home.

156

Ojas munched on his biscuit thoughtfully, allowing Bindiya time to absorb this information. 'I always thought I would be a rubbish businessman and a fantastic dad. Turns out I was completely wrong there too ... I ended up being a fantastic businessman and a rubbish dad,' he said, staring at the cup in his hand.

'Oh,' said Bindiya, leaning over to put a hand on his arm, her heart welling up with emotions.

Ojas took a deep breath. 'When Samar was seventeen, Diya suffered a renal failure. She had a kidney transplant which at first seemed to have been a success. And then her body rejected the new kidney. It was horrible to see her wither away slowly ... Samar felt we should get another transplant done, redo the whole surgery. Doctors advised against it because Diya's body was too weak to take on another six-hour operation. Most importantly, Diya insisted that she did not want another surgery, dug her heels in and refused to budge. That left me in a very difficult situation. Samar was adamant that Diya should not give up like this and Diya was stubbornly refusing to even consider another surgery. There were three of us. One wanted surgery, another did not. I was to decide.'

'Oh,' said Bindiya, unable to quite imagine how tough this would have been for Ojas. 'And you chose?'

'I decided that Diya should have the dignity to decide what happens to her body.'

'And Samar ...?'

'He felt we – no, I – did not give his mother the second chance she should have got,' said Ojas, a faraway look on his face. 'It was not pleasant.'

'Didn't you try to explain ...?'

'He withdrew into a shell. Try as I might, I couldn't reach out him. My own son was lost to me. There was, however, one heated conversation where he told me that he didn't think I was any better than a murderer.' Here Ojas paused to steady his voice and then continued. 'If you didn't know Samar, you could say that he was being too melodramatic but ... you know how Samar is ... intense. Intense in his love, intense in his anguish and intense in his hatred. There is no grey for him – it's all either white or black.'

Bindiya stared at Ojas who looked like he had aged a decade in the last few minutes.

'Diya and Samar were very close, so close that I felt that they were connected in more ways than science could possibly explain ... He never got over his mother's death and continues to hold me solely responsible for it.'

Bindiya sighed deeply. Every life has a story, some sadder than others. Every story has a hero, some braver than others.

'In a way I'm okay with it ...' Ojas said, shrugging.

'How can you be okay with it?'

157

'Sometimes, Bindiya, it's almost therapeutic to have someone to blame. It converts the pain into anger and anger can be much easier to deal with ...'

'Hmm ...' said Bindiya, nodding.

'He is hurting, Bindiya, still hurting. I wish Diya's death was the last tragedy that happened to him, but it was not. He is now just a shadow of the man he used to be ...'

'Oh ...'

'Sometimes,' said Ojas, looking thoughtfully at Bindiya, 'around you, he seems to ... to ... open up. I think it's your smile. You know your smile is a lot like Diya's? Open and honest.'

Bindiya's heart skipped a few beats. Ojas Uncle thought she made Samar happy?

'Anyway let's get going, Bindiya dear. I don't want to bore you with more of this stuff,' said Ojas, getting up.

Ojas did not refer to Diya or Samar during the rest of the afternoon but hardly a minute went by when Bindiya was not thinking of them. All she wanted was to hold Samar close, the way he had held her that night, and tell him that everything would be okay.

Finally, it was in the peace of a jolting auto ride back home that the tears started to flow. She wiped them hurriedly but they wouldn't stop.

'I miss you, Samar,' Bindiya mumbled to herself and then she stopped short, surprised. She missed Samar. She was crying because she missed Samar so much. She missed his voice, she missed the way he looked at her, she missed the way his fingers felt around hers, she missed his precious smile. She missed how he tried hard not to smile. She missed him. Missed him enough to sit in an auto and cry for him.

Was this love? Had she fallen for a super rich business

tycoon completely out of her league and ten years older than her?

31

'Team,' said Malika, walking into the room, 'we need to head to the conference room. Samar and Madhav want to give us an update on the deal via teleconference.'

From the corner of her eye, Malika saw Bindiya's head turn sharply towards her at the mention of Samar.

'Now?' asked Atul.

'Yes, now. They're already connected and waiting,' she said hastily. 'Let's move it, team.'

Bindiya was getting up too, suddenly nervous, her face pale. Would Samar say something to her? Would he let her know in some way that it was all okay between them? That there was something between them?

'Ms Saran, could you be a dear and take this package to Shashank? You know he sits in Tower Two? Then see if you want to join this meeting?' Malika said. Innocent. Conniving. Machiavellian.

Bindiya looked blankly at Malika.

'Ms Saran? Will you please?'

'Oh ... um, yes,' Bindiya said, knowing fully well that she couldn't say no to Malika and that Malika was doing this to simply get her back at Bindiya.

Having handed Bindiya the package, Malika gave a satisfied smile and walked out of the room. That had been fairly easy – the girl had no spine.

Samar, sitting in the plush Zorawar Group office in Montreal, stared at the screen in front of him, watching the team troop in, one after the other, waving or nodding to him. None of them mattered, except for that one face, the real reason for this video call.

And she was nowhere to be seen. Was she okay? Was she sick? Was she ...

Bindiya burst in, panting, red in the face. And Samar breathed again. For the last fifteen minutes he had felt like a diver in the deep sea struggling for air, but now he could feel oxygen fill his lungs.

Bindiya, who had run all the way from Tower Two to the teleconference room, faster than she had ever run before, stared at the screen, not blinking. Samar! Her eyes found his.

'Ah, Ms Saran, how are you doing?' asked Madhav.

'I am okay, Sama ... I mean, Madhav. I'm doing great.' She looked down in embarrassment.

160

For the next twenty minutes, Madhav did the talking and Samar did the staring. She was thousands of miles away standing alone in a corner, as far away from Malika as possible. Alone. Fidgety. Uncomfortable. Not sure where to look.

He stared as Bindiya brought her hand up to rub her nose. He had seen her do that at that first meeting she had been late for. It had then, as it did now, reminded him of a pup he had briefly owned as a child. White fur and a pink, wet nose. Adorable.

Even as the meeting ended and the monitors beeped off, Samar was staring at the spot on the blank screen where Bindiya had been, thinking sometimes of the pup with a pink, wet nose and sometimes of the shy smile.

✻

'Why don't you just call?' asked Madhav.

'Call whom?' said Samar, flicking through the presentation.

The two of them were being chauffer-driven across Montreal for an important business meeting.

'Can you stop pretending?'

'I don't know what you are talking about.'

'Be a little easy on yourself, Samar, give yourself another chance. A second chance at love?'

'Let's discuss the meeting.'

'You're just playing with her, Samar. And with yourself.'

'Can we now discuss the meeting?'

'Did you see the way she was looking at you?'

'No, I was busy.'

'Do you know that she loves you?'

Startled, Samar looked at Madhav. 'I am no longer capable of love, Madhav. It's best for you and for her to understand that,' he said shortly and went back to his presentation.

161

❀

Over the years, Samar had grown to hate nights. He spent them reading, writing, working … sometimes even cooking. Sleeping little. Sleeping uneasily. Sleeping vulnerably. Tonight he sat in the state-of-the-art kitchen and looked out at the snow that was falling in a gentle, whisperless patter.

Bindiya would have loved this, he thought to himself. The image of her standing in a corner of the videoconference room, rubbing her nose with the back of her hand, flashed in front of his eyes. It broke his heart and it made him smile.

It's 1 p.m. in India. I can call. Listen to her voice.

He missed Bindiya's voice. And her smell. And her long, slim fingers. And the way she felt like cotton wool in his arms. And the startled look. And the horrified look. And the shy look. And the mad hand movements that always accompanied her words. And the hair. And the eyes that danced with mirth. And the small, shy smile.

The small, shy smile. The one that crinkled the sides of her eyes. The one that always reached her eyes. The one that made it difficult for him not to smile back.

Samar knew he would feel a lot better if he were to call Bindiya. He picked up the phone, stared at it for a few minutes – and then dialled Naina's number.

They spoke for half an hour about the meetings he had lined up for the next day.

❋

A travelling businessman leads a lonely life of meetings, unfamiliar beds and buffet breakfasts.

162

The more Samar tried to push Bindiya out, the more resolutely she seemed to make herself comfortable in the corner of his mind.

A rainy day and he would wonder if Bindiya liked the gentle pitter-patter of raindrops as much as he did. A beautiful flower and he would wonder if Bindiya would like to pluck it, maybe put it in her hair? A pretty poem and he would wonder if the words would sound as lyrical to her as they did to him. A beautiful painting in the hotel lobby and he would want to show it to her.

Letting your heart fight your brain is but a lost battle. The heart is often stronger and, more often than not, the winner.

He pushed her away and she fought to stay in. He pushed harder and she fought back harder.

On the eve of his return to India, Samar sat down in a pub and bought himself a cheap beer. He left the pub when it started to get a little crowded, put on his ear plugs and, instead of hailing a cab back to the hotel, began to run. Cocooned from the world by the music he neither liked nor recognized, he could finally think.

'What do you want to do?' he asked himself.

'Pick up the phone and call her.' Pat came the reply. 'Hear her speak, listen to the random questions and ...'

'Bindiya might want to be with the man she thinks Samar Chauhan is. Are you that man? A man or the shadow of a man?'

There was so much in his past that was ugly and excruciatingly painful. He needed to get over it himself first before he could bring anyone in to share his life, leave alone a naïve girl, ten years his junior.

'No,' the voice in his head said, loud and clear, 'don't drag her into this bog – she'll never be able to get out.'

'What about that look in her eyes when you pulled her into an embrace before leaving for Canada?' the other voice in his head asked him.

'She'll get over it,' he said out loud and ran faster, 'and getting over that one hug will be a lot less painful.'

During that one-hour angry run, Samar sealed Bindiya's fate.

163

❋

Back in Mumbai, Samar went out of his way to ignore Bindiya, fully aware the whole time of the questioning, pained look in her eyes. The first time he saw her approaching him, a bright, expectant smile on her face, he abruptly turned around and busied himself in conversation with someone. He heard her steps falter, and when he looked at her from the corner of his eye, the smile had vanished.

He refused to even look at her when he addressed a group of people a few days later but noted how she had receded to the back by the time his monologue ended. Malika, on the other hand, stood right next to Samar throughout, a hand resting slightly on his arm, a subtle reminder of who had the upper hand.

Bindiya messaged him on the office intranet. He stared without blinking at the 'Hi Samar, can we talk please? Did I do something wrong?' that had appeared on his screen but he did not reply.

A few days of such behaviour, and Bindiya got the message loud and clear. A couple of days before IC's last day at the Zorawar Group, Samar saw Bindiya walking towards him in a narrow hallway. For a moment panic struck him but now it was Bindiya who looked away, her face draining of colour at the sight of the man who had not too long ago held her in his arms. Clutching her laptop, she stuck her chin to her chest and walked past.

'Evening,' she mumbled.

'Evening, Ms Saran,' Samar replied.

Her eyes, for the brief moment they met his, were no longer questioning; now they just held a quiet sadness that Samar hated.

'I should have never let it get to this,' he mumbled angrily to himself. 'I don't care. I shouldn't care.'

The worst thing about telling yourself that you don't care is realizing how much you actually do care.

32

News that the Zorawar Group had won the deal came in on the last day of the project. A clean, happy end to the year-long process. As Samar announced the win, his eyes searched the crowd for Bindiya. When he could not spot her, a cold hand gripped his heart. It was Bindiya's last day at the Zorawar Group; had he already seen the last of her?

The IC team were the undisputed stars of the win. They had been handpicked to help the Zorawar Group for the project and how well they had delivered! There was no way Bindiya was going to be allowed to miss the celebrations. Three people had to literally pull her away from her desk and drag her to the pub. Too tired to resist, Bindiya had come but nothing would allow her to be happy at the moment.

She sat listlessly in one corner, distant and aloof, powerless in the face of the noises that created havoc in her head. It had been a month since she had slept a full night, spending them tossing and turning, thinking about Samar. She felt foolish for having believed in something that had never even existed. To be honest, she had never really expected anything to happen; Samar belonged to a different world of the rich and the famous. Then why did it still hurt?

In more ways than one, what Samar had done was nothing new; people, men, left her, without explanation, reason and warning all the time. Why had she expected Samar to be any different?

Because of the way he had looked at her, a little voice in her head said.

Bindiya shook her head. Malika had been right all along – Bindiya did not matter, she had never mattered.

She caught sight of her expression in one of the mirrors that decorated the wall around her and did a double take. Was that terribly sad, despondent girl Bindiya Saran?

Her mobile phone rang. The number was familiar. Rehan?

'Hi,' she said into her phone, not sure she should have picked it up in the first place.

165

'Bindiya, I need to see you,' came a serious voice.

'No. I am sorry, Rehan. I don't want to see you.'

'Please, Bindiya, please.'

'No ...'

'Bindiya, I am sorry for everything. Just meet me one time, so that I can say sorry to you.'

'No, I am out ...'

'I know where you are. I am downstairs in the garden. Can you please come for just two minutes? Please let me say sorry to you, please, please, please?'

He sounded very polite, a far cry from the man who had been sending her nasty texts.

'Uh ... I mean ...'

'Please Bindiya, after all that I've done, I really, really need to apologize, just so that I can sleep at night. Please give me the opportunity to say sorry. It will just take two minutes.'

'How did you know I'm here in the pub? Are you following me?'

'Just to say sorry, please ... please,' he pleaded.

'Um, okay, okay, I'll be down there in a minute,' she finally said. He had been her boyfriend for a couple of years and deserved two minutes of her time. Bindiya took her glass of rum and coke with her as she walked downstairs, for a moment forgetting Samar.

Bindiya had seen the shed from a distance. It had some trendy barrels near it to give it the look of a barn. People came down here for some fresh air or a smoke. For the moment it was deserted.

'Hi, Rehan?' Bindiya called out.

'Hi Bindiya.' The voice came from behind her, making her jump. Bindiya turned around and came face to face with

Rehan. He was a shadow of his former self, only skin and bones, and his eyes were bloodshot.

'Heyyy girl,' he now slurred.

'Are you drunk?' she asked, shocked.

'No ... I'm not drunk,' he said, inching closer to her. A waft of putrid, alcohol-ridden breath reached Bindiya.

'Rehan, you need to go home ...'

'I want you back, Bindiya, come back to me,' he said, his arms wide open for an embrace.

'Shut up, Rehan,' said Bindiya, pushing him away, suddenly aware of how deserted the shed was.

Rehan had serious anger management issues when in his senses and god only knew what he was capable of in this inebriated state.

She had turned around to flee when a strong hand grasped her wrist. She gasped and Rehan pulled her close.

'Come back to me, you bitch,' he snarled, his mouth inches away from her ears. As another wave of putrid breath hit her, Bindiya felt hair rise at the back of her neck.

'This is not good, this is not good.' She realized she was mumbling to herself. 'Let me go, Rehan, I'll scream like mad if you don't,' she said out loud.

It felt like a flash of blinding light struck her next. Disoriented, she looked around and then realized, with utter shock, that Rehan had just slapped the living daylights out of her.

'Wha...what?' she mumbled, dazed, bringing her hands to her cheek which had begun stinging now. Before she could make sense of what had just happened, Rehan shoved her into one corner of the barn and pinned her to the wall

'So, this Samar guy. Are you fucking him? Are you his girl? Are you Samar Chauhan's girl now? Is that what you want now? Money? Do you think he's hot? Do you like him better

RUCHITA MISRA

than you liked me? You hated it when I kissed you, didn't you?' he spat at her. 'Do you like it when Chauhan kisses you?' he asked, working himself into a fury.

Bindiya closed her eyes in terror as she felt Rehan wrap his hand in her hair. And then she nearly passed out as Rehan smashed her head into the wall.

'Rehan, stop!' Bindiya screamed wildly, feeling the world around her swim. Surely her screams could be heard by everyone within a mile? Why wasn't anyone coming to her help? Okay, wait, where was this whimpering sound coming from? Was that her? Where were the screams?

'Samar Chauhan's girl. Rich Samar Chauhan. Head of Zorawar Group Samar Chauhan. Are you his girl now?' Rehan thundered on, pulling her away from the wall and readying to smash her head in it again.

'No, Rehan!' she screamed, expecting her head to hit the wall again any instant now.

Nothing happened. No wall slammed into her face. Rehan's hand had lost the grip on her hair.

Bindiya turned around and almost fainted with relief.

'No,' snarled the suited Samar Chauhan, fists smashing into Rehan's face without any mercy. 'One.' Another unforgiving hit. 'Messes.' Another punch that resulted in a gush of blood from Rehan's nose. 'With.' Another hit and Rehan fell down. 'My.' And a final huge hit. 'Girl,' he finished.

My girl.

33

In a matter of a few seconds, Rehan was a crumpled, weeping, snivelling, bleeding mess on all fours.

Surat and another man Bindiya did not recognize appeared from nowhere and rushed forward.

'I'll take care of him, Samar,' said Surat, rolling up his sleeves to reveal bulging muscles Bindiya hadn't noticed before.

'Thanks, Surat,' Samar said, an unmistakable edge to his usually even voice. 'This guy should not forget tonight in a hurry.'

When Samar turned around to face her, Bindiya, still dazed and shocked, felt her heart fill with inexplicable dread. It took her a moment to understand why. At the moment, Samar was like a raging dragon, breathing fire on anything he set eyes on – if you went too close, you could get singed.

With one long stride he was next to her and had wrapped his fingers around her wrist in a steel grip. 'In the car,' he said in a dangerously angry, low baritone that sent shivers down Bindiya's spine.

'Please,' he added when he saw Bindiya hesitate.

With one hand on the steering wheel and another on the gear, Samar drove at a hundred kilometres an hour, all the while saying nothing, simply glaring at the road in front of him. He whizzed past other cars narrowly missing some, all regard for rules forgotten. A couple of drivers honked their horns in protest but it was obvious that there was precious little that Samar Chauhan cared about at the moment.

Even though she was now in the safety of Samar's car, Bindiya, still in a state of shock from her encounter with Rehan, dared not breathe. She stole a look at Samar and hurriedly looked down at her hands; Samar was red with anger and seemed to be breathing fire from every pore. She had seen him angry before but never like this. Bindiya also knew that his anger was directed not just at Rehan, but also at her for having let things come to this.

Bindiya gingerly touched her temple, where a dull, warm ache had been steadily growing, and when she looked at her fingers, she gasped. They were red, covered in her blood.

'Samar,' she heard a small, frightened voice say.

Samar turned around face her, his brow furrowed in anger. His expression, however, changed the moment his eyes fell on her face.

'Oh shit,' he cursed. Without bothering with an indicator, and again narrowly missing hitting another car, Samar careened his Mercedes-Benz to a stop on the side of the road.

He opened his door, rushed out and a second later, had opened her door and was kneeling on the dirt road track. 'Oh you poor thing,' he mumbled as he tenderly used his fingers to comb out her hair from the wound.

'That bastard,' he mumbled again, not taking his eyes off her forehead. Bindiya stared at Samar, whose face was just a few inches away from hers, noticing the flecks of light brown in his irises. Softened into gorgeous beauty, as they were now, Samar's eyes riveted Bindiya.

He took out a pristine white handkerchief from his pocket. 'Keep this pressed against it,' he said. Their eyes met for a split second. Hers teary and his very worried. 'I'll take you to a hospital, okay? Everything will be okay.'

Bindiya nodded, clutching the handkerchief to her forehead but feeling very relaxed and safe. With Samar beside her, she was home and everything was already okay.

Samar rushed Bindiya to a hospital that looked like a five-star hotel to her. He barked orders, angry and impatient, as if he owned the place. Bindiya would later find out that he did.

'I need a doctor right now. NOW!' he growled at the manager of the private hospital who had broken into a sweat.

It was only when the senior neurosurgeon had examined

170

Bindiya, assured Samar that she was fine but would need a few stitches to close the wound and clarified that she would certainly not need to be admitted that he showed any signs of relaxing.

An hour and four stitches later, Bindiya found herself back in the car with a now calmer Samar.

'Can I speak with your mum, please? I need to tell her about the medicines you should be taking for the week.'

'Er ... um, no, please don't.'

'What? Why?'

'She's not in Mumbai, Urvi and Mum are in Bangalore for Urvi's interview. If they find out about this, they'll both panic. Urvi needs to just concentrate on her interview—'

'Who's at home then?' cut in Samar.

'No one,' said Bindiya meekly, adding hurriedly, 'but I'll be fine. I'll just go to bed right away ... and ... I am feeling okay now. It's okay ... I'm fine ...'

Without bothering to reply, Samar pulled out his phone and dialled a number.

'Kaka,' he spoke into the phone to his house help of over three decades, 'I am getting a friend, Bindiya, home for the night. She has hurt herself ... no, she's fine now but there is no one at her place. It's best she stays with us tonight. Can you also please let Dad know about this?'

'No,' interjected Bindiya, quite shocked. 'I ... n ... no, thanks but I don't want to ...'

Samar paused his conversation briefly to give Bindiya a stern look that promptly silenced her stuttering.

Even though it was close to midnight by the time they reached Samar's house, the household was wide awake and waiting in the lobby. Ojas Uncle, Kaka and a couple of other servants came rushing out when they heard Samar's car pull into the driveway.

171

'Is she okay? Is she okay?' asked Ojas, hurrying down the stairs towards the car and taking Bindiya gently into his arms.

'I am okay ...' Bindiya said, smiling weakly.

'Oh my darling little girl, of course you are not!' Ojas exclaimed, caressing the top of Bindiya's head, careful not to touch the bandage. A lot had happened through the night and so far Bindiya had borne it all without breaking down. Yet, all it took was a kind look and a gentle word from a dear friend like Ojas Uncle to bring her close to crying.

And with that the fuss marathon began. Someone got her a comfortable nightdress. Someone else brought her a glass of warm milk. Kaka's wife Geeta was called. A room was set up for Bindiya and it was decided that she should not sleep alone; Geeta would keep her company.

His bit done, Samar now had retreated to the door of the main living room and was watching the goings-on with a content look on his face. Ojas was feeding Bindiya with his hands. Bindiya sat there, tears gathering in her eyes.

'Oh, does it hurt, darling?' Ojas asked, alarmed. 'Should I give you another painkiller?'

'No,' she said, shaking her head. 'I am fine, Ojas Uncle. It's been a long night.'

She was fine. She had to be fine. It was the first time in decades that a fatherly hand was feeding her. Her soul could sense the love Ojas had for her and it wrapped itself in that happy, warm blanket of affection. How could she not be fine?

34

Samar did not even attempt to sleep; it would be a wasted effort, he knew. He was sure that the images from the last couple of hours would never leave him. That man with his hand wrapped in Bindiya's hair about to smash her face into the wall, Bindiya's wet eyelashes fanning wide, surprised, scared eyes. Bindiya looking up at him and then at the blood on her fingers, half scared, half surprised.

Samar promised himself again that the guy, whoever he was, would regret what he had done to Bindiya for the rest of his life.

Restless, Samar began to pace his plush bedroom. He felt an urge to just see Bindiya, make sure she was sleeping peacefully.

Samar walked to Bindiya's room and soundlessly pushed open the door, intending to only peep in and expecting to see the sleeping forms of Bindiya and Geeta kaki.

Two women in peaceful slumber were *not* what met his eyes.

173

For starters, Bindiya was awake. Bathed in the glow of the small bedside lamp, Bindiya was sitting cross-legged on a corner of the bed, wrapped in a thin blanket, her frail body racked with silent sobs. Next to her, Geeta kaki was fast asleep.

Samar, shocked – or maybe not really shocked, for in his heart he had somehow sensed Bindiya's state, hurried into the room. When Bindiya looked up and saw him appear by her side as if from nowhere, the last threads of control she had been hanging on to deserted her.

'Samar,' she whispered in a fragile, teary voice. And with that, like a baby that wanted its mother to hold her, she extended her arms towards Samar.

'Bindiya,' muttered Samar, aghast, as Bindiya sobbed as if her heart was breaking, gasping for air in bursts.

'Come out with me,' he whispered and then helped Bindiya get up.

The mess that she was, Bindiya struggled to walk, weighed down by the tears that would not stop. One look at her and Samar knew what had to be done. He bent low and scooped her in his arms.

The warmth and strength of Samar's arms around her soothed Bindiya and she curled herself against his chest as he carried her to another room and put her down on a leather couch. Samar did not bother to switch on the lights, letting the glow from a street lamp filter into the room through the window and bathe everything in a dull yellow.

He sat down next to her and, without saying another word, wrapped his arms around her, held her tight and rocked her to and fro. Bindiya sobbed, then cried and then howled, the pain finding a way out through her tears. She clung to Samar in the darkness of the room and buried her face in his neck.

Samar remained silent. He did not ask her to stop crying; instead he simply held her as tight as he could, sometimes caressing the back of her head, sometimes pushing her hair behind her ears, but mostly just holding her tight.

A little while later, when the tears stopped, Bindiya pulled back so that she could face Samar.

'Thank you, Samar,' she mumbled in a tiny, teary voice. Her face looked so innocent, so delicate and so fragile that it broke Samar's heart.

'Not a problem, Bindiya,' he said softly and pulled her back into a hug.

They stayed like that for an eternity. Her sobs had died down, yet she clung to him and Samar let her, finding an odd relief in the comfort he was able to provide her.

'Bindiya,' said Samar after a while, 'who was that guy?'

'Rehan ... my ex-boyfriend ... we broke up last year ...'

'Has this happened before?' Samar asked, anxiously biting

his lower lip. The question had been gnawing at him since he had first spotted Bindiya that evening, her face white with terror, looking pleadingly at Rehan. He had been there this time but ...

'Not really,' she said in a matter-of-fact voice. 'Rehan is very short-tempered, so he ... um, in a fit of anger he would snatch my phone and throw it ... or you know, would say rude things ... but ... except ...'

'Except?'

'Except for the night we broke up.'

'What happened that night?'

'He wanted something I wasn't ready for, one thing led to the other and ... and ...'

'What did he want?' Samar asked, taking Bindiya's face into both his hands.

Bindiya paused for a second too long.

'Oh,' said Samar, getting it. 'And then? What did he do when you refused?'

Images from that night flashed before Bindiya with painful clarity.

'What did he do?' Samar's eyes bored into Bindiya's, willing her to answer. Rehan, Samar decided there and then, would never find a job in the country.

'He tried to force himself on me,' said Bindiya in a small, sad voice, looking down. 'But ... but nothing really happened. I just slapped him really hard and ran away. In fact,' she said, looking up now, 'that was the night I was supposed to submit my Excel sheet to you and I did not, and everyone kept calling my phone and then you called me the next day to shout at me.'

'I am sorry,' he mumbled in the darkness. 'I wish I had known.'

Bindiya smiled at a memory that now came back to her.

175

Sitting in Samar's office that day, waiting to be sacked, she had vaguely considered telling Samar all that had happened. Something in her had known, even then, that Samar would care.

'You are the last person who is at fault in this case, Samar,' Bindiya said gently.

'I'll kill him,' he said in a low, dangerous voice that, for a moment, frightened Bindiya.

'You'll do no such thing, Samar,' she said, taking his hand in hers. She moved back a little so that she could look at his face. The two stared at each other in the relative darkness of the room. Try as she might, Bindiya could not take her eyes off Samar. Samar put a hand on her cheek. Gentle. Tender. Soft.

176

With his thumb, Samar traced Bindiya's eyebrow, completely lost in the perfection of the arch. Though she was trying to smile, there was a sadness in her eyes that was not lost on Samar.

'Bindiya, tell me what is going on in your mind?'

'Nothing,' she said, vehemently shaking her head.

'Then why this?' said Samar, wiping off a tear that had just begun its journey down her cheek.

Bindiya clasped her hands around him and buried her face in his chest again, holding him tight.

'Come on,' he prodded in a gentle voice.

'Were you angry with me, Samar, these last few days?' she asked. 'I ... I am sorry if I did something to upset you. I swear I did not do anything deliberately. I say silly things ... but ... I ...'

And she was crying again. Bindiya's body shook with tears and Samar felt utterly helpless. He had hit the man who had hurt Bindiya; what was he supposed to do with the other man who had done pretty much the same, in other ways?

'No ... forget it, Bindiya,' he said, distressed. How ridiculously selfish he had been.

'But ... you never even sent me your phone number ...' she said, brushing away tears with the back of her hands.

'I'll do that right now,' he heard himself say. *Stop. Don't do this.*

'And you ... I was waiting for your call the whole time you were in Canada ... and then, when you came back ... you ...'

'Shh,' said Samar, leaning in, his forehead now touching Bindiya's. 'I am sorry Bindiya, I've been horrible. And no, I am not upset with you ... I was fighting my own demons.'

'Everybody,' she said, rubbing her red nose with her hand, 'decides to ... one day ... just walk away. And,' she now pretend-hit Samar across his chest, 'they don't realize how much it can hurt.'

Samar held her tighter.

177

'Most people who matter leave me and go, Samar. If you want to go, go now, please, go before I wrap my heart all around you,' she said slowly.

Leave her now. 'I won't go, I promise,' he whispered in her ear, holding her tighter and closer.

'I want you to know something,' she said, after a few seconds, her voice calmer now.

'I don't need to know anything, Bindiya.'

'But I need to tell you this,' she said more firmly than usual. 'You need to know before you decide to stay.'

For most of us, at some point or the other, life feels like a pack of cards, delicately balanced into a pyramid and at the mercy of fickle forces beyond our control. A little flick somewhere and the pack of cards tumbles into a mess. Then you have to pick up the cards, one by one, slowly, choosing the sturdier ones and leaving behind the rest to build your pyramid again. Sometimes, you pick up the cards on your own, in the silence of the night, in the loneliness of your room. And sometimes, you pick them up with someone you trust.

'A decade ago,' she said, 'we were a happy family. We lived in San Francisco. Mummy and Daddy were one tight unit and Urvi was the happiest little toddler you could find on the face of this earth. We were a small loving family; things were very normal ... Daddy used to travel for most of the year and I remember him bringing back expensive gifts to make up for his time away. Then one day, he came back from a trip without any gifts. Instead he pulled Mum into the bedroom and told her, calmly and quietly, that he no longer wanted to stay with us. Mum cried and cried and he wouldn't tell us any more till later that night when Mum was a little calmer.'

178

Bindiya grew silent, lost in the memories. 'He had a family in Canada, a full family. A wife and two sons we knew nothing about.'

Samar looked up now, startled.

'And then, just like that, almost as if an evil witch had waved her magic wand over us, our whole world collapsed. We were no longer a family. Dad was a villain and Mum would not stop crying. Mum left the US, with the two of us and a suitcase. Nana and Nani were in Mumbai and we came to live in a house next to them. With time, you would think, things would have improved,' said Bindiya. 'They did not.'

'Oh,' said Samar.

'Over the next few months, I realized that I was losing Mum ... almost like she was a painting that was fading away in front of my eyes and, try as I might, I couldn't bring back the colours. First, she stopped smiling. Then she stopped talking. Then she stopped sleeping ...'

Bindiya now rested her head on Samar's shoulders, as if

exhausted from all the memories. Samar rested his chin on Bindiya's head, quietly listening to the sad tale.

'Dad came over too. He wanted a divorce; Mum refused. Mum wanted me and Urvi to stay with her in Mumbai; Dad refused. Dad fought for the divorce, Mum fought for us ... the fights were bitter. And loud. And angry. I would bury my head in between my knees for hours, trying to silence the noise, but they would not stop. It was odd, I suppose, because before Dad told us about his other wife, I had never seen them fight, but now it was as if they couldn't stop.'

Samar tightened his arms around her and she fiddled with the cuff of his shirt, lost in the time the memories were coming from.

'It had started with the colours but soon I began to lose bits of the painting itself. She stopped eating, she stopped cooking for us ... I was no doctor but I knew something was horribly wrong. I also knew I had to hide it from the world. I didn't know why I had to hide it, but I had no doubt that had to be done. And I did.'

179

Bindiya shrugged her shoulders, surprised at how the little girl had done it all. 'Mum had begun to truly scare me when one day, Dad turned up, unannounced, and was shocked to see the state of the house. He got in the doctors who diagnosed Mum with extreme clinical depression. Dad took Urvi and me with him to Canada. Mum wailed and shrieked and howled and he still took us away ...'

Samar gently stroked her back, shocked at the story Bindiya was telling him.

'Then one day, Daddy and his other wife rushed into my room and asked me to pack my bags. They told me that Mummy was hurt; but I knew in my heart that they were lying. I worried that she had died. I called up Adi's mum and begged her to tell me the truth and bless her, she did. Mum had tried to take her life because she couldn't live without Urvi and me. I screamed and shouted at everyone that day and stopped only when Dad's wife slapped me shut. I knew Mum needed me and I had to go be with her. Daddy said I could go, but I would have to leave Urvi behind.'

So that explained it, the out-of-place mother-like air floating oddly around the young, seemingly carefree face, Samar thought.

'I had to come back to be closer to Mum who had been institutionalized. Mum no longer recognized me, and Urvi would call and cry on the phone, desperate to be home again. The unfairness of it all broke my heart, Samar, it broke my heart but I didn't give up.'

I might be a lot of things, Samar, but I am not a quitter. Her passionate words from their meeting came back to Samar with greater meaning.

'Mum spent about eight months in the home during which time I stayed with Nana and that is when, just when I thought I was going mad myself, dealing with Mum's illness and listening to Urvi's cries, Nana enrolled me in dance class. The dance classes, they saved my life and I understood how art can heal the soul.'

So that was why she had picked Ujala for her CSR and was spending hours teaching dance to little girls who had mentally ill parents. Bindiya, Samar now realized, had been one of those girls!

'When Mum was a little better and back home, Daddy came to get her to sign the divorce papers. Mum agreed on two conditions. One, Dad would never try to meet us again, and two, he would let Urvi come to live with us. And that is how we restarted life, very grateful to be together again.

'People have called Mum and me many names. That Dad left us for another woman has been a stigma that we haven't been able to shake off, not at school, not at office and not in relationships. I know it's something that others will continue to find pleasure in reminding me of. And that is what I am, Samar, a girl with a father but without one.'

Samar remained quiet. A cold, damp hand had caught his heart at the beginning of Bindiya's story and had clutched at it tighter and tighter as the story had progressed. He now saw Bindiya's bright smile and silly antics in a completely different light.

'You may be a girl without a father, Bindiya, but I don't think that alone defines you. More than anything else, you are a girl with a powerful spirit and anyone who cannot see that should not matter,' said Samar. 'Tell me, why is it that you thought you deserved someone like Rehan? Be honest.'

181

Bindiya took a deep breath. 'I put up with Rehan's behaviour because I was afraid that he would leave and I know how painful that can be,' she said.

'And?'

Bindiya remained silent.

'And? Go on?' Samar prodded.

'I thought if Rehan left, I would never again find anyone who liked me ... after all, my own father didn't love me enough to stay on.' Bindiya's lips trembled as she said these words and her large eyes welled up with fresh tears. Samar knew this was difficult; the truth can be painful.

'Because, Bindiya?'

'Because I am so broken, Samar.'

Broken.

He then used his index finger to gingerly lift Bindiya's chin. 'You are beautiful,' he said.

'I am broken,' she insisted.

'And who says broken can't be beautiful?' Samar asked softly, gazing into her eyes. 'You are so beautiful, Bindiya, that I can barely take my eyes off you.'

For a moment the two of them stared at each other, breathing each other in, acutely aware of the darkness around them. He held her face in his hands and slowly leaned forward. He stopped when his lips were inches away from Bindiya's. She leaned forward to meet them, and they kissed.

It was the shadow of a kiss. It was the whisper of a kiss. It was the scent of a beautiful poem. It was the burning sun.

'When I saw you first, I tried so hard not to stare at your lips,' said Samar in a whisper, staring into her eyes. 'They look as if an artist has just painted them.'

A small, shy smile appeared on Bindiya's face.

'And do you know what else I found difficult to peel my eyes away from?'

Two large eyes looked questioningly at him.

Samar leaned in and tenderly kissed the side of her left eye. 'Your pug nose!' he said, grinning, trying to lighten the intense air around them. Bindiya's face broke into a smile and Samar pulled her into a tight hug again. Bindiya wrapped her arms around him and the two stayed like that for a while, rocking gently, like leaves swaying in a gentle breeze.

Bindiya had never known that being in a man's arms could feel this way. Safe. This safe. As if nothing in this world could harm her. Samar kissed her again and then again, each time more gently, slowly and tenderly than before.

They lay on the couch, and Bindiya fell into a deep, contented sleep, nestled in Samar's strong arms, her tear-stained face resting peacefully against Samar's rising and falling chest.

Samar stayed awake the whole night, barely taking his eyes off Bindiya's face, sometimes caressing her cheeks and sometimes kissing her forehead. She had a past that was not all beautiful, yet Samar could not imagine anyone more beautiful. He hoped desperately to be able to make life beautiful for her, unaware of the storm the universe had begun to brew for them ...

35

'So, does my little chidiya,' asked Ojas over his cup of chai, a knowing smile spread across his face, 'want to tell me something?'

Bindiya almost spluttered out her tea and Ojas laughed loudly, hastening to offer her a paper napkin. She put her cup on the table and hugged herself tightly.

'More often than not, Bindiya,' said Ojas thoughtfully, stirring the chai, 'and much like friendship, you end up finding love in the most unexpected of places and with the most unexpected of people ...'

'Yes.' She had to agree.

'You are the best thing that has happened to him in years,' Ojas said, his face serious. 'You don't believe me, do you?' he asked after a moment.

Bindiya smiled and shook her head.

'You'll know when the time comes,' he said. Both Bindiya and Ojas smiled. Ojas got up, came over to Bindiya's chair and kissed her on her forehead. 'You are my angel,' he said.

❀

Madhav sat Naina down. 'What's going on, you think?'

'With?' Naina asked, grinning.

'Our very own Satan. I heard he smiled twice yesterday.'

'I saw it happen.'

'So it's not just a rumour?'

'No, sir!'

'How many people has he shouted at in, say, the last month?'

Naina pretended to study some notes in her little notebook. 'About ... let's say ... zero!'

'Are you serious?'

'Very much so, sir.'

'Do you think Satan is on his way to becoming vaguely tolerant of us, the lesser mortals?'

'There is that danger, sir,' she said gravely.

'And to what, Ms Naina, would you attribute this sudden change in temperament?'

'A little bird, sir, who used to work for us till a few weeks back.'

'Ah, I thought so too.'

'She calls every once in a while.'

'During the day?'

'Yes, sir.'

'And Satan actually receives personal calls during the day?'

'Answered a couple even during meetings.'

'Unbelievable!'

'I understand the lady was fretting about his eating habits and the fact that he works so late in the night.'

'And what did Satan say?'

'His reaction can best be described as an indulgent smile.'

'Holy smoke! Another smile, did you say?'

'Yes, sir.'

'And what, Ms Naina, is your personal opinion of the little bird?'

'I've had the privilege of having some meals and golgappas with her, sir, and I think she's absolutely delightful,' she said.

'I think so too, Ms Naina, I think so too,' said Madhav, smiling his widest.

❋

Partly because he had been so busy and partly because of his anxiety-ridden mind, Samar had not slept in fifty hours. Yet when Bindiya shyly asked him if he wanted to meet, he found himself saying yes.

A small, rickety bench in a remote part of the beach, a few metres away from the dilapidated restaurant that, according to Bindiya, served the best Malabar chicken for the meagre amount of twenty rupees.

The stars and the moon shone brightly at them. Bindiya sat on the bench, dressed in a simple, white salwar kurta, her open hair flowing in the wind. Samar sat on the sand next to her feet, facing her. And stared.

Not at the gorgeous girl in front of him but at the gentle, happy soul that radiated the goodness of the world from within that body.

'Don't sit in the sand,' she said softly, running a finger through his hair.

'I like it like this,' he said. The salty winds from the sea carried its muffled grumblings to them in gentle waves. Their eyes locked, hers speaking, his trying to read. 'What are you thinking?' he asked.

She smiled. 'That you are a wonderful man, Samar.'

Samar smiled. He wrapped his arms around her waist and put his head in her lap, as she continued running her fingers through his hair. It took him less than five minutes to fall asleep.

185

Surat stood at a distance and tried hard to look away, yet such was the tenderness of the moment that his eyes would stray back to the two every few minutes. She sat still, delicate yet strong, caressing his forehead. Tall and broad, clad in a sharp business suit, he sat at her feet, his arms wrapped around her waist as if he were a child.

They are odd together, Surat thought. They are perfect together, another voice in his head said.

And then he wondered if she knew.

36

'Let's go?' asked Bindiya, bounding into the sombre teak of Samar's office, hair flapping around comically. 'Dinner at our favourite Jai Mata Di dhaba?'

Samar took a moment to study her carefully. Big, clunky laptop bag on one shoulder, a more lady-like bag on the other, a simple, smart top, well-fitted trousers and that fake Rolex watch (the one that Samar had been asking her to get rid of forever) glinting on her slim wrist.

And that smile. The one that made it difficult not to smile back. The one that reminded him of rainbows he had chased as a happy child in the mountains. The one that made everything okay.

'Our favourite?' he asked with the slightest raise of his eyebrows. He glared at Bindiya who had now covered her mouth and was giggling like a schoolgirl. Perhaps because the economic divide between them was so massive, or because of what Malika had once said, or perhaps just because she was Bindiya, Samar had realized Bindiya was very conscious of never letting him spend any money on her. Much to his chagrin, she insisted on paying half of any bill they incurred and would never let him buy her anything. Samar had tried reasoning with her but to no avail. Aware that Bindiya was pretty much the sole earning member of her family, Samar now readily chose dhabas over posh restaurants so that she wouldn't have to spend much on their dates.

Samar was picking up his coat when his phone rang. 'Excuse me,' he said to Bindiya and spoke briefly into his phone.

'Bindiya, I need to speak with Madhav about something important. I'll be back in a minute?'

Bindiya nodded.

'You'll be okay here?' he asked, looking around. It was past eight and he knew the office was quickly emptying.

'Yes,' she said.

'I'll be back soon.'

'I'll wait for you,' she said with a smile.

Samar nodded vaguely, his mind already on the issue he had to discuss with Madhav.

❦

At about 11 p.m., Madhav finally shut his laptop.

'Enough for the night, Samar, I think we are ready for our discussion with the ambassador tomorrow,' he said, taking off his spectacles. His green eyes studied his friend's face, which was still focused on the screen in front of him. When Samar immersed himself in work, there was not much you could do to bring him out.

'Samar,' he prodded further, 'dinner? It's getting really late.'

He saw Samar freeze. 'Dinner,' he gasped, horror on his face, his eyes flying to his watch. 'Fuck! It's eleven!'

'Samar?' Madhav called out but Samar had already pushed aside his laptop and dashed outside. He ran all the way to his office.

He burst in and stood there panting, taking in the scene. Bindiya was sitting on the leather sofa next to his desk, reading a book. Sensing him at the door, she looked up, a slightly surprised look on her face.

'There you are,' she said softly, as if nothing was amiss.

'Bindiya! I am so sorry!' he said, rushing in and going down on both knees, gathering her in his arms.

'Why?'

'I was gone for hours, that's why!'

'It's okay, Samar,' she said, wrapping her arms around his neck.

'No! It's not!' he said, frustrated. 'Scream, shout, tell me that I'm a jerk. For god's sake, you've been waiting for three hours!'

Bindiya pulled back a few inches so she could look at Samar's face. His brow was furrowed, eyes clouded and face tense.

'It's okay, Samar, three hours is nothing,' she said.

'Bindiya!' said Samar restlessly, confused at her behaviour and angry with himself, 'I am sorry, I forgot all about you ... I ...'

'You forgot something you said to me and that's okay. You didn't forget me, I wouldn't let that happen.'

Samar stared at her. 'Why didn't you call or just leave?' he asked, brushing away some hair from her face, yet again failing to understand the bundle of contradictions this girl was.

'Because I had said I would wait,' she said, shrugging her shoulders.

'And you waited even if it took me three hours to come?'

'I would have waited thirty hours,' she said, nodding.

188

Samar remained silent, his eyes searching Bindiya's face.

'I will always wait for you,' she said softly, looking into his eyes.

Samar pulled Bindiya into a hug, moved by the conviction with which she spoke. 'Say that again,' he whispered in her ear.

'I will always be here, waiting for you.'

'Again?' He could barely hear his own voice.

'I will always be here, waiting for you.'

'Once more, please?'

'I will always be here, Samar, waiting for you.'

'Always?' asked Samar, his chin resting on Bindiya's shoulder.

'Always,' she said, gently rocking Samar back and forth.

She held him, surprised at the vulnerability she sensed emanating from one of the most powerful businessmen of the country, and felt her throat tighten.

189

❀

'Do I look okay?'

X-ray like, his eyes scanned her from top to toe, taking in the scared face and nervous wringing of hands. 'Only fools are never fearful, Bindiya' he said with a small smile. 'The trick, however, is to not let it show.'

'And how do I do that?'

'By understanding that, more often than not, fear harms more than it protects.'

'Eh?'

'Tell yourself that this fear, even if it's as silly as that of meeting some people you think are important, will harm you more. Push it in a corner. Stomach in, chin out, straight back, smile on the face,' he said.

Samar looked on as Bindiya comically sucked in her stomach, jutted her chin out and smiled a wide smile.

'Let's go in, Mr Chauhan,' she said haughtily, offering him her arm. Samar laughed and grabbed her hand.

Invited to the annual dinner hosted by the minister of industries for about a hundred of the country's top businessmen, Samar had asked Bindiya to be his guest for the evening. When the shock of being asked to accompany him had subsided, a big problem had raised its ugly head. What should Bindiya wear? After due deliberation, she picked out a Satya Paul sari from her mother's wardrobe. Bold prints set against black, the chiffon sari was a stunner. When Samar had first seen her that evening he could only stare.

'What?' she had asked, innocently.

190

You, Bindiya Saran, are walking in beauty. Not just the kind that comes from a beautiful face, great figure and expensive clothes, but the kind that comes from a gentle, generous soul. I see in you all that is good in this world. Everything around you seems more beautiful because of you.

'Nothing, you scrub up well,' he had said, shrugging.

Confident and suave, Samar shone like a star that evening. His succinct but impactful presentation on the Zorawar Group was met with thunderous applause and the minister would not stop fawning over him. Bindiya stood by Samar's side, absorbing it all, basking in Samar's glory.

After dinner, when the lights dimmed and gentle music filled the air, Bindiya found herself being wordlessly guided to the dance floor. And when Samar placed his hand lightly against the small of her bare back, Bindiya tried very hard to ignore how it burnt.

Samar stepped forward, his warm, mint-fresh breath hitting her cheeks and her head reeled. She looked up at his face, a few inches away from hers, and almost tripped when she found his eyes boring into hers.

Get a grip – stop behaving like an idiot.

'You remember I told you about Jayprakash Marath,' he asked, his voice sounding like molten lava.

'Hmm ...' she mumbled dreamily.

'Hey,' said Samar, leaning further in, his eyes drilling suspiciously into hers, 'you don't remember him.'

'I probably do.'

'Do you? Okay ... who's he then?' he challenged playfully.

'I can't tell you now,' she said.

'What? Why?'

'I can't think,' she fumbled.

'Why?'

'You are too close.' The words were out of her mouth before she could stop them. Instantly, colour rose in Bindiya's cheeks. Her eyes darted everywhere, avoiding his.

'Aah,' Samar said, a slow smile of understanding beginning to play on his lips, 'are you suggesting that your brain freezes when I am this close?'

Bindiya nodded, feeling remarkably stupid.

'And what happens when I come closer?' he asked, leaning further in, eyes not leaving Bindiya's for a moment.

Bindiya gulped and mumbled something incoherent.

'And closer?' he asked, now just inches from her face.

Bindiya dared not breathe, half afraid, half hoping that Samar would kiss her, but he leaned even further in only to whisper, 'Let's get out of here?'

Without waiting for Bindiya to answer, not that she would have been able to say no, Samar clutched Bindiya's slim wrist and led her out of the ballroom.

As they left the room and the guests behind them, Bindiya

191

thought she caught someone's eyes. Angry, accusing eyes. Was that Malika, she thought fleetingly, before her brain refocused on Samar.

It was much later in the night, pretty much towards the end, that Bindiya left Samar's side to head to the ladies', blushing yet again as images from the few stolen minutes in the back garden came back to her. There was something about having Samar close to her that drove her to madness sometimes. All those books she had read and the stories her friends had told her of times with their boyfriends paled in comparison when it came to Samar. There had been an urgency when he had kissed her in the privacy of the garden. And then he had suddenly pulled away.

'What happened?' Bindiya had asked.

'If I don't stop, I won't be able to stop,' he had said, all the passion from a few minutes back evaporating into thin air, eyes and face back to being expressionless.

Bindiya had stared at him, not sure she had understood him and blushing deeply when she realized that she had.

Bindiya was so lost in her thoughts that she did not notice the woman standing in front of her, blocking her way to the ladies'.

'How much?' a cold voice asked, waking her up.

Bindiya looked up and saw Malika Oberoi standing in front of her. The usually stunning Malika, invincible in the boardroom, had the look of someone who had been defeated in the biggest battle of her life.

'I am sorry?'

'Oh, so we are being all innocent now, are we?' she asked with acerbic coolness.

'I am sorry, Malika, I don't think I understand.'

'How. Much. To. Leave. Samar?' Malika's eyes were cold but helpless.

Bindiya felt anger raise its head inside her. 'What do you mean?' she said.

'While I don't know why Samar is with you, because all you seem to have is youth and a good body, two things any whore in the city would be able to provide him with, I know exactly why you are with him.'

Bindiya stared, aghast.

'Money. Money and money,' Malika continued. 'Isn't it what all you girls are after?'

Bindiya clenched her fists, focusing hard on not losing control.

'Samar should have better sense than to stand in a roomful of the most prominent people in the city and hold your hand and look into your eyes like a love-struck puppy.' She spat out the words.

'Malika ...'

'Shut up, Bindiya Saran, I know girls like you very well. You will regret this sooner than you would like to think. Listen to my advice, name a figure, take the money and leave. Now.'

As the tears began to pool in Bindiya's eyes, Samar's words from the ladies' the other day came back to her. It was high time she learnt to give it back. She had, for far too long, resorted to tears in the face of Mallika's vitriol and now Samar's words rang in her ears. *You stay put, look them in the eye and give it right back to them a hundred times worse.*

Bindiya's hands shook with fear but she cleared her throat. It was, she told herself, finally time to stand up for herself.

'No!' Bindiya heard herself thunder. 'Now you shut up, Malika Oberoi!'

For a moment Malika just stared, shocked at Bindiya's audacity.

'The truth hurts, does it?' Malika challenged.

193

'Let me make this clear once and for all. I. Do. Not. Care. About. His. Money. Save your breath.'

'Don't kid yourself, you silly girl, of course you care only for his money. All girls do!'

'In that case,' Bindiya said, 'you take the money, Malika – you are a girl too. I just want my Samar.'

'My Samar?' Malika laughed. 'He never even belonged to his dad or even Kaasi ... what makes you think he will ever belong to you? He's a bitter, angry man, Bindiya ... a coward at best. Do you think it's brave to scream and shout at people? No! It's the façade he hides his demons and the truth behind.'

'If he's so horrible, then be happy he's not interested in you and go find yourself a more suitable man,' Bindiya retorted. 'There are plenty of fish out there for you.'

194

Malika stared at Bindiya and then, as something inside her gave way, her face crumbled. For too long she had fought for Samar's affections and in the process she had become someone she no longer knew. She was known for being fair and confident, not the emotional wreck she was fast becoming. Over the last few weeks, as the proximity between Bindiya and Samar had grown, Malika had found herself becoming more and more dependent on alcohol. Samar was slipping away, and slipping away fast, and Malika did not have it in her to watch it any more.

Unaware of the turmoil, Malika was going through, Bindiya watched in surprise as Malika's voice grew desperate. 'Bindiya, please, let him go ... leave him alone, please. I've spent the last fifteen years loving him ... please ...'

Bindiya looked at the pitiful figure in front of her, taken aback.

'Malika, Samar can leave me for you and I'll accept his decision, but I will never leave him.'

'Bindiya, you are pretty, young. You'll find a hundred men … I have spent my entire life waiting for this one man, please let me be with him,' she pleaded.

'Malika, I am not stopping you or Samar from doing anything you want to do. I'm just telling you of the one thing I can't do.'

'Bindiya, please …' said Malika, tears welling up in her eyes. 'I want him and I won't get him unless you back off.'

'That,' replied Bindiya, straightening up, 'is the difference, Malika. You want him because you don't have him. I simply love him.'

As fireworks exploded in Bindiya's head, she turned around to walk away from Malika, for once victorious, and then stopped dead.

Samar stood there, face expressionless and hands in his pockets. How much had he heard? 'You were gone for so long, I thought I would come and check to make sure everything was okay,' he said casually. 'Oh, hi Malika,' he said, looking over Bindiya's shoulder. 'How are you doing?'

'I am doing great, Samar,' said Malika brightly.

Samar dropped Bindiya home that night. In the back of the car, Bindiya sat thinking; she loved Samar. Did she love Samar? She had never uttered those words to herself, too scared of the consequences of giving love a second chance, but in front of Malika, in that fit of anger, it had all come tumbling out.

'I love Samar,' she said to herself in wonder.

She sat there, lost in thought, when she felt a warm hand clasp hers. She turned around to look at Samar and realized that the edges of his face had somehow become softer. He looked younger. Happier.

She smiled.

'Sit closer to me, please,' Samar asked simply.

195

She slid across the car seat, rested her head on his shoulder and went back to her thoughts. Comfortable silence, as can only exist between two people who know each other very well, reigned in the car.

37

That one thing was eating at her insides. The two men she was ridiculously fond of did not speak to each other, and they were father and son!

Bindiya was sitting at the kitchen table with Ojas, discussing the US elections, when Samar walked by.

'Samar,' Bindiya asked brightly, 'come join us! And tell me who you would have voted for had you been a US citizen?'

Samar cast one look at her, and then at Ojas.

'Come on, Samar,' Bindiya pleaded. 'Sit with us?'

'I am busy,' he said briefly and left the room.

Ojas caught Bindiya's pained expression and smiled. 'It's okay, Bindiya, I know what you are trying to do,' he said kindly. 'Nothing will change between Samar and me. When you have lived in a particular way for a long time, it becomes a habit, one that is dangerously difficult to break.'

'But Ojas, Samar should ...'

'No, Bindiya. I am at fault. I may or may not have made a mistake, but I definitely failed my son by not being able to reach out to his broken heart ... and this is my punishment.'

'Ojas Uncle ...' Bindiya said, crestfallen.

'Come on, my little chidiya, let's see how the kids have done in the test,' Ojas said kindly but firmly.

'Do you think Urvi will make a cup of her masala chai for me?' Samar asked, stuffing his hands in his pockets.

'No.'

Bindiya laughed at Samar's shocked expression, enjoying herself to the fullest. She loved it when she was able to ruffle his feathers like this.

'Because she's not in Mumbai right now, no one is home,' she said, closing the door of the car behind her. Samar had invited Bindiya as his guest for an event he was speaking at. Bindiya had sat in the sixth row, right behind someone she had seen on TV, and watched in amazement as Samar delivered his speech without even once glancing at either the presentation or the placards Naina had kept ready for him. Bindiya gulped in wonder as Samar rattled off figures, told a story, cracked a couple of really good jokes, all the while looking, Bindiya thought, ridiculously sexy.

197

'Stop laughing,' said Samar, pretending to be cross.

'I can make masala chai as well,' she said, winking.

'Please do the honours then,' said Samar, smiling a relaxed smile. Bindiya caught herself gazing at him with what she knew was a lovelorn expression, and straightened her face. Really, what was getting into her?

Once inside the house, Bindiya went straight to the kitchen and made Samar his chai. Back in the living room, the two sat down on the sofa in companionable silence.

Then Samar put down his cup and held her by the shoulders. Bindiya looked up quizzically at him. 'Bindiya,' he said, his eyes serious, 'I'm going to the US for a few days.'

'Yes, I know ...'

'You know how we are thinking of entering the clothing retail business in the US. I have some meetings set up with successful entrepreneurs in that area ...'

'Okay,' she said slowly, not sure where this was going.

'One of them, I've been told, is a gentleman from San Fransisco named Jai Saran.'

Bindiya's smile disappeared. Her lips quivered but she didn't say anything. Seeing her wordless reaction, Samar wrapped his arms around her and pulled her in. 'Do you want me to cancel the meeting?' he asked softly.

Bindiya, her face buried in his chest, shook her head.

'Do you want to come?' he asked again after a pause, fully aware that he was treading on thin ice.

In Samar's arms, Bindiya stayed eerily still, as if she had stopped her body from even breathing.

'Bindiya?' he tried again after several moments of complete absence of any sound or movement from Bindiya.

'Twelve,' came a soft voice a few seconds later.

'What?' he whispered into her ears.

'Twelve years. It's been twelve years since I saw him last,' she said, looking up finally with such torment on her face that something inside Samar writhed in agony.

'I know, Bindiya ... I know. I'll cancel the meeting but I ... I felt I had to ask you ... I am sorry, I did not wish to ... to ...'

Bindiya buried her face in his chest again, almost as if words no longer mattered. 'What he did was horrible ... everyone around me was so hurt ...' she said after a while.

'And that is why you don't want to meet him?'

'No.' She shook her head. 'Parents are people too and just like you and me, can make mistakes ... and really, we all deserve a fair shot at happiness. If he wasn't happy with us, a part of me – not the one that had to deal with Mum later, but some other part of me – thinks he was right to leave us to be with people who made him happy. Maybe there's nothing wrong with making changes in your life that might make it happier. After all, we all just get one life to live. I just wish he did it in a better way.'

Samar looked at Bindiya in amazement.

'I forgave my father many years ago, Samar,' she said.

'Why?' Samar heard himself ask in wonder.

'I realized I can't change what happened but if I forgave him, I could change the future, for myself, for the better.'

'Yet you don't wish to meet him?'

'I might have forgiven Dad but Mum has not ... I don't think she ever will and it will upset her if I met him ... so.' She now looked up and Samar noted that her face had cleared up. 'Out of respect for my mother's feelings, I will not meet him.'

She gulped and then added, 'I'll never meet him.'

A moment of silence in an atmosphere laden with thoughts.

'Bindiya?'

'Hmm?'

'Was it horrible then? Right after your dad left?'

'Yes.' She smiled. 'But it's very un-horrible right now.'

'You are such a nutcase,' said Samar, laughing. 'What do you want me to do?'

'To have the meeting ... carry on as you would have had he not been my father ...'

'I am sorry, Bindiya, for bringing this up. I'll make it up to you,' he said, mentally kicking himself for having even started this discussion.

'Actually, you can do something right now to make up for it,' she said.

'And what is that?'

'Pick up the phone, call your father and ask him how he is doing,' she said.

Samar stared at Bindiya, aghast. 'So let me get this straight.

199

You don't want to meet your dad and I accept your decision without question, yet you want me to speak with my dad ... when you know what he did?'

'What did he do, Samar?' she asked gently.

'He. Killed. My. Mother.' Samar spat out the words, his eyes burning fire.

'Samar,' said Bindiya, keeping her voice low and calm, 'you know that's not true.'

'He. Killed. My. Mother. Bindiya. You refuse to even meet the man who hurt your mum, how do you expect me to forgive the man who killed mine?'

'For two reasons,' she said, caressing his arm. 'One, Ojas Uncle did *not* kill your mother. And two, it's the strong who have the power in them to forgive, and you *are* strong.'

'Bindiya,' Samar said angrily, 'you don't know what happened, so pl—'

'Samar, if we have the right to live life the way we want to, we do have the right to die the way we want to as well and that is what your mum did. What is wrong with wanting to die with dignity? Ojas Uncle tells me that your mum spoke to you at length before they decided not to go in for another surgery, to explain her choice to you. It was her choice, Samar – Ojas Uncle had nothing to do with it.'

'Exactly,' said Samar, his face clouded. 'He did nothing to change her mind and for that I'll never talk to him again.'

'Samar, by not talking to Ojas Uncle, who are you punishing? Him or yourself?'

'Bindiya, I am not up for this conversation,' Samar said, now getting up, his face red with anger. Bindiya got up with him and turned him around so they stood there facing each other.

For a moment, fire blazed.

Then Bindiya breathed out. 'Samar, who are you angry with?' she asked in a soft voice, tilting her head to one side.

'Bindiya ...'

'There was nothing the twelve-year-old Bindiya could do to save her parent's marriage ... there was nothing the twenty-year-old Samar could do to save his mother. Forgive him. Please.'

'Stop this rubbish, Bindiya,' came the low growl.

'You couldn't have done anything to save her—'

'Bindiya ... please ... I don't want to—'

'Samar, there are times when we are helpless no matter how powerful we might one day become. You have to accept such things as god's will and believe that god has a plan. I wasn't able to save my parents' marriage and—'

'You did something bigger and better, Bindiya, you did ... you got your family back together again.'

'And you set up a million charities that help patients and their families. I helped two people for the most selfish reasons. You help hundreds and thousands for the most selfless reasons.'

'I would trade with you any day ... to save the two people who mattered ...' Samar slumped back into the sofa, defeated, lost. Again.

One look at Samar's eyes and something inside Bindiya's heart broke. She climbed onto the sofa and hurriedly gathered him in her arms.

'Samar,' said Bindiya, tearing up, 'losing your mum was the worst thing that could happen to you. You pretend to be all Hulk-like, but you are not. You have the most sensitive, gentlest heart I have ever known. You look at me once and you can see everything that's going on in my head. You gave me a chance when anyone else in your position would not have.

201

You pulled Naina out of the slums and gave her an education. Surat tells me he'll take a bullet for you in his chest, not because he is your bodyguard, but because you have helped him in ways that have put him in your debt for the rest of his life and he isn't talking about money—'

'Bindiya,' Samar broke in, his voice cracking, 'I begged Mum again and again to fight. Once more. For me ... but she didn't ...'

Samar, the powerful, scary Samar Chauhan, looked as vulnerable as a little boy, and Bindiya's heart broke with each word he said.

'Mums are people too. They can't always be strong and sensible. Look at mine – she fell apart like dry sand that cannot hold any shape when she heard about my father ... but you know what, it's okay. God gives you problems; He gives you strength to deal with them too. Forgive, Samar, forgive and let the pain go ...'

Samar's eyes were hard and his face was set. The only thing that spoke loud and clear of the sheer pain he was going through was the lone tear that had begun its journey from his eyes. Bindiya, her heart broken into a million little pieces, placed a hand on his cheek and with the other wiped it off.

'Samar, unless you forgive, you won't be able to love. Unless you forgive, you won't be at peace ... You are hurting ... always hurting – hurting so bad that I ... I can feel it even from a distance. I felt it the day I set eyes on you ... I sometimes feel I can touch your pain. And I hate it. I hate to see you sad. Please, Samar, for my sake, if not for anything else, forgive Ojas Uncle for not fighting, forgive your mum for not fighting for you, and please, please, please forgive my Samar.'

By this time Bindiya was sobbing and when she saw tears

stream down Samar's face, it was like a dam inside her had burst. She sobbed into his chest for him, for his pain, for the emptiness in his life. They clung to each other, vulnerable on their own, strong together.

'Parents don't stay forever, Samar,' she said, very aware of a deep sense of regret searing through her own chest. 'A day will come when you'll be desperate to talk to Ojas Uncle and he won't be there any more.'

Samar remained silent but Bindiya felt him clasp his hands tighter around her.

'Some day, Samar?' she asked hopefully a little later. 'Maybe when you are more ready, you'll give your father a second chance?'

Samar combed some hair out of Bindiya's tear-stained face and smiled a weak smile.

'Some day?' she asked again.

'Some day,' he said and kissed her forehead.

The grandfather clock struck one and Samar got up to leave.

'Stay the night,' Bindiya heard herself say as she stared into the brown flecks of his exhausted eyes. 'Er ... I mean, can you stay?'

'I don't want to be without you,' he said simply.

'Then don't be without me,' she said. She got up and switched off the lights in the living room, leaving on a lamp in the far corner. She came back and gently guided Samar to the sofa, propping a comfortable cushion under his head. She then lay next to him, her face a few inches away from his, their noses almost touching.

For now the world consisted just of Bindiya and Samar. Nothing else mattered. Nothing else existed.

Samar's fingers found hers and clasped hungrily around

them. His other hand went behind her waist, crept easily under her shirt and rested firmly against her shoulder blades and the strap of her bra. His hand against her skin. Gently he pulled her in and they stayed like that, close, snug and staring at each other in the semi-darkness. Silent.

'There's another thing I want to tell you ...' he said in a whisper.

'Is it good or bad?' she asked, using her free hand to caress his soft hair.

'It is sad.'

'Then not tonight,' she whispered.

'Okay,' he whispered back, a slow smile returning to his face.

'Close your eyes now?' she asked.

He did not.

'I'll be right here when you wake up. Like this, looking at you ...'

Samar clutched her hand tighter and pulled her closer. Close enough to sense each breath she took and feel each flutter in her body. 'When I hold you,' he said, staring into Bindiya's eyes, 'I don't just hold you; I hold everything that can ever matter to me.'

With that, Samar's eyes, heavy with sleep, slowly closed and, continuing to hold Bindiya, he fell into a deep sleep. And for the first time in twenty-odd years, Samar Chauhan slept through the night.

When his eyes flicked open at seven in the morning, Bindiya was there, just as she had promised, bathed in the sunlight that streamed in from the window, her hand wrapped around him and her body pressed against his, eyes open and full of love, her soul still rejoicing in the words Samar had said the night before.

When he smiled, a relaxed, happy smile, Bindiya felt that it had to be the most beautiful thing she had ever seen.

❋

Samar went to the US the next day and had his meeting with Jai Saran. Jai had been nervous about meeting the business tycoon he had heard so much about but nothing had prepared him for the slaughter that awaited him in the boardroom. Even Naina, used to Samar's harsh ways, was taken aback by the relentless fury of the salvo of difficult questions that Samar hurled at Jai.

'It was almost as if he had a personal vendetta against me,' Jai said to his wife later that night, a very puzzled expression on his face. 'I'm so worried he'll destroy my company.'

Jai would be proved right. He would never quite understand how it happened, but two years later he would find himself filing for bankruptcy.

Meanwhile, Bindiya went about her days with a big smile plastered on her face.

Oblivious, entirely oblivious, of the storm the universe was brewing up for her.

Oblivious that in less than a week's time Bindiya and Samar would part ways.

38

Malika sat in the little Iranian café and drummed her fingers, thinking hard. For forever now, all she had wanted was for Samar to love her back. The more Samar tried to tell her that they worked best as friends, the more Malika wanted him to

205

take her in his arms, kiss her passionately and tell her he was crazy about her. Yet he had turned a blind eye to her and fallen for that silly Saran girl. That had now made Malika hate Samar as much as she loved him. Almost like she wanted to cut him into pieces and then hurriedly put him together again, even before he started to hurt. From feeling hopeless, then desperate, Malika was now madly in love *and* seething with anger.

Malika's mother had tried to reason with her. 'You are successful, beautiful and talented. God has given you so much – be happy with what you have and forget about Samar.'

'Who says I can't have it all? I love him and I will have him.'

'You are not chasing him because you love him,' said her mother, looking at her daughter as if seeing her in a new light.

'What do you mean?'

'You want him for the worst possible reason,' her mum replied.

'What?'

'You want him just because you can't get him,' she said, 'and no good ever comes of that.'

Malika rolled her eyes at her mother and walked out of the room.

She might have won many a war in the boardroom, most of them alongside Samar, yet Malika knew she had lost the most important battle of her life to Bindiya. The desperation with which she had begged Bindiya for Samar at the gala dinner had killed some part of her spirit. And it hurt and seared and burnt her everywhere even now. Why Samar had chosen Bindiya and not her was beyond Malika; she was now too angry to care, but her love had been spurned and some one had to pay for it for her to begin to heal.

'Malika ma'am,' Ajai from the IC Group said nervously, coming up to her table and bringing her back to the present.

'Oh hi, Ajai, thanks for coming,' Malika said, smiling.

'How can I help you, ma'am?'

Malika smiled. *Of course you can help, Ajai, you are with Bindiya in her new assignment.* 'A tiny little job for you, Ajai,' she said.

The meeting lasted a total of ten minutes. Ten minutes that Malika hoped would change her life. And Bindiya's. And Samar's.

❋

When Samar walked into his house at nine, a lot earlier than usual, sounds of laughter reached his ears. Without thinking, he found himself walking towards it.

Kaka and Ojas were in the kitchen, huddled over a phone.

'And then I literally fell off the chair laughing. It was *so* funny,' came Bindiya's voice from the phone, breaking into fresh peals of laughter. Kaka and Ojas, who were already doubled up with laughter, hooted in agreement, back-slapping each other like lads on the street.

'Good for you, my little chidiya,' said Ojas indulgently. 'Next time he acts funny, just break his head.'

Samar shook his head. That girl was crazy and the rest of his family was steadily acquiring some of her madness.

'Samar beta,' said Kaka, seeing him. The laughter, Samar noted, died that instant.

'Hi Samar,' squealed Bindiya on the phone. 'I'll call you in a bit when I have some time,' she added in a fake busy tone, mimicking Samar's voice and words.

Samar smiled. 'Yes, sure,' he said.

With Bindiya gone, the three men stared at each other. Awkward. Silent.

207

Odd, Kaka thought, how Bindiya's mere voice made the house happier.

Ojas cleared his throat, shuffled his feet and turned to go out of the kitchen. He knew Samar would breathe more comfortably if he left.

'Um,' mumbled Samar.

Ojas turned around and saw Samar standing there looking awkwardly at him. He fiddled with the knot of his tie, an old habit, something he did when he felt uncomfortable.

For a moment father and son looked at each other.

'Uh.'

'Yes?' asked Ojas, his heart thumping. Did Samar want to say something to him?

Samar stared at the lines around his father's eyes. When had they appeared? And the hair, had it grown white overnight? And the ...

One day you'll be desperate to speak with Ojas Uncle and he won't be around any more.

'Do you need anything, beta?' asked Kaka in an attempt to diffuse the awkwardness.

Samar's eyes lingered on his father's face for another moment before he turned to look at Kaka. 'No, thank you,' he said and walked out without saying another word.

❋

The sound of the ringing phone woke Bindiya up at 4.30 a.m.

'Are you ready?' the golden voice reached her ears, waking her up instantly. Bindiya eyed her watch and wondered how anyone could sound so sexy at four bloody thirty in the morning?

'What?' she squawked.

Samar laughed. 'Get off your bed! The car's waiting outside.'

'Why? Where am I going?' she mumbled, rubbing her eyes, and then it struck her. It was Samar's birthday! A couple of days back, when Bindiya had asked Samar what he wanted for his birthday, he had simply said 'a day'.

'Take a lifetime,' Bindiya had said theatrically.

'Your life should always only belong to you, Bindiya, and lived exactly the way you wish to – just give me a day,' he had said, his face serious.

'Oh my god,' Bindiya now squealed as her brain kick-started into motion, 'you never told me we were going somewhere ...'

'Half an hour, Bindiya Saran,' Samar growled.

Bindiya giggled. She had learnt to no longer be intimidated by his growls; Samar's bark was, as they said, a lot worse than his bite.

'What do I pack?'

'We have everything you need – just get out of your bed. Surat is waiting outside. I have spoken to your mum and promised her that I'll get you back by midnight.'

'Do you have any idea where I am going?' she asked Surat once she had jumped into the vehicle. Surat smiled and winked but said nothing.

'So now you'll also be all secretive with me,' she said, pouting, but Surat just laughed and said, 'Orders, ma'am.'

When the car finally stopped at the airport Bindiya got her first clue. They were going away from Mumbai! But where? Her eyes fell on Naina who was standing outside, waiting for her. Was all of Samar's personal staff at the airport?

'Where am I going?' she blurted, the moment Naina peeped into the car.

209

'Wait and see,' said Naina, grinning and pulling Bindiya by her arm. 'Samar is in the lounge, let me take you to him.'

'Why is everyone being so secretive?' Bindiya wailed, secretly enjoying the suspense.

The two walked briskly through the busy airport terminal to the first-class lounge, and then across it into an exclusive waiting room. There, laptop open in front of him, eyes intent on the screen, sat the birthday boy, hard at work.

'Happpppyyyy birthday once again, Samar!' Bindiya shouted and threw her arms around Samar.

Naina grinned. Samar rolled his eyes but laughed nevertheless.

'Thank you! Let's go now!' he said. 'We're already behind schedule.'

'Where are we going?' Bindiya asked again.

'Shut up, Ms Saran,' said Samar sternly, which made Bindiya giggle.

'My documents?' Bindiya asked as they reached a gate.

'All taken care of,' Naina said, grinning like the Cheshire cat.

Much to Bindiya's shock, it was not a scheduled flight the two got on. Instead, a gleaming private plane, capable of seating five, waited for them on the tarmac.

'Are you kidding me?' was all that Bindiya could manage as she climbed into the plane.

It was only once the aircraft had taken off and a woman about ten times better dressed than Bindiya had placed champagne in front of them that she finally turned around to face Samar. 'Samar,' she said, a frown on her face.

'Yes?' he said, looking into her eyes in a way that made her forget what she had been so determined to say a few seconds back. Damn that stubble! And the rolled-up sleeves! And the eyes! And the eyelashes! And ... arrggghhh.

'Bindiya?' Samar prodded her, an amused expression on his face.

'Um, ... what *is* going on?' she said hastily, trying to regain some authority in her voice.

'What do you mean?'

'You are behaving like it's my birthday! All these secret plans, whisking me away to I-don't-know-where on a private plane! It's your birthday, not mine! I am supposed to be doing things for you, not you for me!'

Samar pushed back the hand rest between their seats and pulled her closer. A waft of his perfume reached her but she tried hard not to let it distract her.

'Bindiya,' said Samar, his voice serious, 'as my birthday gift I asked you for a day.'

She nodded.

'And you agreed?'

She nodded again.

'So let's just spend this day the way I want to?'

'But ...'

'No, no buts.'

'Samar ...'

'Bindiya, I listen to you when you insist on paying half our bill each time we go out – whether it is at Jai Mata dhaba or the Hyatt. We have been to ... what ... maybe six movies and you have paid for me most of the time. I am ten years older than you, head of one of the largest companies in the country and was born with I don't know how many silver spoons in my mouth. You've just started working and pretty much fend for your family! But for reasons beyond me, you hate it when

I spend a penny on you. I know it's, in some weird way, about your pride. I don't get it, Bindiya, but I know it's important to you and that is enough for me to respect it. If for three hundred and sixty-four days a year, I do as you like, for one day, on my birthday, can we do things the way I'd like them to be done?'

Large, surprised eyes stared at Samar. Eyes that had softened as Samar spoke.

Samar leaned forward and kissed her lightly on her lips. 'Can we?' he asked gently.

'As your birthday gift you want me to let you splurge on me?'

Samar smiled. 'Yes, that's one way of putting it. It will make me very happy, Bindiya.'

It was only the sweetest thing anyone had ever done for her. Programmed and accustomed only to giving, she stared at Samar. A thousand thoughts raced through her mind, and try as she might, she could not find the right words to express what she wanted to say.

'I want you to be happy. Let's do everything the way you want to do it, Samar,' she said, resting her head on his shoulder. Samar smiled and then switched his phone off, something Bindiya had never seen him do before.

39

Bindiya and Samar spent the day on a remote, breathtakingly beautiful island in Thailand.

'With just a day and no time for visas, this is the best we could manage,' he said, shrugging when their speedboat finally stopped near the island, but Bindiya was already staring around, open-mouthed.

White sand, aquamarine blue sea and the verdant green in the distance. How could anything be lovelier? 'Samar,' she said, awestruck, 'this is gorgeous!'

'You like it?' Samar asked, looking at her eyes which were shining with excitement.

'I love it!' Bindiya shrieked, kicking off her sandals and running towards the beach. The island, the obsequious manager of the resort informed, Bindiya, was only eleven kilometres long and almost invisible even on the map of Thailand. The resort was spread across the island, and Samar and Bindiya were the only guests.

'Off season?' Bindiya asked, as she propped herself up on the sand.

Samar shook his head. 'There were a few guests. I understand we offered them extra money, reservations in a seven-star and some perks, and they all agreed to move out.'

Bindiya rolled her eyes at Samar. 'Why?'

'So that we could have this place to ourselves, Bindiya, that's why,' said Samar.

Bindiya opened her mouth and then shut it. The rich and their ways, she thought to herself with a chuckle but straightened her face when she saw Samar looking at her.

'So what do we do now?' she said, excitedly tapping her foot.

'First, we try and be still,' Samar said sternly but Bindiya could see his eyes laugh, 'and then we hit the water!'

Samar pulled off his shirt to reveal a surprisingly muscular torso that Bindiya had to force her eyes away from. A tray with several swimsuits and bikinis appeared in front of Bindiya.

'Can I just swim in my shorts and tee?' Bindiya asked.

'Do whatever makes you happiest, Bindiya, it's just us on the island,' he replied.

The next couple of hours would later become a sun-soaked, happy blur. Samar was surprisingly and endearingly playful. He dunked her in the sea, taught her to catch waves, hoisted her on his shoulders and marched into deep waters. Bindiya laughed and squealed and delighted in the attention he lavished on her, clinging on to him literally for dear life at times. Someone got them some snorkelling gear and they spent the next few hours snorkelling, pointing out brightly coloured fishes to each other.

At about four in the evening, they plonked themselves on the sand, deliciously exhausted. When Samar extended his arm, it felt most natural for Bindiya to rest her head on it. They lay together, in silence, breathing deeply, wide grins plastered on their faces.

'The best birthday ever,' said Bindiya.

Samar laughed, squinting in the sun to look at her.

'And I am now hungry!'

'Room number one is yours. Why don't you change and meet me at the beach at five?' said Samar, getting up as a staff member miraculously appeared from nowhere to escort Bindiya.

'Change into what? This is the only set of clothes I have.'

'Just go to your room, Bindiya,' said Samar, gently pushing her away. 'Everything has been taken care of.'

And everything had indeed been taken care of. There were some boxes on her bed and a little hand-written note. 'On you, all of this will look prettier,' it said simply, in Samar's cursive.

Intrigued, Bindiya opened them one by one and stared in amazement. The largest one contained, in a cloud of butter paper, a simple white, floaty dress. Bindiya picked it up and gasped when she saw the label. Alexander McQueen.

Her mind flashed back to that night in Kufri when Malika had worn a black Alexander McQueen dress.

'Malika's dress looks lovely. The rumour is, it's an Alexander McQueen,' Bindiya had conspiratorially told Samar.

'Is that your favourite designer?' Samar had asked.

'Yes, though, it'll be a good few decades before I earn enough to buy a dress that expensive,' she had said, laughing, 'but when I do, it won't be black.'

'Which colour would it be?'

'White,' she had said, smiling. 'Floaty, dreamy white.'

The second box she opened contained white strappy shoes, with red soles. Christian Louboutins. She had seen this pair in a shop at one of the hotels she had been to with Samar.

'They are beautiful!' she had gushed.

'Then let's get them for you!' Samar had said, moving towards the entrance of the shop. Bindiya had, however, pulled him back.

'Noooooo.'

'Why not?'

'I don't wear such expensive shoes, Samar,' she had said, 'and no, I don't want you to buy them for me.'

The third box contained a silver glittery clutch from Prada that she knew she had seen somewhere though she couldn't quite place it for a moment. Then she remembered.

Samar had come to drop Bindiya home and had stopped for a few minutes to chat with Urvi who had been flipping through a fashion magazine.

'Bee didi has such horrible taste,' Urvi had squealed in delight even as Bindiya tried to snatch the magazine away from her. 'She says that when her salary hits fifty lakhs a year, she'll buy this clutch to celebrate!'

'Really?' Samar had said and peeped in for a look, barely

215

catching a glimpse of the page before Bindiya, horrified and embarrassed, had snatched away the magazine. 'Prada?'

'Or Prada-Shrada as Bee didi likes to call it.'

Bindiya laughed out loud when she opened the fourth box. It contained a sparkling, brand-new, collector's edition Rolex. Samar had had enough of the fake one she often sported on her wrist, Bindiya thought to herself.

Still smiling, Bindiya now spotted a fifth box that had been hidden behind one of the larger boxes. It was very tiny in size and earthy gold in colour. 'Zariin Jewellers' was printed on it. When Bindiya opened it, she gasped and then bit her lower lip when she realized what the box contained. Glittering back at her was a pair of earrings, but they were not just any earrings. Bindiya fingered the earrings, incredulous, thinking about the night after her dance performance when Samar had first shown her his mother's picture – she had been wearing the same earrings Bindiya now held in her hands.

With silent tears streaming down her face, Bindiya sat down on the edge of the bed, overwhelmed. Without saying a word, Samar had let her know many things she knew he would need a lot more time to actually say. From her bag she took out the birthday gift she had got for him. She stared at it for a few moments, then placed it next to the pile of gifts from Samar, the topmost of which was the small blue jewellery box. The value of his gifts, both monetary and emotional, was unbeatable. She shook her head sadly, feeling small, and then called up Samar.

'No,' he said, instead of 'hello'.

'What no?'

'I'm not taking any of it back. Get ready and come out.'

'Okay, okay,' said Bindiya, laughing and wiping away her tears.

216

When Bindiya walked to the beach, a stunning sight met her eyes. Against the backdrop of waves crashing against the beach, a white shabby-chic table and chairs had been set up under a fluttering white canvas canopy. Paper lanterns flickered in the wind, reminding Bindiya of butterflies, and rose petals had been strewn across the white sand leading to the table.

Samar, in a smart tux, was waiting by the dinner table, oddly suave in the rustic surroundings. He got up when he saw her.

Bindiya was a vision in white. The hazy cloud of the dress billowed around her, and her elegant chignon added yet another touch of class. Samar could only stare at her as she walked up to him.

When she stopped close to him, Samar, as if in a trance, reached out to finger one of the earrings she was wearing.

217

'The Zariin Jewellery box … ' Bindiya left the sentence incomplete, words failing her. They were not needed; he knew she had recognized the earrings.

'Zariin was her favourite,' he said with a small smile.

'These earrings are beautiful,' she said in a voice that made him shift his gaze to her face.

'So are you. Inside and out.'

'Are you sure you want me to keep these?' she asked softly.

'Yes,' he said simply.

'And now let's eat before it begins to rain,' said Samar, looking at the clouds which had been gathering over the last hour. He had but finished his sentence when the first drops of rain began to fall and as if on cue, the winds picked up speed.

'It's a storm!' someone shouted.

The winds began to howl and lightning ruthlessly parted the grey clouds. About ten people appeared on the scene with hurriedly mumbled promises of making an equally elegant setting for dinner indoors. Samar followed them towards shelter but had not taken ten steps when he realized that Bindiya was not with him. He turned around and saw that she was still standing next to the canvas which was now dancing madly in the wind, staring at the sea with an expression of amazement on her face.

Samar stuffed his hands in his pockets and watched from a distance as Bindiya took in the beauty of the storm. He saw her spread her hands wide, as if embracing the winds. She twirled and, when she looked back him, smiling, Samar's heart filled with a kind of joy he had not known in years.

She laughed when leaves, lifted up by the winds, hit her face. She turned her face heavenwards when bigger drops began to fall from the sky. Samar found himself smiling when Bindiya squealed as the winds played havoc with her dress, trying desperately to keep the skirt wrapped around her legs.

He came running to Bindiya. 'Let's go in, Bindiya,' he said, covering both of them with his coat.

'Samar,' Bindiya said, her eyes oddly serious, 'stay please.'

'Wh ...'

'Sit down,' said Bindiya. Samar agreed. He sat on the wet sand, cross-legged as the winds growled around him, feeling oddly calm in the midst of the noise. Bindiya hopped over his legs and came to sit on his lap, facing the sea.

'Look at the sea with me? Please?' she said.

Samar wrapped his arms around her stomach, rested his cheek against hers and stared at the now angry waves crashing against the beach. Rain pelted around him and the winds howled angrily. The two sat there, wrapped in silence.

Bindiya now turned around to face him, her face inches from his. She placed both her hands on his cheeks and whispered, 'I have something for you.'

Samar smiled. 'We discussed my gift. I don't want anything else from you.'

'It's a very small thing, Samar.' Samar looked quizzically at her. 'I want us to make a memory for you.'

'A memory?'

'Yes, a memory … See the colour of the sky?'

'Grey?'

'See how it's darker grey in bits and almost silver in others?'

'Yes …'

'Paint it in your mind. Now look at the water … Do you see how the aquamarine now looks dull blue?'

Samar nodded, staring at the waves.

'Do you see the white surf of the waves crashing against the shore?'

'Yes.'

'Memorize it … Can you hear the winds howl?'

'Yes.'

'See how it's scary and beautiful at the same time … much like life?'

Samar nodded.

'See my face … the arch of my eyebrows, my lips, my cheeks …'

'Your eyelashes are wet.'

'And?'

Samar traced his finger along her face. 'And your hair is … is … beautiful even like this …'

'And?'

'You are so close to me …'

'Do I feel close enough?'

'You never feel close enough,' said Samar simply and pulled her in tighter.

'Can you memorize how being this close feels?'

'You are shivering,' he said, wrapping his jacket tightly around her.

'Memorize this ...'

'You shivering?'

Bindiya smiled. 'Yes, you have to memorize everything, how else will you make a complete memory?'

The two stayed like that for a few moments. Then Bindiya opened her purse and pulled out a colourful loom bracelet.

Yellow. Green. Red. Blue. Pink. Orange. She had made it herself and had used every colour she had never seen on Samar.

'This is for you.'

Samar grinned. A handmade loom bracelet – the little gift had Bindiya stamped all over it.

'I love my birthday gift,' he said, kissing her forehead.

'Now back to memory-making.'

'Oh, there's more memory-making?'

'Yes, there is. Now see, I am tying this bracelet around your wrist ...' she said, laughing as she slipped the band on to his wrist. It looked comically out of place next to Samar's collector's edition Rolex.

'All this is part of your gift.' Bindiya now reached out and put her hand on his mouth, stopping him from speaking any further. 'Now,' she said, looking a little nervous, 'I wanted you to make the memory because I want you to remember everything about this moment. How I am in your arms, wrapped in your coat, how I look, how the waves sound, how the wind feels ... everything. Shh,' she said when she sensed he was about to say something. 'I just want you to listen. To hear me out. I don't want you to say anything now, I don't want you to say anything after I finish speaking. I just want you to know. To listen. To remember.'

Samar's eyes, large and expressive, looked on from above the hand that covered his mouth.

'Samar,' said Bindiya, gulping for she understood the gravity of what she was about to say, 'I love you.'

Samar's stunned eyes stared back at her.

'No ... no, don't say anything ... just listen to me, please,' she pleaded when Samar reached out his hand to pull hers away from his mouth. On hearing her plea, Samar immediately released her hand. 'It's easy to understand why I love you. With you by my side I feel like I can conquer the world. You are my strength, my courage, my confidence, my everything. When you hold me, Samar, everything feels okay ... when you look at me, everything about the world around erupts and then it all melts into oblivion ...'

Samar's eyes stared unblinkingly at the girl in front of him.

221

'What I cannot fathom is the amount of love I feel for you ... I love you so much, Samar, that loving you hurts. When your eyes cloud, my heart breaks, it actually breaks. Do you understand? Do you have any idea how that feels? A thought, a sad thought across your face like when you stand and stare at a mother and her son eat candy outside the theatre it can make it impossible for me to breathe. I love you so much that I am ... I ... am ... You are my biggest strength, Samar and, by far, my biggest weakness now.'

'Bind ...'

Bindiya pressed her hand harder against his mouth. 'I love you more than I ever thought I could love anyone, Samar, and it's liberating to feel such love for someone ... I want you to know this. I don't expect anything from you. I don't want you to say anything in return. No, that's not what I want. I love you too much to want anything from you. I don't know if you love me, hell, I don't even need you to love me in return. My love is enough for two,' she said, smiling through the tears that had begun to pool in her eyes. 'But I want you to know. I want you to have this memory of a girl sitting in your lap on a beautiful beach telling you how much she loves you. I want you to have this memory to go back to whenever there is darkness around you. I want you to have this one memory of such pure love that it will see you through your darkest hours.'

Something inside Samar's heart lurched in an incomprehensible mixture of yearning, pathos and gratitude. His brow now furrowed and, seeing tears streaming down Bindiya's face, he felt his own eyes well up.

'I simply want you to know that I love you with all my heart. I love the good in you, the bad in you and the ugly in you. I ...' said Bindiya and turned the bracelet on his wrist inside out and read to him words that were woven into it, 'love you, Samar.'

Samar stared at the bracelet and the words that had been cleverly woven into it in red thread. 'I love you, Samar,' it said. And then he stared at Bindiya. At the girl who had just opened her heart to him.

Slowly she released her hand away from his mouth. 'Please, don't say anything ... please,' she whispered, now looking down at her hands.

Samar did not say anything. He simply stared into her eyes, looking, searching, finding, cherishing. He pulled her chin up with his index finger and leaned forward to kiss her, long and slow. The rain, steady and relentless, poured around them in a curtain of water, cutting them off from the rest of the world.

When, without another word, he picked her up, effortlessly, as if she were a baby, she did not resist.

222

When, a few minutes later, in her room, he gently laid her on her bed, she did not resist.

When he lay next to her, smelling of the rain and the beach, and pulled her into his arms, kissing her tear-stained cheeks, she did not resist.

And when he, gently, tenderly, wordlessly, unzipped her dress, she did not resist.

40

Samar held Bindiya close to him during their flight to Mumbai, barely letting go of her hand.

Back in the car that Surat drove, Bindiya rested her head on Samar's shoulders, breathing him in, images from the last few hours coming back to her in welcome flashes. She tried desperately to bottle these images in her head, safe, to be brought out again and again in the future.

His body, strong, lithe and powerful.

His eyes, serious and intense.

Samar himself, heartbreakingly gentle.

He had treated her with such tenderness that you would have thought she was made of glass. When he had touched her, every bit of her had erupted. And when he pulled away, her heart had ached.

'Consider it a glorious gift from the universe if it allows you to fall truly and madly in love with someone,' Adi had said once to Bindiya and it was now that she fully understood what he meant. Being in love with someone, without being shackled by doubts or expectations, was oddly liberating. It made Bindiya feel like a giant bird soaring high in the cloudless sky.

'Are you okay?' Samar asked, touching her hair, half concerned for her, half afraid of the fragility of the girl who stared at him with all the love of the world in her eyes.

That too. 'Are you okay,' – he had asked her that so many times. Bindiya smiled, both at his question and the memories. 'I am fine, Samar,' she said and wrapped her arms tighter around him. The car stopped and Bindiya stared dismally at the familiar red-brick building of her house looming in front of her. Really? So quickly? Where had the day gone?

'I don't want you to go just yet,' Samar whispered into her ears.

Surat hastily parked the car some distance away from the house and left them to 'get something from somewhere,' which made Bindiya smile. Samar and Bindiya sat there, as close as they could get yet not close enough, unwilling to let the night end.

'When do I see you next?' Samar asked, touching her cheeks with the back of his fingers, eyes focused on the tiny mole just below her eyebrow.

'When you come back from Beijing.'

'Please take care of yourself while I am away?'

'And when you are back, then?'

'Then I'll take care of you,' said Samar, smiling.

'Okay,' said Bindiya, grinning.

'Call me if there is anything?'

'And if there is nothing?'

'Call me anyway,' he said, laughing, surprised yet again at how easy it was for him to laugh with her ... and it was a laughing Bindiya that he dropped off at the doorstep.

❀

Bindiya, Ajai and Varun sat in the cafeteria of their new client's office, talking over a cup of chai. Ajai and Varun were deep in discussion and Bindiya was distracted, Whatsapping with Adi who had finally starting behaving normally with her.

It was Adi she had been talking with last week when, completely out of the blue, it struck Bindiya that she and Samar had not used protection of any sort in Thailand. Horrified, she had excused herself and was hurriedly Googling for what to do when Samar had happened to call. Bindiya had been unwilling to tell Samar what was troubling her, but she had to just say 'hello' into the phone and Samar had just known that something was terribly wrong. He questioned her relentlessly till he got the truth out of her and within half an hour of the call, one of Mumbai's leading gynaecologists had spoken to Bindiya and advised her on the morning-after pill.

'I am sorry,' Samar had said briefly afterwards. 'It was my fault. I should have taken care of it.'

No, Bindiya had wanted to reply, no, no, no. It was not a 'fault', nothing about this had been a 'fault'. It had been the most beautiful experience of her life!

'Next time I'll be careful,' Samar had added after a pause.

Next time. Bindiya blushed deeply.

'Mr Mukherjee is a good boss,' said Varun, bringing Bindiya back to the present.

'Hmm ... yes, much easier to get along with than Satan from Zorawar,' Ajai remarked.

'Oh yeah, I have heard so much about him,' said Varun. 'Shame I was not on that project.'

'One of the hardest projects I ever did!' said Ajai.

'So I heard,' said Varun.

225

'Samar Chauhan such an interesting man,' said Ajai, eyeing Bindiya to make sure she was listening and not engrossed with her phone.

'Why?'

'Many reasons actually – brilliant at work, very highly regarded professionally ... but ... but, you know, all the stuff about his past ...'

Bindiya cleared her throat, suddenly uncomfortable.

'What about it?' asked Varun, leaning forward.

'You do know about his wife, right?' asked Ajai.

And with that one word, Bindiya's world began to collapse. She looked up slowly, hands turning icy in a second, and faced the two men.

'Whose wife?' Bindiya heard herself ask.

'Samar's wife ... surely you've heard about her?'

For Bindiya, the earth stopped moving. 'He's married?' she asked in a voice that was surprisingly devoid of emotion.

'Was,' said Ajai.

'Was?' Bindiya repeated.

'Yeah, she died, and Samar Chauhan was accused of murder,' Ajai said. Varun gasped dramatically. 'Didn't you know?' asked Ajai, looking at Varun and then carefully at Bindiya. Malika had asked him to note Bindiya's expression when he revealed Samar's past and describe it to her.

'He murdered his wife?' Bindiya found herself asking.

'Yeah,' Ajai said, shrugging.

Bindiya brought her hand to her mouth and then ran out of the cafeteria, desperate for some air, afraid that if she stayed inside even a second longer, she would collapse.

41

Bindiya was not quite sure where she was going, but she hoped it was to the Zorawar Group HQ where she knew Samar would have headed straight from the airport. She had to meet him; something, she thought, had to be done to steady her wildly beating heart. Why was her body reacting to this information in such a manner? Did some part of her truly fear that Ajai was speaking the truth? Did some part of her know? Had always known? Did this explain the anger in Samar's eyes? Could he kill? Had he killed? Was he a murd ... no, not her Samar, that wasn't possible.

Bindiya gripped the window of the auto, afraid that she would blank out. The auto rattled on and, restless, Bindiya pulled out her phone.

Stop overreacting, she told herself, trying hard to rein in her emotions.

'Samar Chauhan + wife + murder' she typed into the browser and then crossed her fingers. 'Nothing's going to come up and you can go back and hit Ajai on the head,' she mumbled to herself. However, to her utter shock and dismay, it took Google merely 0.08 seconds to throw up a page full of links.

'Mining magnate and marriage disaster,' screamed one website.

'Kaasi Chauhan, murdered in cold blood!' said another in font size 14.

Kaasi. Why was the name familiar?

Helpless tears cascaded down Bindiya's cheeks as she read on. By the time the auto stopped at the Zorawar head office, Bindiya knew she couldn't read another word.

According to the reports – and maybe they were all

wrong, Bindiya thought in desperately – Samar had married a girl called Kaasi when he had just turned twenty-four; four years, Bindiya thought, after his mum passed away. Too soon, a voice in her head warned.

It had been a marriage of convenience, a report had said, Kaasi was the daughter of Ojas Chauhan's best friend, also a well-known industrialist, and the marriage had meant deeper ties between the two prominent business families. The handsome Chauhan heir, said another report, clearly was not the prince charming Kaasi would have hoped he was – they hadn't been married three years when, because of extreme mental torture supposedly inflicted on her by the ruthless Samar Chauhan, Kaasi had the first of many nervous breakdowns.

228

Instead of caring for his wife, Samar Chauhan threw Kaasi into an institution for the mentally ill, in effect abandoning her. Kaasi pleaded with Samar to take her home with him but he stoutly refused, preferring a carefree life to taking responsibility for his ill wife. A women's association tried to help Kaasi but they were quickly and effectively shushed by the powerful Chauhans.

Kaasi Chauhan was found dead about two years after she was admitted to the mental institution. Details from the suicide note clearly stated that Kaasi was sure someone was out there to murder her and speculation was rife that the Chauhans had arranged for her murder.

The charities for the mentally ill that Samar supported. His involvement with Ujala. The time with the little girls. In a morbid way, it all made sense now, and Bindiya felt physically sick. Ujala was Samar's penitence, his way of ridding himself of the guilt.

Bindiya closed her eyes, continuing to hear her heart thud.

After the disaster Rehan had been, she had allowed love a second chance. And look where that had taken her.

Life, you bitch.

❀

'Bindiya,' Samar said, taking three long strides across his office to come to her, 'are you okay? Naina said that you wanted to meet me now?'

'Yes, I need to speak with you,' Bindiya heard herself say.

'What's wrong?' he said, his eyes serious now. He took a step closer. She stepped away. Puzzled, Samar stared. 'Bindiya ... is ...'

'I need you to answer three questions for me,' she said in a voice devoid of emotion. Samar stared at the inanimate girl, barely able to recognize her.

'Oh okay ... sure ...'

'Were you married before?' she asked, staring straight at him. Bindiya saw Samar's expression change and the little hope she had carried in her heart vanished. She knew the answer even before Samar said it.

'Bindiya ... listen,' he said, putting a hand on her arm.

'Yes or no?' she said, angrily pushing his hand away, surprised at the magnitude of emotions she felt surge inside her.

'Yes.'

Bindiya's expression did not change. 'Did you admit your wife to a mental asylum soon after your marriage?'

'Yes,' he said, his face expressionless.

Bindiya looked down now, trying to gather all the strength she could muster for the last question.

'Did you kill her?' she asked quietly, a moment later, her eyes boring into Samar's.

229

Samar's eyes grew cold and hard; his breathing became heavier and dark clouds of fury coloured his face. He took a few steps towards her and stopped only when he was inches away from her.

In that one moment, for the first time in many months, Bindiya felt petrified of Samar.

'You want to know if I murdered Kaasi?' Samar asked in a low, dangerous growl.

Bindiya stood still.

'Is that what you think? Well, yes then, I killed her. Happy now?' he spat out the words, turned around and left the room.

Bindiya stood in the middle of his office, stunned. Had Samar just confessed to killing his wife? Had she fallen in love with a murderer?

230

42

Bindiya fled from Samar's office, unable to control the tears that flowed unabated down her cheeks.

'Bindiya, wait!' Naina shouted, placing a hand on her shoulder.

'No, Naina, no,' Bindiya mumbled and ran out of the building.

She did not go to work; instead, Bindiya headed home. Sunaina's stream of questions, on seeing the red, tear-stained face of her daughter, fell on deaf ears. Bindiya ran to her room, locked it, flung herself on the bed and tried her best not to go online to search for the murder trial of Mrs Kaasi Chauhan.

Crying yourself to sleep is the worst way to sleep. So, when loud knocks on her door woke Bindiya up, it was from a very uneasy, fitful sleep. Her head already splitting with the worst ache she had ever had, Bindiya opened the door and froze when she saw who stood at the door.

The one person, try as she might, in whose face she wouldn't be able to shut the door. Ojas Uncle.

'Bindiya,' he said gently, 'can I have a moment please?'

'Ojas Uncle ... I ... no ... I ...'

'Just five minutes. I promise, I won't take longer,' he said.

Damn it. Wordlessly, she opened the door wider, allowing him entry. From the corner of her eye, she saw Sunaina sitting at the dining table, a worried expression on her face. She looked as if she had been crying. There were three cups in front of her.

Ojas Uncle shut the door behind her and then looked at her. 'I thought you knew about Kaasi.'

'How would I?'

'Because, really, everyone does,' he said softly.

'Everyone does what? Everyone knows that Samar murdered his wife?'

Ojas Uncle pursed his lips. 'Is that what you think?'

'Who cares what I think?'

'Bindiya,' said Ojas Uncle, his voice calm, 'as with any discussion of such nature, there are two lines of thought that can dictate your behaviour. One, you can stand here with the aim of being rude and difficult, and nothing will come of this. Two, you can have this discussion with the aim of hearing me out and maybe you'll end up feeling better. Which one would you prefer?'

Bindiya remained silent and, feeling a tad ashamed of herself, looked down.

'I take it that you'll go for the second option,' said Ojas Uncle, smiling kindly.

He gently pulled Bindiya by her arm and the two of them

sat down on her bed. 'Naina called me, so I know something has happened, but I want to know the details from you,' he said.

'Ojas Uncle,' she began, after pausing to think for a few moments, 'Samar had a wife. And ... and ... he kille ... she died, Ojas Uncle, and the Internet is full of stories about how Samar ... ki ... killed her ... and after reading about all of this, I don't even know what to think. I was hoping Samar would give me an explanation, but he just said that I was right and that he had indeed murdered his wife. I ... I ... I've been so foolish. In all the time we've been together, he never even mentioned his wife! What else has happened in his life that I know nothing about?' Pitiful, angry, helpless sobs broke through again.

Ojas took a deep breath. 'The truth is, Bindiya,' he said, 'Samar was married to Kaasi and we lost her.'

Bindiya stared at Ojas with utter dismay written all over her face. 'It is better to be hurt by the truth than be comforted by a lie, darling,' said Ojas Uncle. 'But we have never ever tried to hide his marriage. Everyone knows about Kaasi and Samar is in no way responsible for her death ...'

'Ojas Uncle, but ...'

'Bindiya please, now let me speak for five minutes and then you say what you need to say?' asked Ojas, placing a gentle hand on her head.

Bindiya nodded.

'Mukesh and I studied together. He was my best mate, the one guy I went to for everything. Mukesh married Jaya and when I married Diya, the four of us became inseparable. Then Samar happened and then, when three years later Jaya gave birth to Kaasi, a girl that we all desperately wanted, it was like we couldn't have asked for anything more. Samar met

Kaasi the day she was born and decided with the innocence of a three-year-old that Kaasi was his baby. It was so sweet to watch.' Ojas smiled at the memory.

'As the two families were very close it was only natural that the kids spend a lot of time together. Even when Kaasi, as a small baby, had been crying for hours, the howling would stop the minute she spotted Samar, and she would start smiling. Our family pandit even claimed that the two were born under the same star and would always be together. And he seemed to be right, for as they grew older, they became inseparable. I wondered sometimes what a thirteen-old-boy found in common with a nine-year-old girl but they never seemed to be short of things to chat about. She knew all about his soccer matches and he knew everything about her friends. We sent Samar and Kaasi's brother to Eton and Kaasi, along with her sister, went to Welhams – different parts of the world, yet Samar and Kaasi's friendship never changed. When they all trooped back home for their holidays, you wouldn't think that Kaasi and Samar had been apart for even a day – they knew so much about the other. Kaasi worshipped him.In her eyes he could do no wrong. And Kaasi was Samar's best friend, with Kaasi's brother coming a close second. The three of them, Mukesh's two and Samar, were thick, always together. I have seen many friendships, Bindiya beta, but quite frankly, none as beautiful as that of Kaasi and Samar.'

Kaasi and Samar. Not Bindiya and Samar. Why did that hurt? Bindiya felt a pang of jealousy sear through her.

Ojas Uncle paused and his face clouded as darker memories pushed aside the happier ones.

'There is only one common thing between good and bad times, Bindiya – they both pass. The good times gave way to the worst days we had ever seen when Diya left us. Samar,

233

who was twenty then, took it very badly – you know the full story there. Of course, he blamed me for Diya's death and stopped talking to me. Gradually, in front of my eyes, my only son began to cut himself off from the world. He spoke to just two people, Kaasi and her brother. While they were around, I assured myself repeatedly, Samar would be fine.'

Ojas paused again and gently wiped a tear off Bindiya's face. 'It's not a happy story, Bindiya,' he continued, 'because someone up there had some scores to settle with Samar. About a year after Diya died, Mukesh came to meet me, very worried. He said he wasn't sure all was well with Kaasi and asked if I knew anything. Of course I didn't, but I had a long discussion with Kaasi. She said everything was fine and I made the mistake of believing her. As time passed, I realized that Mukesh's suspicions could be correct for even I had, by then, started to see changes in her. Once an incessant chatterbox, Kaasi now became very quiet. She stopped paying attention to how she dressed, her behaviour in social gatherings started to become erratic. Her smile was vanishing ... and her eyes ... her eyes, they had become fearful ...'

'Oh ...'

'She had been very close to Diya, Bindiya, and we thought that maybe this was her way of grieving. Again, I was wrong. She ...' Ojas Uncle now shuddered.

'She?'

'She started seeing things.'

'What do you mean?'

'She saw people who were not present. They said things to her and did things to her body. And then ... they started making her do things. She was petrified of the demons inside her head and could not, no matter how much we all tried, get rid of them. It was a relentless battle that was sucking life out of my poor Kaasi.' Ojas Uncle closed his eyes and shook his head as if he were in great pain. 'We took her to doctors from across the world and she was diagnosed with schizophrenia. The doctors reassured us that it was not too pronounced yet and that a change of scene could help.'

'Schizophrenia?' she asked, her heart sinking. Memories of her mother's illness and the darkness that surrounded every moment of that time now came back to Bindiya. Samar had been through the same?

Ojas sighed. 'Yes, we did not know it then but Jaya's mother was schizophrenic as well. The illness had skipped a generation.'

'Then?'

'Samar ...'

'What about Samar?'

'He married her.'

'What?'

'Yes, Samar married Kaasi. Samar was twenty-three and Kaasi was twenty.'

'Did he know about Kaasi's condition?'

'Yes, he did. I don't exactly know what his reasoning was because you know Samar had stopped speaking to me by then, but I think I have a fair idea. As her illness began to take over her life, Kaasi, in the moments when sanity prevailed, had become very unsure about her relationship with Samar. Very anxious, very insecure – it ate her up on the inside. She could hardly speak about it without breaking into tears. It had been most precious to her and she feared that Samar would now leave her – to be honest, any other boy would have.'

'But not Samar ...' said Bindiya softly.

'But not Samar,' repeated Ojas. 'He married her ... He loved her before her illness struck and his love did not change.'

'Oh god,' Bindiya mumbled, thinking about what Ojas had just told her.

'There are no greys in Samar's life, Bindiya, no comfortable middle grounds. When he hates, he hates like no one else can, and when he loves, he loves like no one else can.'

'And this is when Samar was twenty-three?' Bindiya asked.

Ojas Uncle took a deep breath and nodded. 'More man at twenty-three than most men could ever hope to be,' he said. 'You know, I think Samar is god's most favourite child but he's also god's least favourite child and possibly both at the same time.'

'So Kaasi did not get better?' Bindiya asked. Yet again, Bindiya found herself looking at Ujala in a new light.

Ojas Uncle shook his head, slowly, sadly. 'Far from it. The episodes became more frequent and dangerous. Kaasi was sure there was someone out there trying to kill her ... it was madness – well, literally madness. And soon, despite the best medical care in the world, her illness took a turn for the worse. Kaasi began pointing fingers at Samar. She would scream and cry out when he came near her and cry helplessly when she felt better. It was sheer torture for everyone. It broke my heart ... it broke his heart ... and it broke her heart too ...

'Kaasi became too unwell to be kept at home and had to be put in the institution where she would at least not harm herself or others. Samar went mad with rage when it was first suggested and he fought tooth and nail to keep her home. In fact, we even made a small hospital wing at home and kept Kaasi there for some time, but it did not work out in the end. At last, they took her, leaving behind a very lonely Samar. I saw Samar die a hundred deaths during this brief time. He would spend innumerable hours in the institution just to be around her. He stopped working, stopped thinking, stopped living ... Really, time just stood still for us then. We had of course been trying our best to keep this under wraps because it was such a personal problem, yet somehow the media heard of it. Many stories were cooked up and carried by a lot of newspapers. It was difficult for me to see my son, who was almost killing himself looking after Kaasi, be called a wife beater. When Diya died, I had thought that nothing could get worse than this, but god had to prove me wrong ... and He did, in the most cruel way possible.'

Bindiya looked at Ojas Uncle, not able to take her eyes off his tormented face.

'Kaasi committed suicide, convinced that someone else would kill her if she did not,' he finished.

There was silence in the room.

'Bindiya,' said Ojas Uncle, looking at the anguished girl in front of him, 'Samar did more to save Kaasi than anyone in his shoes would have. For god's sake, he even married her knowing fully well what lay in store for him. Yet, in spite of all he had done, he blamed himself for her death, just as he blamed himself for the death of his mother ... It was – no, is – a very big burden to carry, and I saw him wilt under its pressure. He threw himself into work and led a very angry, unhappy life for a decade and a half ... till he met you ...'

Bindiya sat still, trying to take in all that had just been revealed to her.

'Samar never said a word about all this to me ...'

'It's no secret that he was married to Kaasi ... we obviously never tried to hide that. Yes, very few people know of the events leading to Kaasi's death, but now you know. I know it hurts that Samar didn't tell you all this himself, but if I have to make a guess, I would say that he must have tried to ... or maybe was looking for the right opportunity to tell you about Kaasi's death.'

Bindiya nodded, thinking, wondering, hurting ...

'If you still have questions, you do know that there's one more person you can speak with?'

'Who?'

'Kaasi's brother.'

'I don't know him, Ojas Uncle.'

'Of course you do, Bindiya, you worked with him.'

'What? I don't understand ... who are you talking about?'

'Madhav.'

Bindiya stared dumbstruck. After a while, she said falteringly, 'Madhav Zorawar is Kaasi's brother?'

'Yes, he is, and you see how thick Madhav and Samar are?'

Bindiya nodded her head. Their friendship was legendary.

'Do you think anyone would be such good friends with a man who was in any way responsible for his sister's death?'

Bindiya shook her head, now looking at the friendship between Madhav and Samar in a new light. Madhav had always seemed so keen for Samar to be with her ... almost as if he were willing Samar some happiness ...

'Bindiya, Samar is given to intense emotions – it is his weakness and his strength. He does not love easily but when he does, he loves with everything in him. He loved Kaasi and now he loves you. He has started smiling for the first time in fifteen years, Bindiya – he has opened his heart again. I want you to – take your own decision, but do that knowing that Samar would never trick or cheat you.'

Bindiya stood still for some time, thinking.

'Ojas Uncle,' she said, and Ojas turned around sharply, surprised by the vulnerability in her voice.

'Yes, darling,' he said, saddened by the tears that had pooled in Bindiya's eyes.

'I wish all of this had never happened to Samar, even if it means me not being with him,' she said. 'Why did god let this happen to Samar after all that he went through with his mum?'

'You know, Bindiya, we err in thinking that happiness is our birthright – it is not. We cannot question god when problems come our way, we just thank Him when they go.'

'I asked him if he murdered Kaasi,' said Bindiya. 'Do you think he will forgive me?'

'Yes, of course he will, darling,' said Ojas.

Bindiya wondered why, deep in her heart, she did not quite believe her Ojas Uncle.

43

Bindiya walked into Samar's office, feeling as nervous as she had felt that day, many months ago, when she had walked in to ask him to give her another chance. Now she was here again, asking him to give them and their love another chance.

She had a bad feeling about this. The cosmos has a way of letting us know that we have crossed a line and Bindiya was no exception.

Bindiya's heart sank the moment her eyes fell on Samar who was sitting upright at his desk. Grey suit, white shirt and grey tie. His face dark, serious, grim – the Samar Chauhan mask was back on. It was the Samar from before she became friends with him, the Samar she did not quite know, the Samar she felt very scared of.

'We need to talk,' she said hesitatingly, fiddling nervously with her fingers.

Samar looked up slowly. His eyes, expressionless and hard, focused on her, sending a slight shiver down her spine. This was not her Samar, this was Mr Samar Ojas Chauhan, rich, successful, no-nonsense.

'We need to talk,' she repeated.

'Perhaps you do, I don't.'

'Because you are the one who's supposed to be mad. You are the one who has just found ... er ... things ... things about me,' she tried to retort confidently.

'No, because I am the one who was called a murderer.'

'Samar, please.'

Samar remained silent.

'Why didn't you tell me?' she tried again.

'I owe no one an explanation, Ms Saran.'

'Samar, it all came as such a shock for me that ... that ...'

'That you decided that I must be a murderer.'

The silence that engulfed the two of them was heavy with anger and pain. When Samar spoke a few minutes later, his eyes were kinder but his voice remained edgy with anger. 'Kaasi is no secret.'

'I know now, Samar, but it was such a shock ... I ... I overreacted ...'

'In that case, I apologize for the inconvenience,' he said.

Anger surged inside Bindiya. 'Samar, stop this, this minute.'

'Let us both stop this, this minute, Ms Saran,' he said in a low voice. 'I don't want to have anything to do with you ever again.'

Bindiya stilled. 'What do you mean?' she asked.

'I. Don't. Want. To. Have. Anything. To. Do. With. You. What part of this do you not understand?'

'You ... you are breaking up with me?' she asked, incredulous.

'I don't want to have anything to do with you, Ms Saran,' he repeated, his voice dangerously patient.

'What? Just like that? Just because I found out about your past?'

'Just because you found about a past where I murdered a wife.' His voice dripped with angry sarcasm.

'Samar, I spoke with Ojas Uncle ... he ... he ... told me everything. I ... I understand now ...'

'Oh, did he now? Daddy dearest to the rescue?'

'Samar ...'

'I have nothing more to say.' His eyes moved back to the computer screen. He was done with the conversation. With Bindiya.

'I don't believe you ... you love me.'

Samar looked at her again and a slow smirk appeared on his face. 'Maybe Malika's approach was correct,' he said. 'How much, Ms Saran, will you take to leave me alone?'

'You are just trying to say hurtful things, Samar, I know ... I know ...'

'Just as you knew that I murdered Kaasi.'

Bindiya stood there, aghast, helpless, unsure. The stone-cold man in front of her was not the Samar she loved. Unbidden, unwanted tears now streamed down her face.

Samar focused his attention on the laptop in front of him.

'I love you,' said Bindiya softly, her voice broken by sobs, 'with all my heart. In fact, I love you more than I ever thought I could love anyone ... Don't do this, please? Please give us a second chance?' she pleaded.

Samar's fingers paused for a moment but he did not look up.

'Maybe it's different in the world of the super rich but in

241

the much simpler world I come from, love is for real. I can't switch it off. I was angry that I didn't know so many things about your past and I know I overreacted but none of it changes the fact that I love you.'

Silence.

'A second chance at love, Samar?'

Silence.

'You know the way out,' he said finally, not looking up.

Bindiya felt strength surge through her. Instead of walking away she marched purposefully towards Samar's desk and planted her palms firmly on either side of his laptop so that he had no option but to stare back into her eyes. 'Samar, I told you once that I would wait for you no matter what you say or do, and that is exactly what I intend to do. Even if you never again think of me, I'll spend the rest of my life waiting for you. If, some day, you decide you want me back you know where to look for me.'

Her tear-stained cheeks, her red nose, the fierceness in her eyes – Samar did not miss anything.

'I am not giving up on us, Samar, not now, not never. If you can be stubborn, I'll match you for it,' she said. For one last, lingering moment Bindiya stared at Samar, but when he didn't say anything, she brushed tears off her face, about-turned and ran out.

For a few minutes, silence reigned in Samar's office. Samar stared in front of him, unblinking. He then picked up a glass of water from his table and smashed it against the wall with all the force he could muster.

Naina came running in and stopped short when she saw the expression on Samar's face. 'Sa … Samar … are you okay?'

'Naina,' he said, staring unblinkingly at the pieces of broken glass that lay scattered on the floor, 'call Madhav,

242

please. He's expecting your call. Tell him that I will head our setup in Latin America. I am okay with being based in Rio for the next couple of years. Keen to leave by the end of the week and will of course help him in finding a replacement for my role here in India.'

'Samar ... I ...'

'Naina, please can you do as requested,' he said, now looking evenly at her.

'Yes, sir ... Bindiya ... I mean ... she—'

'I don't want that name mentioned again in front of me,' he said, roughly cutting her off.

'But Samar, Bindiya—'

'There is no Samar–Bindiya, Naina,' said Samar, looking out the window, his tall, broad body framed in the sunlight. 'There is no Samar–Bindiya any more.'

Epilogue

Found

Fourteen months later.

'I am so nervous it's not funny,' said Anuj, comically wringing his hands.

Bindiya, absently fidgeting with her Rolex, grinned.

The two of them were in Pondicherry, meeting the regional head of a large manufacturing company. For Bindiya this was another, rather inconsequential meeting to be got over with quickly, but for Anuj, this was his first.

'I am scared, Bindiya,' said Anuj, looking at his manager.

'Anuj,' said Bindiya, turning to face him, a kind smile on her face, 'only fools are never fearful. The trick, however, is to not let your fear show.'

'And how does one do that?'

'Tell yourself that fear harms more than it protects,' Bindiya said and then added with a wink, 'And then the drill also helps. Stomach in, chin out, straight back, smile on the face.'

Anuj grinned, already feeling better. 'You know, Bindiya, before I accepted the IC offer, I spoke to a couple of seniors from my B-school about you, and Aditi, who works for you in Hyderabad, told me that I should take this job just to work with you. You are, she said, the oddest combination of the wise and the fun.'

Bindiya laughed. 'I am just repeating something someone said to me a long time back.'

'A friend?'

'A very wise friend,' said Bindiya, smiling.

'You quote your "very wise friend" very often, don't you?'

'He used to say a lot of wise things.'

'Where is he now?'

'I wish I knew, Anuj,' said Bindiya, smiling and getting up. 'Let's go in, and let's rock the meeting!'

Laughing, and not feeling nervous any more, Anuj got up and followed Bindiya Saran.

After the meeting and a hurried dinner, Bindiya retired to her room for the night, looking forward to a long bath and the crisp white sheets of the hotel room. It was only when she had settled in that she picked out from her handbag the magazine she had been dying to read. A delicious little treat after a long, tiring week of travel.

Forbes India, latest edition.

Bindiya sucked in her breath when she looked at the cover. Two men stared back at her, smiling, friendly hands on each other's shoulders. The easy camaraderie that can only come from years of friendship and trust radiating even from the photograph. 'THE MEN IN CHARGE,' the magazine screamed in large font.

Bindiya briefly looked at Madhav Zorawar's green eyes, and then stared at the man standing next to him.

Samar.

It's always sad, Bindiya thought to herself, when life puts

245

you in a situation where you are forced to become strangers with someone you love with such intensity.

She stared at his picture, feeling her heart skip a beat and an unfamiliar tingle run the length of her body. She smiled; the body does not lie. Fourteen months since she had seen him last, and even his photograph had this effect on her. Had she even realized how much she loved him when she had been with him?

This had to be a recent picture. Bindiya squinted and wondered if there was indeed some grey in his hair or just the light playing tricks. Samar's eyes, fierce and intelligent, stared back at her. The same confidence, the same raw presence.

'Fourteen months,' Bindiya mumbled to herself.

In those fourteen months he had never tried to get in touch, and Bindiya, oddly enough, did not grudge him that.

246

The last fourteen months had brought with them some good and some not-so-good experiences for Bindiya and her family. Urvi had finished her MBA course and now had a fantastic job with a reputed investment banking firm. With another stream of income coming in, the financial situation of the Sarans had improved drastically. Sunaina had been offered a permanent role at a small newspaper and she was busy and happy.

Sunaina and Bindiya had had a slightly turbulent relationship in the last few months. Bindiya was now about to turn thirty and still vehemently refused to even consider marriage. Sunaina, who had always harboured a soft corner for the mild-mannered Adi and was aware of his feelings for her daughter, broached the topic of Bindiya's marriage to Adi. All hell then broke loose.

Bindiya now smiled at her own theatrics. Such drama.

'But why, Bindiya?' Sunaina had argued. 'You can't live

your life pining for that year and a half you spent with Samar. He is not here. He ended the relationship. Why can't you move on?'

'Mum,' Bindiya had said, 'every relationship has a life of its own. Its own destiny. Sometimes you get enough love from one person in a short span of time to last you a lifetime.'

'Enough love? He never even told you he loved you, Bindiya. Why are you being so unreasonable?'

'Not everything has to be said for it to be understood, Mum,' Bindiya had said softly and Sunaina could do little but roll her eyes at the daughter she could not understand.

Finally, it had been agreed that since Bindiya did not wish to marry, Sunaina would focus her attention on Urvi's marriage. There had been other, albeit minor, hiccups. Their landlord had asked them to vacate their house in a week's time, and Bindiya, who considered herself to be the man of the house, had panicked. Where would she go with two other women to care for, at such short notice? However, like Sunaina said, god helps when He can. The matter had resolved itself amicably with the landlord coming to them a few days later, looking surprisingly apologetic, almost begging them to stay. Some ups and some downs, yes, but by and large it had all been good.

Lonely and empty, but good nevertheless.

The one area in which the last fourteen months had been fabulous was work. Praise for Bindiya's work at the Zorawar Group had reached the right people; rumour had it that someone very senior at Zorawar had put in a good word, and she had been promoted to associate level with a team of three reporting to her. That meant longer hours at work and a lot of responsibility but those were not things the new Bindiya shied away from.

247

And how Bindiya had shone.

Since the Zorawar Group project, Bindiya had been on three projects and had delivered them confidently and professionally.

'Her work had lacked sincerity, Sumit,' Mohit had said to his colleague with pride in his voice, 'but look at her now. So much confidence and ... such gravitas. Almost as if she needed someone to show her what working sincerely means – and there you go, we have a gem on our hands. I had seen the potential in the very beginning.'

'Mohit,' Sumit had graciously acquiesced, 'you were right and I was wrong about the girl.'

Now Bindiya hastily opened the magazine to the interview of Madhav and Samar. Samar had just set up the Zorawar Group office in Latin America and the story spoke of their success and friendship. There were more pictures and Bindiya devoured them hungrily before starting with the text. Hastily flipping through pages so that she could see all the pictures, Bindiya could not hide her shock when she came to the last page of the article which carried two pictures. In the first picture Samar stood in his garden, smiling, an arm draped around his father.

Bindiya gasped and rubbed the goosebumps on her hands. 'Like father like son,' the caption below the photograph read. 'My father is my rock. It's funny how long it took me to realize that parents are also humans.'

Bindiya brought her hand to her mouth in genuine surprise. Samar and Ojas Uncle were friends now? Each particle of her soul delighted at the mere thought that two of her favourite men were back to being friends now. And it was then that her eyes fell on the last picture, which again had Madhav and Samar together, both of them looking ridiculously confident and self-assured. Bindiya squinted at the picture. Samar had his right hand in his pocket, yet from under the sleeve of his suit could she spot something bright peeping through?

Was it the ... no, of course not ... it couldn't be ...

The landline in her room buzzed.

'Hello,' Bindiya mumbled distractedly into the phone, still staring at the photograph.

'Ms Saran?' a suave voice asked.

For a moment Bindiya's heart stopped beating.

'I am Abhay from reception,' the voice continued.

Oh.

'Yes, Abhay, how can I help you?' Bindiya asked, smiling weakly. Really, why did some part of her always keep waiting for him? When for him, it was all over and had been so for over a year now.

'Madam, there's someone requesting to meet you.'

'Me?'

And then she remembered. Her aunt who lived in Pondicherry had promised to send some home-made food through her driver, Vinay. She had said he would reach her hotel by ten. Bindiya looked at her watch. Ten to ten.

'Oh, yes, yes, I'm expecting him. Please can you tell the gentleman to wait and I'll come down?'

'Sure, madam, he's waiting for you by the beach,' said Abhay from reception, referring to the private beach that the reception opened into.

'That's very fancy of Vinay bhaiyya,' thought Bindiya, smiling to herself as she got out of bed.

Feeling too lazy to take her nightdress off, she pulled a pair of jeans under it and a jumper on top. When she passed by the bathroom mirror she noticed what a royal mess her hair

249

was in, but she felt neither any need nor any inclination to make herself presentable. After all, it was just Vinay.

Hoping she wouldn't bump into Anuj, Bindiya walked down to the reception. She looked around for Vinay and then shook her head. A man in a suit stood at a distance, his back to her, but that was all. Where was the thin, mustachioed Vinay?

'Abhay?' she said at the reception and the smart young man looked up.

'I am Bindiya Saran from Room 365. You told me someone was waiting for me. Where can I find him?'

'That way, ma'am,' said Abhay, pointing in the direction of a man by the beach silhouetted in the moonlight.

Puzzled, Bindiya slowly walked up to the man. Something was not quite right, that man was not Vinay ...

For as long as she would live, Bindiya would try, hundreds and millions of times, to relive this moment but it would never come back to her quite as clearly as she would like. The few seconds it took her to walk across to the man and extend her arm to touch him on his shoulder would be lost forever in the maelstrom of emotions that awaited her.

'Vinay?' she asked hesitatingly, her heart figuring it out a split second before her brain did and beginning to thump uncontrollably.

The man turned around and sharp, intelligent eyes focused themselves on Bindiya's face. Eyes that made her heart skip not one but hundreds of beats.

The earth stopped spinning and time stood still. The moon, the waves, the sand. The gentle hum of conversation from the hotel reception.

Bindiya stared. The goosebumps. The wildly beating heart. The utter shock.

'Ms Saran,' said Samar softly, his face very serious.

Bindiya simply stared, not even attempting words. An immense wall of sheer helplessness crashed over her and tears gathered in her eyes. He was here!

The eyes that stared back at her, she noted through her now blurry vision, were not dry either.

The two of them stood there, one foot apart, staring into each other's eyes, not saying a word, just breathing each other in, drinking each other in …

Samar closed his eyes and shook his head as if preparing himself. 'I am sorry,' he said softly when he opened his eyes.

Bindiya brought her hand to her mouth in an attempt to stop the tears, but failed miserably. As she succumbed to sobs, powerful arms gathered her and a gentle hand guided her to a bench near by. Bindiya slumped on the sand, leaning against the wood of the bench. Throwing herself on the one man she had ever truly loved, she wrapped her arms around Samar and cried like a baby, surprised at the pain that was oozing out of her.

The catharsis of a good cry.

Samar held her tight, the fierceness of his hug crushing her and healing her heart. When, finally, after what seemed both like an hour and a second, Bindiya looked up at Samar, what she saw were red eyes and a wet, vulnerable face.

'I am so sorry,' he mumbled.

There was such sincerity and such pain in his words that something else inside Bindiya gave way and she found herself crying harder than before, this time for the man who now looked so defenceless to her.

Samar placed a long finger under her chin and tilted her face upwards so that their eyes met. 'I am sorry,' he continued, looking stricken, 'for what I have done and for what I am about to do.'

251

Bindiya froze. 'What are you about to do?'

'I am going to be really selfish, Bindiya, and beg you to come back to me.'

'Come back?'

'Yes, come back.'

'How can I come back, Samar,' said Bindiya, her voice breaking, 'when I never left?'

Samar opened his mouth and then shut it, speechless. 'I am being so selfish Bindiya. You should be with a man who's like you and who will keep you happy. Not someone as messed up as I am ...'

'I happen to love my messed-up man more than I could ever love anyone else, Samar,' said Bindiya, now wiping tears with the back of her hand.

252

'I wanted to tell you about Kaasi, all about her, so many times, Bindiya. I wanted you to hear it all from me, in my own words, though I was sure you knew – everyone knew. Weird things stopped me – you were smiling this one time and I didn't want you to stop smiling. Then this other time, you yourself stopped me from saying anything. When I spent the night with you in your home, I told you I wanted to tell you something that was sad and you said you didn't want to hear it then ... and I didn't insist.' He shook his head in frustration. 'I never for a moment thought that you didn't know anything ...'

'It's okay, Samar, it's absolutely okay. I overreacted too—'

'Bindiya,' said Samar, holding her face in his hands, gently brushing away her hair, 'I carry a lot of baggage ...'

'It's okay, Samar, baggage is okay, resentment is not. Resentment debilitates, it cripples. If resentment is a part of your life, you won't be able to move forward.'

'Everyone tells me to move forward! I can't move on, I can't forget!'

'Moving forward is not forgetting, Samar,' said Bindiya. 'It is simply letting go.'

'Letting go of what?'

'Resentment.'

'And what do I do about the anger inside me, Bindiya? There's so much of it that I feel scared of myself sometimes.'

'When we are faced with a difficult situation, Samar, the easiest recourse is anger. And since when did my Samar start choosing the easier way out?'

Samar looked at Bindiya, his eyes telling her that he had no hope for himself.

'Forgive, Samar, please forgive. I beg you, please forgive. Forgive god for taking away your mum and Kaasi. Forgive Ojas Uncle for letting your mum go, and most importantly, forgive yourself,' she said, gently caressing Samar's cheek. 'Forgiveness is huge, Samar, so huge. It's the only thing that will set you free ...'

'I have lived with anger far too long, Bindiya, I can't change myself.'

'You may not, but maybe together we can?'

'I am so broken, Bindiya,' he said.

Bindiya leaned forward and planted a kiss on Samar's forehead. When their eyes met, Bindiya's were very calm. 'You might be broken, Samar, but to me you are beautiful.'

Samar stilled and Bindiya knew her words, borrowed from Samar from a long time back, had hit home.

'My hair is such a mess,' she said, grinning, trying to diffuse the heaviness around them.

'It's gorgeous,' he said and leaned forward to pull off her hair tie so that her hair fell around her like a sheet of shiny black paper. Samar raked his fingers through her hair, lost in thought.

'For fourteen months you didn't even think about me!' said Bindiya teasingly.

Samar pulled back with a small smile. 'You can't be further from the truth,' he said simply, without giving her details of how he had kept a close eye on everything that had happened in Bindiya's life in that time. Urvi was good but Samar had made a few calls to make sure she had at least twice the package someone in her place would have got. Sunaina's surprise job appointment had been the result of another very quick call. Anything to make sure that his Bindiya did not have to worry about being the only earning member of her family. Then that little issue with the landlord. Surat had taken care of it even before he told Samar about it.

'Why did it take you fourteen months to come to me?' Bindiya asked. 'When it should have been fourteen days or hours at most? I know I crossed a line that day but why couldn't you forgive me, Samar? Why didn't you just shake me by my arm and explain things? Why did the anger last so long?'

'It didn't,' said Samar quietly, now looking at the waves that were crashing gently against the beach.

'Then why?'

'Bindiya,' said Samar, 'I was very angry, possibly unreasonably, that you had even considered I could have harmed Kaasi, even in a fit of anger. It was almost like you did not know me, like we were strangers, like you were the media from back then that had cooked up stories. And then, by the time my anger subsided, I thought that maybe it was best for you to not be around me. I carried heavy baggage and you deserved someone better. I stayed away for as long as I could only, and only for your sake. And then I couldn't bear to be away from you any longer and I had to come here.'

'It's okay, Samar,' she whispered.

'No, it's not,' he said.

Bindiya now reached out and crawled into Samar's lap. They sat there, against the cool wood of the bench, foreheads touching, wrapped in a tender embrace, breathing each other and the salty air in. Samar leaned forward and kissed Bindiya, slowly, gently, as if time had ceased to matter ... he kissed her lightly on her lips, her cheeks, her forehead and her neck, his kisses as gentle as snowflakes.

'I have thought about you every minute I've been awake in the last fourteen months,' whispered Bindiya, biting her lips to stop herself from bursting into sobs again. Samar grabbed her hands and that was when her eyes fell on it.

Her multi-coloured I-love-you loom band.

'You are wearing my loom band,' she said, smiling through her tears.

'I never took it off.'

Bindiya rested her head on Samar's shoulders, just glad to be with him, wondering if this was all a dream she would wake up from any minute now.

'Bindiya?' muttered Samar.

'Yes?'

'I breathe easier when I am with you.'

Bindiya looked up and her eyes met Samar's.

'Each time I meet you, I see something else in you that I had not seen before and fall in love with you again.'

Love.

Bindiya stilled. Did he mean to say that he loved her?

'You know, Bindiya, there are just two women I have ever loved before, and god took away both of them from me. If I tell you that I love you ... who knows ... wh ...'

255

Bindiya, biting her lower lip hard to stop the tears that she knew were ready to burst forth, sat up straight and clasped Samar's face in both her hands. When she spoke, there was an urgency, a desperation, in her voice.

'No, Samar, nothing will happen.'

'How do you know?' he asked helplessly.

'I promise, Samar, I promise nothing will happen to me.'

'And if anything happens to you, Bindiya, I swear I'll burn the whole world down,' said Samar and Bindiya had no doubt he meant his words.

'Okay, no ... I mean, not okay,' said Bindiya, laughing and crying now, her face a few inches from Samar's. 'Just say it, Samar, please. *Please.*'

Silence.

'Please? I won't let anything happen to me, Samar.'

Silence.

And then Samar leaned forward a few centimetres so that their foreheads touched again.

'I love you, Bindiya,' he said, his voice relieved, resigned.

Binidiya's shoulder sagged as she leaned into Samar. A sob, long in the waiting, escaped her before she could bite her lips once more and stop it.

'Say that again, please?' she whispered, barely able to keep her voice steady.

'I love you, Bindiya,' Samar said.

Bindiya was openly sobbing now, tears flowing down her face unchecked.

'Say that again?'

'I love you, Bindiya,' Samar said and he pulled her into another fierce hug.

As if on cue, the skies parted and the first drops of rain began to fall on Bindiya and Samar, who looked up, smiled and snuggled in closer, entirely unaware how the same raindrops had danced around them when they had first met each other many, many years ago, on the day Kaasi had died, on the day this had all started.

Samar and Bindiya.

Then lost but now found.

Acknowledgements

Prof. Ram Chandra Shukla, my grandfather, for a lifetime of words that have encouraged and inspired.

Rachana Misra and Nisha Kant Misra, my parents, for making me believe that no dream I dare to dream is too big to be realized.

AVM (retd.) Shyam Bihari Bajpayee, AVSM, and Amita Bajpayee, my in-laws, for their continued love and support.

Nikhil Agrawal whose faith in my writing never falters.

Ridhi Dandona, Ankita Bhatia Dhawan, Alan Cartwright and Rekha Devarapalli for their feedback which helped me shape the story into its present form.

Shraddha and Gautam Misra for their continued support for my books.

Manasi Subramaniam, Amrita Talwar and the rest of the HarperCollins team. This book has been a 'labour' of love and I cannot thank you enough for being the most accommodating publishers I could have hoped for.

Diva Kant Misra and Neharika Neeraj Kalra, my brother and sister-in-law, for being the most enthusiastic cheerleaders of my books.

And last but not the least, my boys, Siddharth and Shikhar. Siddharth, for being more friend than husband, and Shikhar, for teaching me what love truly is.